From The Ashes

Ashes

MINISTRY OF CURIOSITIES
#6

C.J. ARCHER

DEDICATION

For Joe who doesn't complain when I'd rather be writing or think I'm strange for hearing voices in my head (much).

CHAPTER 1

Yorkshire, December 1889

"Miss Holloway! Stop slouching!" Mrs. Denk's cane smacked across my back. I felt the bite of it against my skin, even through all the layers of clothing. My breath left my body and my eyes watered. I arched away from her. "Young ladies do not have round shoulders."

I gritted my teeth until the sting lessened. "I am not a lady." Instead of straightening my back, I tipped my head forward so that the book balanced there slipped off and crashed to the floor. It landed open, bending some pages and stretching the spine.

Air hissed through Mrs. Denk's nose. Whenever she became angry, her heavy breaths hissed through her nose. The headmistress and deportment teacher at the School for Wayward Girls seemed to become angry a lot—mostly with me.

I expected her stick to come down on my back again, but it did not. She stepped into view. The other girls in the old banqueting hall shuffled away, clearing space around us. They sensed confrontation, and if there was one thing the girls at the so-called school hated, it was confrontation, particularly with the formidable Mrs. Denk.

Out of the corner of my eye, I saw the girl I shared a room with, Alice, shake her head, warning me not to cross the headmistress again. I tried to convey with a look that I would be all right, that Mrs. Denk wouldn't harm me, only attempt to frighten me with her sharp tongue and punishments, which were nothing compared to what I'd experienced in years past. I must have failed, because Alice looked worried, and she wasn't usually a worrier.

"Pick that up." The tiny lines around Mrs. Denk's mouth whitened with the pursing of her lips. The rest of her face was otherwise smooth, a remarkable feat for a woman who must be in her late forties. Some of the other girls speculated that she'd done a deal with the devil to keep her skin youthful, but if that were true, she should have asked the devil to stop her hair from going gray too. Mrs. Denk rarely showed emotion, except for the occasional tightening or flattening of her lips, and that was more likely the reason for the lack of wrinkles. I would never think of a wrinkly face as something to be lamented again, but rather a sign of a passionate nature and a full life.

I bent to pick up the book, not because she'd ordered me to, but because I didn't like to see a book damaged, even a dull one about the art of being a lady. Instead of returning it to my head, I placed it on the occasional table that made up part of the obstacle course through which I was attempting to maneuver.

"Return it to your head and continue with the exercise," Mrs. Denk said in her crispest tone, which had more than one girl trembling.

Once again, Alice shook her head at me. We'd only known one another ten days, but she already had my measure. Most likely because I'd clashed with Mrs. Denk from my first day. I didn't like a bully, and the headmistress was the worst kind—a bully in sheep's clothing. At least Lincoln had never pretended to be anything else.

I swallowed down the lump in my throat that formed whenever I thought of him, which, unfortunately, was often. Instead, I summoned the anger that was never far away. Not anger directed at him—it was no longer as sharp or hot—but anger at myself for allowing him to treat me as he had.

"No," I said with more calmness than I felt. I knew I presented a tough exterior to Mrs. Denk and the other girls and teachers, but inside, part of me quailed when she held the cane in both hands and her eyes brightened with a cruel gleam. If it weren't for my anger fueling me, I wouldn't have tested her patience so, but I found I couldn't quell my anger any more than I could accept her authority over me. Every order she gave, every attempt to turn me into a ladylike figure of grace and poise, triggered my rebellious streak.

Where had the bloody thing been when Lincoln had bundled me into the coach and sent me away from Lichfield?

Mrs. Denk's lips pinched even more. Her nostrils flared and the hissing breaths became a wheeze. "Put the book back on your head, Miss Holloway. *Now.*"

"I don't see the point of this." I flung my arms wide to indicate the banqueting hall that probably hadn't seen a banquet since the castle's medieval days.

"The point is that your guardian sent you here so that you would become a lady."

I snorted. "I doubt that's the reason he sent me. And do not call him my guardian. He's not. No one is."

7

Before she could counter me, I added, "I am not, and never will be, a lady, Mrs. Denk. No matter how many times you force me to walk with a book on my head, or how many times you make me enunciate my vowels, or whip me with your cane. I'm a gutter rat. A ne'er do well. A homeless waif." A discarded fiancée, I might have added, and an abomination against God, as my adopted father had once called me. But I did not. Speaking those words out loud hurt too much, and I didn't want tears to well when standing up to Mrs. Denk. She was the sort of woman who fed on the weaknesses of others and used them to her advantage.

One of the other girls gasped, and another suppressed her surprise with a hand over her mouth. The rest simply stared at me. No doubt it was the first clue they'd had regarding my background. Despite speculation and gossip behind my back, I'd not told them anything about my past, since they had not asked me directly. Only Alice had, and I'd told her my story, leaving out the part about my necromancy and the specifics surrounding my going to live with Lincoln at Lichfield Towers. Of the girls in our deportment class, she alone showed no shock at my words. She simply frowned and warned me with her eyes to stop pushing Mrs. Denk toward her limit.

The air whistled from the headmistress's nose at a particularly high pitch. "Your dramatics are tiresome, Miss Holloway. It's no wonder your *guardian* sent you here, where he no longer has to listen to them." No doubt she put the emphasis on "guardian" to goad me further. "Pick up the book and return it to your head. You're wasting my time and that of the other girls."

"They're all rather good at walking around with books on their heads already," I said. "All except me, that is, and I refuse to be party to your ridiculous exercise."

Some of the girls tittered nervously.

Mrs. Denk bristled, drawing herself up to her full height. She was considerably taller than me, and not a slender woman. Her bust resembled a shelf, rising and falling with every hiss. "Place the book on your head," she said through a clenched jaw.

"Or?"

She brought the cane down on my upper arm.

"Bloody hell!" I cried, wincing. "You're mad!"

She attempted to strike again, but I was ready and caught the cane in my bare hand. Fiery pain, worse than a thousand bee stings, branded my palm. I wanted to cry out and cradle my hand, but refused to show any vulnerability. Bearing down against the agony, I pulled the cane out of her hand, bent it over my knee, and snapped it in two.

Her eyes widened. Her mouth flopped open. It was worth the pain to see her shock. "How dare you!"

"Now, now, Mrs. Denk. Don't get too upset or your corset will burst." I nodded at her heaving chest. "I'd say the structure is dangerously close to its limit already."

Her smooth face reddened and scrunched, forming grooves where before there'd been none. I shot a victorious grin at Alice. She bit her lip in an attempt to contain her smile. A smile that nevertheless quickly vanished.

Mrs. Denk's hand came down on my cheek. I reeled back, clutching my stinging face, too surprised to make a sound. The other girls' gasps echoed around the stone walls. Alice covered her mouth with both hands, her pretty gray eyes huge.

Mrs. Denk grabbed my arm at the point where her cane had struck me. Her bruising grip rubbed my sore flesh. "Come with me, Miss Holloway. I have a very special punishment in store for you."

She marched me out of the banqueting hall to the sound of the girls' horrified whispers. I couldn't catch many of their words, but one sounded clear as a bell: oubliette.

Alice had told me all about the oubliette, the narrow dungeon beneath the castle too small to lie down in and accessed via a trapdoor in the castle floor. She'd claimed it was a special punishment reserved for the worst prisoners in the castle's violent history, and for those "wayward" girls too wicked to socialize with the rest of the students at the school. None of the current students had seen the oubliette, but Mademoiselle LeClare, the French teacher, told them of a girl who'd died within its damp, lonely confines in her time as a student here. I asked her if the girl had simply fallen in or if she'd been thrown in by the headmistress, but Mademoiselle LeClare hadn't been forthcoming with the particulars. The girls believed the worst, however. Rumors of the student's ghost haunting the castle didn't help. I'd not seen any female spirits floating around the castle, however, only a man dressed in blood stained clothes and chain mail that clinked musically as he walked. It alerted me to his presence, allowing me to avoid him. I didn't want anyone there to know that I could see ghosts, let alone summon them at will.

We passed through the old kitchen with its yawning fireplace, our footsteps echoing in the disused room. Mrs. Denk pushed me through the doorway to the stairs, not stopping at ground level but descending into the stale, damp depths of the castle. I could have escaped Mrs. Denk's grip using the moves Lincoln taught me in our exercise regimes, but a spell in the dungeon would save me from classes for the rest of the day, so I decided against a fight. Besides, it would probably only be for a few hours to try and scare me into submission. I could pretend to be contrite if I grew bored.

The stairwell became too narrow for us to walk side by side. My hair skimmed the rough stones overhead and Mrs. Denk had to hunch over. The stairs opened up to a large room with a vaulted ceiling, supported on columns wider and taller than the generously proportioned headmistress. It was colder than the rest of the castle, something I'd not thought possible. The only fire allowed in the school was in the dining room attached to the new kitchen on ground level. Not even Mrs. Denk had one in her office. I knew, because I'd been sent there every day since my arrival.

She finally let me go, but blocked the exit to the stairs. I considered tackling her, but suspected that would only lead to further punishment. I didn't want my food rations to be cut. They were already less than what I'd become accustomed to at Lichfield, although so much more than the meager morsels I'd managed to steal each day living on the streets. If I was to build my strength for a spring-time escape from the school, I would need to eat as much as I could and stay healthy.

"Mr. Fitzroy won't come for you," she said without a sympathetic note in her voice. "They never do. It's best if you learn that now rather than later."

"For once, I agree with you. He's not the sort of person who changes his mind once it's made up." Especially when there was no one to help him change it. Seth, Gus and Cook couldn't manage it. They still feared him, and even if they struck up the courage to challenge him for sending me away, he didn't care enough about their opinions to change his mind. That was the problem—he didn't care enough about anyone. Even me, as it turned out.

I suppressed the rising well of sorrow by biting on my tongue.

"Is this it?" I asked, looking around. The wall glistened with damp and something scratched in the dark corner. I could just make out a large stone slab positioned near one of the columns, and a set of rusty chains hanging from rings attached to the wall. Leg irons puddled on the floor nearby. "No oubliette? How disappointing."

"I am not an unreasonable woman, Miss Holloway," she said. "But I do not tolerate willfulness in students."

There were a dozen responses to that, but I suddenly couldn't be bothered with any of them. I wasn't going to change her mind, or soften her stance. She believed that discipline and routine would fix our so-called waywardness. While that may be true for many girls, it wasn't true for those of us sent there because of our supernatural abilities.

It had taken me a week before I'd seen evidence of inhuman characteristics in the girls, but once I noticed them, I saw more. I counted six out of the eighteen students, and another two I wasn't yet sure about. It had begun with the medium whose gaze followed the ghost as he walked past, but there was also a fire starter, two who could move objects with their minds, and another two whose hands became suddenly and inexplicably hairy when they were upset.

Then there was Alice, a seer, or something of that nature. Or so I suspected. She had strange dreams that were so vivid it took her a few minutes to fully waken. In that dreamlike state, she rambled about all manner of strange things, mostly about a queen trying to kill her.

"You will remain here until you learn to co-operate," Mrs. Denk said, spinning on her heel.

"Will I be fed?" I asked.

"Once per day."

"Per day? You intend to keep me here overnight?"

"If that's what it takes to instill some obedience into you."

"And if it doesn't?"

"We shall see."

"What if I'm still disobedient in a week? A month? Will you keep me in here without exercise or company, or even light?"

"It never takes long, in my experience."

"I'd wager you've never met anyone like me before."

I thought I heard her snort, but I couldn't be certain. Such an unladylike sound from the very dour Mrs. Denk was highly unlikely. It was far too emotional for the wooden matron.

"What if I die down here?" I asked, rather enjoying myself now. It was petty and juvenile to make a nuisance of myself, but it felt bloody good. It wasn't just her I was annoying, it was Lincoln too, in a convoluted way. God, how I wished I could be a thorn in his side once again, just to get some measure of satisfaction, even if it was petty and small-minded. "What if the welt on my hand festers?" I showed her my palm, still burning from the strike of her cane. "What will you do then, Mrs. Denk?"

"Do be quiet, Miss Holloway," she said on a sigh.

"And if I'm not? Will you send me back to my guardian?"

She stopped and rounded on me. Her hands linked in front of her, a picture of demure, albeit expressionless, piety. "I don't think you understand, Miss Holloway. Girls are sent here with the understanding that they will never return to the homes they knew beforehand, no matter what transpires. You are unwanted. Cast off. Forgotten. I do not send anyone back to the place from which they came. Ever."

Each word struck me with the force of a hammer blow. I'd not realized I'd held out any hope of Lincoln collecting me until now. My hope had been small, but it had existed. Now it lay shattered at my feet. He'd sent me here to remove me from his life as thoroughly as a surgeon amputating a limb. There would be no return, even after I escaped from the school. I didn't want to be somewhere I wasn't welcome. I would have to make another life for myself, away from Lichfield, perhaps even away from London. It was a decision to make another day, when my head was clearer. It was too wooly to think straight now.

"So if you wish to remain under this roof—or any roof, for that matter—you *will* learn obedience and anything else your small mind can take from your lessons," Mrs. Denk went on. "If not, the world is a very large, very frightening place for a young woman with no home, no friends, and no means to support herself except for her..." Her gaze lowered to my rather insignificant chest. "...natural attributes."

I stumbled back until I smacked against the stone slab. My legs felt weak and I gratefully sat. Mrs. Denk didn't smile in triumph at the effect her words had on me. Her expression didn't change.

"The oubliette is back there." She nodded toward the black depths behind me. "So mind your step." She turned and climbed the stairs.

The door slammed closed, cutting off what little light reached the dungeon. The lock tumbled. I was a prisoner.

CHAPTER 2

The scurrying of tiny claws over stone didn't help my taut nerves. Living in burned-out basements and abandoned warehouses for years had instilled in me a hatred for rats, beetles and lice that I doubted would ever lessen. While I didn't particularly like being alone in absolute darkness either, I could have borne it better if it weren't for the direction my thoughts took me. They inevitably returned to Lincoln.

He was not a flexible man, and his mind was unlikely to change. Waiting and hoping for rescue was futile. I knew that. I'd known it since I was thirteen, but I admit to having forgotten the lesson in recent months. Comfort had bred complacency, and that had made me forget that the only person I could truly rely on was myself. If I wanted to escape from the School for Wayward Girls, I would have to do so under my own steam.

Despite my anger and frustration, I missed him terribly. I both hated and loved him, which I gave up trying to understand. My feelings regarding him were in turmoil, but my feelings regarding my situation were clear. I wanted to see my friends again. I wanted to be home with them, and Lichfield was my home. I belonged there. Thinking about what I'd left behind filled me with sorrow so black and deep I doubted I'd ever be free of it.

Damn him. Damn him for making me feel this way, for giving me everything my heart desired then ripping it away from me. I'd removed my engagement ring before reaching the school to avoid awkward questions, but I longed to fling it back in his face. If I ever saw him again, I'd—

Stop! Stop considering the future.

I mustn't think too far ahead, and I certainly mustn't allow myself to hope that I would go home again. There was only here and now—the darkness, the loneliness and the scurrying rats. I had to get out of the dungeon first, and then I would turn my attention to breaking free from the school in the spring. What came after that...I would just have to wait and see.

The scratching suddenly sounded very close. I sprang off the slab, pushing myself up with my hands. Pain sliced across my palm where Mrs. Denk's cane had seared my flesh. I swore at the top of my lungs and shook out my hand, but it didn't help. It hadn't hurt this much before.

Think of something else. Think of escaping in the spring.

I heard scurrying again and kicked out but didn't connect with any living creature. If only my imp could remove the creatures for me, or, even better, get me out of the dungeon. But the cat-like creature living inside the amber sphere hanging around my neck only obeyed me when saving my life. Perhaps I could convince it that rats were a direct threat to my person.

I leaned against the column with a sigh, not wanting to sit down and risk something burrowing into the folds of my skirts. My stomach growled. I'd not eaten since breakfast and I must have been in the dungeon several hours already. I needed to use the privy, too. A horrible thought struck me. What if Mrs. Denk decided to leave me down here? Who would stop her? No one dared cross her, not even the other teachers. I could starve to death. Or die from boredom.

My imagination conjured up all the ways in which I could die and calculated how long each would take. It wasn't the happiest way to pass the time, but at least it meant I was no longer thinking about Lincoln.

More time passed, but I couldn't fathom the length. More than a day? Two? I had to squat in the corner to relieve myself, holding my skirts high to keep them clean. I pictured rats sniffing at my hind quarters and quickly finished and returned to my column in the center of the dungeon. I found my way by feel, my good hand skimming over slimy stones as cold as ice. I shivered as the freezing air seeped through my clothing and skin to my bones. Forget starvation. I would die from the cold before lack of food.

My legs grew too weary to hold me up so I squatted and finally sat. I don't know when I gave up worrying about rats, but I found I no longer cared if they ventured closer to inspect me. I was sure I felt their tiny claws over my hands, their twitchy noses near my ear. The only thing that roused me from the slab of stone was the sensation of something crawling through my hair.

I scampered away, only to smack into another column. I'm ashamed to admit that I squealed. *Pathetic.* The old Charlie would have fallen about laughing if one of the lads in the gang had screamed when a rat ran through his hair. This Charlie was so much weaker. At that moment, I hated her.

I stood. The old Charlie *and* the new must make her own luck. I felt my way to the stairs and tripped up the first step, landing hard on my hands and knees. I grunted, as pain spiked through my palm, but managed to suppress it enough to continue up to the top. I banged on the door with my fist then waited.

No answer.

"Anyone? Is there someone there?"

Nothing.

I banged again and shouted as loud as I could, but there was no response. I felt utterly removed, as if the nearest person were miles away. If the teachers and students abandoned the castle, I would never know.

I leaned back against the door and closed my eyes. Tears leaked from beneath my lashes. I was thirsty, hungry and helpless. Damn Mrs. Denk to hell, and damn Lincoln too.

The tinkling of metal had me opening my eyes again. How long had they been shut? I couldn't see a thing, not even the wispy ghost whose chain mail made the sound.

"Is anyone there?" I asked the darkness.

The tinkling ceased. Had he stopped or simply floated through to another part of the castle?

"I can see you, Mr. Ghost," I ventured. "Well, not now, it's too dark, but I've seen you wandering the halls of the school."

"School?" The rough masculine voice was closer than I thought.

I grinned. So he *could* hear me. Thank goodness he wasn't completely mad and unaware of my presence.

"'Tis not a school," he went on, with equal parts pride and arrogance lacing his tone. "'Tis Inglemere. My home."

"You owned this castle?"

"Aye, but I'd wager it was some time ago. Time has no meaning now. I am dead," he added, as if it would be news to me. "Are you the one they are all a-twitter about upstairs?"

"I suspect so. Charlie Holloway, at your service."

"Sir Geoffrey Falstead. A pleasure to make your acquaintance, Mistress Holloway. It is not often that I meet a seer of spirits. You are only the second."

"We're a rare breed."

"It is a comfort to talk to someone again. I miss company. I miss laughter and serious discussion alike. I miss music. These walls used to echo with it," he murmured. "No longer. Ever since that woman arrived, the air here has grown stale."

"Mrs. Denk has that effect on air. If you miss company so much, why do you stay? Why not cross over?"

"I swore to protect Inglemere. The day the siege began, I promised the folk that I would watch over it, even from my grave, if that became necessary. It did, as it happened. I died that day."

"I'm sorry," I said quietly. "Truly I am. But the siege was a long time ago, Sir Geoffrey, and your contemporaries have all passed. You can go now."

"It's my duty to protect the castle." He sounded offended. "I do not shy away from my duties, Mistress Holloway."

"No, of course not." I would not press him on the point. Some ghosts wanted to remain in this realm, and it was their choice to do so. Usually they wished to resolve an issue before moving on, like seek revenge on their killer, or wait to see if a loved one found happiness again. Very few remained indefinitely. "How much do you see on your wanderings?" I asked him.

"Everything. I see all the comings and goings. That woman bought the castle after my line died out, sadly, but there was little I could do except haunt it. I slammed doors, moved furniture, and flung objects about, but nothing I did frightened her. She remained. One of her students was the first medium I encountered. She acted as an intermediary and the leader and I came to an agreement. I could stay here, quietly, and she would not alter the castle according to the plans she'd drawn up. I agreed." He sighed. "What more could I do? I had no power to stop her, only frighten her students. I will not leave. Ever."

"You're very noble, Sir Geoffrey, and very loyal to Inglemere. I admire you for it."

"Thank you, Mistress Holloway. The dungeon is rarely occupied, hence I have few reasons to venture down here, but I heard them speak of you in hushed tones, holed up in this place forsaken by God and your mistress." He sighed. "It's no better down here now than it was in my time. Are you cold?"

"Extremely." Here was a hope. If I could only get him to *do* something. "You came down here to check on me? That's very kind of you."

"It is my duty," he said rather stiffly. I wished I could see him, as I suspected he could see me in the dark. "I came after hearing a maiden beg that woman to release you."

"Alice?"

"I believe that is her name."

"Good for her. I knew she was the bravest person here. What did Mrs. Denk say?"

"She sent Alice to her room without food."

"Oh." I drew up my knees and rested my forehead against them. "Poor Alice. When was that?"

"Time has little meaning for me. Dawn is making an appearance now."

Some time ago, then. Mrs. Denk truly didn't care for my welfare. Perhaps she really would leave me in here to die. "Sir Geoffrey, will you do something for me?"

"That's why I came. No gentle woman should be imprisoned down here. It's fit only for traitors and Frenchman. How can I help?"

"Is there another escape route? A secret tunnel perhaps?"

"No. One entry and exit, via the stairs."

"Damn." I could force him to enter a dead body from the church graveyard I'd spotted beyond the trees, and then frighten Mrs. Denk into handing over the key, but that would require a wait. Besides, there was another way. Perhaps. "Can you give a message to the medium?"

"There's another medium here aside from yourself?"

I didn't tell him I was a necromancer, and that there was a difference. "Her name is Meredith. She's about my height and her hair is dark with tight curls. She likes to wear pink. You'll find her in the third bedchamber from the old kitchen."

"The servants' quarters," he said absently. "I will fetch her, but she may not be a medium. She does not acknowledge me."

"She will if you talk to her directly. Tell her she must get the key from Mrs. Denk somehow and slip it under the door."

"And if she will not do it?"

"Tell her to fetch Alice. Alice has more courage. She'll do it." It begged the question, however—why hadn't she already tried to get the key and freed me? Or had she tried and failed? "Thank you, Sir Geoffrey. I appreciate you coming here to help a damsel in distress." If a little flattery insured he did his best, then so be it.

"I can't spend much time convincing her," he warned me. "I must continue on my rounds. The perimeter must be secured, the battlements made ready. The French army lie in wait just beyond the trees and may attack today."

Oh dear. So he was mad after all. I supposed it was unlikely that a spirit could reside here for so long, alone, and not have lost part of his mind.

Chain mail rattled and then suddenly ceased. He'd vanished. I waited. And waited. It felt like hours. To take my mind off my hollow stomach and icy bones, I sang every song my adoptive mother had taught me as a child, and when I finished those, I began again, and again, getting louder and less tuneful each time.

"Cease this infernal noise!" shouted Sir Geoffrey finally.

"You're back!" I didn't tell him I'd almost given up. The hint of madness hadn't instilled much confidence in me. "Do you have news?"

"The French draw near."

"I meant news about my escape. Did you speak with Meredith?"

"I did. After she calmed and rallied her wits, I followed her to see the other maiden, Alice. Alas, Alice is asleep and cannot be woken."

"Asleep!" That explained why she hadn't come to assist me. "Did Meredith shake her?"

"She did, and shouted at her, and poured water over her feet." He sounded agitated, his concentration not on the conversation.

"Why her feet?"

"She didn't want to ruin the maiden's hair."

I rolled my eyes. "And then what happened?"

"Nothing. She slumbered on."

Poor Alice was in one of her deep sleeps again, tortured by dreams of the queen chasing her, I suspected.

The chain mail rattled, moving farther away, then drew close again. He must be standing right in front of me. "Forgive me, Mistress Holloway, I must leave now. This is the safest place for you at present anyway."

"What are you talking about, Sir Geoffrey? What's happening?"

"The French will unlikely negotiate."

I clicked my tongue. If I could grab hold of a ghost, I would have strangled him. I was so close to freedom, and yet so far away. I needed his help. Without him or Meredith or Alice...

"Can you speak to Meredith again on my behalf?" I asked. "Urge her to come down here on her own. Tell her Mrs. Denk hasn't fed me in over a day."

"The head woman is busy. I don't like her, but she has more than your wellbeing on her mind at present."

"What could possibly be more important than my life?" I shouted.

"The French."

I groaned. It was hopeless.

"They're setting up siege equipment," he went on. Once again, the rattle of the chain mail grew distant. "It may be a long, drawn-out battle. The castle isn't well defended anymore, and I doubt a gaggle of schoolgirls will be of much use to me. But I must try. Inglemere will not fall! Not as long as I haunt its corridors." His voice faded and the chain mail stopped rattling.

"Sir Geoffrey?"

No response.

I felt my way around the walls, and stumbled from column to column. "Sir Geoffrey, are you there?"

No answer. He was gone.

I crumpled to the floor and burst into tears, but they didn't last long. Crying would not get me out, although it made me feel a little better. All I could do now was wait, either for Mrs. Denk to come to her senses or for Alice to waken. She couldn't sleep forever, and surely Mrs. Denk wouldn't abandon me altogether. She was cruel but not a murderess.

I tucked my arms against my chest and drew my knees up. It did nothing to warm me, and I shivered uncontrollably. My teeth chattered and it felt like ice slid along my veins. If I remained in the dungeon much longer, I would surely die from the freezing damp.

Would my imp consider that life threatening? I closed my fist around the amber. "I release you." When nothing happened, I repeated the instruction in French, as my mother had told me to do. "*Je libère toi.*"

Again, nothing. I sighed. Perhaps it was a positive thing that my imp didn't consider me to be in imminent danger.

A light tap on the door had me spinning toward the staircase. Had I imagined it?

There it was again, louder. No, not a tap. It was the clank of solid iron on wood. A key? I scrambled across the floor on hands and knees so as not to trip up the bottom step in the dark. My sore palm stung, but I didn't care. "Mrs. Denk?" I would promise to be good from this point on. Well, until my escape from the school. And I would keep that promise too. I didn't want her keen eye on me, watching my every move while I planned my exit.

The door opened a crack, letting in a sliver of light. "It's me," came a girl's voice. "Meredith. Charlie?"

"Meredith!" Thank God. She'd plucked up the courage to rescue me after all.

The door widened and her face appeared in shadow. She held up a candle and squinted into the dimness.

"I've come to get you out. We need you." She glanced behind her and beckoned me to come.

I climbed the stairs and took her offered hand. "Thank you. I was beginning to think I'd die in there."

Her rosy pink lips flattened. "Sir Geoffrey told me Mrs. Denk hasn't fed you. My God, Charlie, that's awful." She stepped away and studied me. Her pert nose wrinkled. "You look terrible."

My dress was dirty, particularly at the knees and hem, and my hands filthy. No doubt evidence of my tears still marked my face too, and I hated to think what my hair looked like. "It's been an ordeal. Thank you for rescuing me. Now, I must face Mrs. Denk. Or escape the castle altogether." I bit my lip, unsure how to proceed.

Her eyes widened, and she glanced anxiously behind her again. "You can't do either, I'm afraid."

A thunderous bang boomed above us, followed by crashing that seemed to go on and on. High pitched screaming followed, only to be drowned out by Meredith's wail.

She flattened herself to the floor and threw her arms over her head. Her candle went out, and she began to cry.

"What was that?" I asked, joining her on the floor.

"They're attacking!" she cried. "Sir Geoffrey said they would. I thought him mad, but I should have listened to him. I should have warned Mrs. Denk not to go out there, and now she's gone too, possibly dead! And we have only a ghost to help us and a few girls and teachers with no military experience. We're going to die, Charlie!"

The entire world had gone mad in one solitary evening. Or had I fallen through a portal to an alternate realm? "Meredith, what *are* you talking about?"

Someone screamed again. It was quickly followed by several more screams, including Meredith's. Another booming crash brought an eerie silence over the castle, however. My stomach plunged. I preferred the screams.

"Meredith!" I shouted, shaking her. "What's happening?"

"The French army is attacking the castle! We're under siege!"

I sat back on my haunches and stared at her. Either she was mad, or I was. There was only one way to find out. I got to my feet, hauling her up as I did so. She sobbed loudly. "Tell me everything that has transpired overnight." I took her hand and dragged her with me.

She planted her feet and pulled back. "I'm not leaving. If the castle falls down, it's safest down there in the dungeon."

"Not if the entrance is blocked by rubble. Trust me, Meredith, the safest place is far away from here. Where are Mrs. Denk and the others?"

"Mrs. Denk left early this morning to negotiate with the army." Her face crumpled. "She didn't return."

"So...it really is the French army, or are you simply repeating what Sir Geoffrey said?"

She hugged her body. "I don't know if they're French or not," she cried. "All I do know is, there are hundreds, if not thousands of soldiers surrounding the castle. Some are mounted, most are on foot. One holds a banner with a red heart on it."

"That is not the French flag."

She swiped at her tears. "An emissary asked for Alice."

"Alice! What has she got to do with any of this?"

"I don't know," she wailed. "But Mrs. Denk refused to hand her over. She demanded to know the meaning of their presence, and the emissary simply stated that

Alice was wanted for treason against their queen and country."

"Which country?"

"I didn't hear."

"What did Mrs. Denk do then?"

"She claimed the entire thing was ridiculous. She thought the locals were having a lark, or a mock battle on school grounds. She was furious, and marched out to confront them and demand they leave. Sir Geoffrey warned her not to, but she couldn't hear him, of course. Only I could, and..." She burst into a fresh round of tears. "...and I didn't pass on his warning...and now she's dead!"

I took her in my arms and patted her back. "We don't know that," I said half-heartedly. My mind reeled with all sorts of scenarios, but one thing became clear. Alice was the key. She'd dreamed about a queen chasing her, and here was the army of a queen on our doorstep, demanding her return.

Alice's dream had come to life.

It was ridiculous, and yet I'd seen some strange things in the last few months. I'd be a fool to dismiss any theories, no matter how fanciful.

I heard Sir Geoffrey shout, but I couldn't make out his words, followed by more screams from the girls. They must be extremely frightened. Meredith whimpered.

I grasped her shoulders. "You must wake Alice." If my theory was correct, then Alice had it in her power to stop the army, simply by waking up. If they were a figment of her dreams, then they would disappear if she wasn't dreaming. If my theory was wrong, however...

"What are you going to do?" Meredith asked.

"Pass on Sir Geoffrey's instructions to the girls. He knows this castle's strengths better than anyone, and

I'd wager he's seen more battles than all of us combined." I picked up my skirts and ran up the stairs. "Go!" I shouted.

I passed a girl in the grip of hysteria on the stairs. I tried stopping her, but she was determined to reach the dungeon. I waited to make sure Meredith didn't succumb to the temptation too, and when I saw her following me, continued on my way up to one of the towers at the top of the castle keep for the best view.

What I saw took my breath away. A large gap yawned in the crenellated battlements. Going by the rubble and the matching gap on the other side, the tower had been blasted by a great force.

I picked my way through the mess, careful not to slip on the icy surface, and peered over the edge. "Dear God." A sea of soldiers dressed in red and white amassed on the frosty lawn, a giant catapult on wheels in their midst. Mounted soldiers ranged behind and to the side of the main army, sunlight glinting off their swords. Most of the soldiers were on foot, either carrying swords or long bows. It was these archers who now removed arrows from their quivers.

A movement to the left caught my eye. Sir Geoffrey! He drifted down to the tower, his attention on the army below. He hadn't seen me.

"Take cover!" he bellowed. "Incoming!"

A hail of arrows arched upward like a flock of swallows then changed course and plunged from the sky. "Jesus!" I ducked back down the winding staircases, out of the way. An arrow slipped down the stairs and came to rest beside me.

Sir Geoffrey's spirit suddenly manifested in the stairwell. His craggy features creased into a frown. "You got out."

"Meredith rescued me," I said on a breath. "Sir Geoffrey...is this truly happening?"

He nodded grimly. "The castle will be lost. We don't have any weapons, and the maidens cannot be expected to fight."

"Where are they?"

"Cowering in their beds."

I could hardly blame them. "Tell me what to do."

Another rainfall of arrows sprinkled onto the tower above. "The main gatehouse has fallen and the French are in the bailey. The catapults have done some terrible damage to the walls."

"So I saw," I said heavily. "Oh, Sir Geoffrey, I'm sorry."

He squared his shoulders, causing his chain mail to ripple. "I heard their commander give orders for the battering ram to be fetched. They'll be inside the keep soon."

"I can't believe it," I muttered, finally digesting what my eyes had seen moments before. Those soldiers were real. Their weapons were real. We'd been thrust into a medieval battle.

Medieval warfare was a bloody, brutal business.

Sir Geoffrey tried to touch my shoulder, but his hand went straight through. He stared at it, as if he'd forgotten he was a spirit. "You must prepare yourself and the other maidens for the worst."

"What do you think the worst will entail?"

The look he gave me was filled with bleak horror. "The French have no morals."

I swallowed. "Alice is our only hope now. I'll try to wake her."

"What can she do?" he called after me as I raced back down the narrow, curving stairs.

"I'll explain later." If it worked.

I almost propelled into Meredith, heading in the opposite direction. I caught her shoulders and steadied her. "Well?" I pressed. "Did you wake Alice?"

The huge dark pools of her eyes filled with fear and sickening horror. She shook her head. "Charlie..." Her voice trembled. "Charlie, she's gone. I can't find Alice."

CHAPTER 3

"What do you mean, she's gone?" I shouted at Meredith. "She can't be gone! She was asleep." And if she woke, wouldn't the army disappear?

"I can't find her." Tears streamed down Meredith's face. She hugged herself, and looked as skittish as a kitten.

The thick walls of the castle blocked the sounds of the army's preparations and Sir Geoffrey's barked commands. I could no longer hear screaming. It felt as if Meredith and I were the only two people alive.

"Have you searched the castle?" I asked. "She must be somewhere."

"I performed a quick search, but not all of the school is accessible anymore. The boulders flung by the catapult damaged some of the walls, and I was too afraid to go onto the towers."

"Is anyone hurt?"

"I don't think so. Some are hiding in the dungeon, thinking that's the safest place."

If we couldn't leave, it may well have been, but it could also act as a trap. "Well done, Meredith, but now you must help me find Alice."

"Why?"

"She's the key to this."

Her tears stopped. She blinked at me. "You're not going to hand her over to them, are you?"

"No! I can't explain it, but I think if she wakes from her dream, the army will disappear."

Her brow creased. "That's nonsensical."

"There are a great many things in this world that don't make sense, Meredith, but I've discovered that it doesn't make them any less real. Take Sir Geoffrey." I glanced back up the staircase to where I'd last seen him.

"Yes," she whispered, wiping her cheeks. "You're right. We'll find her."

I gave her a quick hug. Trembles wracked her, but at least she'd stopped crying. "We'll enlist the help of as many girls as we can. Alice must be here somewhere, either sleepwalking or in a trance."

A thud from below stopped us both short. Meredith grasped my hand hard. "What was that?"

"The battering ram. They're trying to get in. We must hurry. Rally as many as you can from the dungeon. I'm going to begin my search on the towers."

"You can't go out there, Charlie!"

I squeezed her hand. "Go, Meredith. Have courage."

I ran through the grim corridor to the dayroom and drawing room beyond, up another tight flight of winding stairs to the tower. This one was near the back of the castle, a part I'd not yet seen. The spectacular view of the barren winter landscape was marred by the ring of soldiers stomping their feet in the cold. Their numbers weren't as thick as at the front, but getting past them would be impossible.

The tower sported no damage like the ones at the front of the castle and it was easier to move around, although I had to be careful not to slip. My indoor shoes weren't made for the slick conditions.

There was no sign of Alice so I returned inside. I wasn't aware of how cold it had been on the tower until I was out of the breeze. The castle couldn't be called warm by any stretch of the imagination, but my bones no longer felt frozen as they had in the dungeon. Racing hither and thither had its benefits.

Below me, the battering ram once again thumped into the thick double doors at the keep's entrance. I'd loathed the heavy iron bolt and wooden crossbar when I'd first seen them upon my arrival—they only added to my feeling of imprisonment. But now I appreciated them enormously. I wondered who'd slid them closed over the doors after Mrs. Denk left. Perhaps it was Meredith, acting on Sir Geoffrey's instruction.

A sprinkling of terrified screams followed the thump. Good. It meant Meredith had convinced some of the girls to join her in searching for Alice. I would never consider her cowardly again. She may be terrified, but she was forging ahead with the task set for her, despite her fears. *That* was a true measure of courage.

I continued my search across the top of the castle, running up and down stairs until my thighs burned and sweat dampened unmentionable places. The battering ram continued its rhythmic hammering, to the tune of screaming. I rushed past girls in the corridors, searching for Alice in each room, under beds, in cupboards. With every slam of the battering ram, their cries became more and more desperate.

Alice had to be somewhere in the castle. If I were her, and someone was after me, where would I go?

The battering ram slammed into the door again. Wood splintered. Girls screamed. If the army wasn't already inside, they would be soon. Once they were in, would they act like the animals Sir Geoffrey described, or would they leave us alone and go in search of Alice? Did they even know what she looked like?

What if I pretended to be her and gave myself up?

It might work, if they'd never met her. It could buy us some valuable time to continue the search.

I headed past a terrified teacher down to the ground level. It was mostly deserted, the girls having fled as far away from the door as possible.

"Charlie, where are you going?" Meredith called from the main staircase leading up from the castle's central court. "It's too dangerous down there. They'll be through soon."

"I'm going to speak to them."

"No! You shouldn't! Come with us. We're going to lock ourselves in the old kitchen."

I waved her off and hurried to the door. Some of the wooden panels were damaged, and the hinges loose. It wouldn't hold for long.

"One!" came a shout from beyond the door. "Two!"

"Wait!" I cried. "Stop at once! I'll give myself up if you promise to leave everyone in here alone."

"Who are you?" demanded the harsh voice.

"Alice."

Murmurs followed my pronouncement. "Show yourself."

Damnation. If he wanted to see me, that most likely meant he could identify Alice. We looked nothing alike. She was beautiful and fair, while I had brown hair and was shorter, plainer. "I want some promises from you before I do so," I called back.

"The Queen of Hearts does not make promises."

The Queen of Hearts? Good lord, what next? "What will happen to me if I give myself up?"

"Execution, of course!"

I stumbled backward. Execution! "With no trial?"

The soldiers laughed. "Give yourself up, Alice! The queen will not rest until she receives justice for your slights against her!" He began counting again in a guttural voice that cracked on the word "One!"

"The white rabbit," muttered a familiar voice behind me. "Must find the white rabbit."

"Alice!"

She stood in her nightgown with nothing on her feet and no wrap around her shoulders. Her glassy eyes looked straight through me.

"Two!" came the order beyond the door.

"Alice, wake up!" I shook her shoulders, but she continued to stare and mutter something about finding the white rabbit. "Alice, you must wake up now!"

"Three!" roared the commander.

The battering ram slammed into the doors. Wood cracked and the hinges snapped. I grabbed Alice's hand and ran toward the dungeon steps.

But it was too late. The army was through and they'd spotted us. The commander's shout of "Get her!" could barely be heard over the soldiers' triumphant cries.

I dragged Alice after me, but she was almost as lifeless as a rag doll. Progress was slow. Too slow. The fastest soldier lunged for her as we reached the top of the stairs.

I shoved her to the side and we both smacked into the stone wall. The soldier's momentum propelled him down the steps. The sickening crunch of bones and screams of pain became lost amid the battle cries of the other soldiers, almost upon us. I bundled Alice against me and closed my hand around my amber necklace.

"I release you, Imp!"

Nothing happened. Everything had gone quiet. I glanced over my shoulder. We were alone. There were no soldiers, no battering ram, and no distant shouts to signal retreat. They'd simply vanished. I leaned back against the wall and expelled a deep breath. *Thank God.*

Alice stirred in my arms. She blinked at me, her eyes clear and bright. "Charlie?" She looked around, nibbling on her lower lip. "Oh. Oh no. Charlie, I'm so sorry."

"It's all right," I muttered between my heaving breaths. "It's not your fault."

"But they came alive because of me." She eyed me carefully. "Because of my dreams. Do you understand?"

"I had guessed."

"And...you believe me?"

"When you've seen what I've seen, you believe the fantastical without question. But this..." I nodded toward the courtyard where the battered doors lay fractured on the ground. "This is quite fantastical indeed. You must tell me everything you know about your gift, but not now. We must see if anyone is injured."

"Gift," she sneered. "I wouldn't call it that.

I took her hand and we headed up the main stairs. "We looked everywhere for you," I said. "Do you know where you went or have you forgotten everything from your...dream?"

"I haven't forgotten. I never forget, although I lack a certain real world awareness while I'm asleep." She sighed. "I was here the entire time, but I drank the potion to shrink myself."

I stopped. "Shrink yourself! You mean...your real body changed too, not just your dream self?"

She lifted one shoulder. "It's a strange magic."

"Indeed."

"I tried to speak to you in my dream," she went on as we headed up to the uppermost level. "But you couldn't hear me. So I went in search of the White

Rabbit instead. He's a guide, of sorts." I gave her a blank look and she sighed. "Never mind."

We met Sir Geoffrey coming down the stairs, an exultant look on his ghostly face. He grinned at me. "We did it, Mistress Holloway! We forced the French to retreat."

I wouldn't dampen his good mood with the truth. "We did, Sir Geoffrey." To Alice, I said, "Sir Geoffrey is the resident ghost here."

She sidled closer to me. "You can see him?" she asked in hushed tones.

I nodded. "As can Meredith. Come, we must find her. She's been very brave throughout this ordeal."

"She has," Sir Geoffrey said with a firm nod. "I ought to warn you, that woman is walking back. She'll be here any moment."

"Mrs. Denk! I almost forgot about her."

"Girls!" came her distinctive shriek from the doorway below. "Girls!" She clapped her hands, the sound echoing around the walls. "To me! Now!"

"How are we going to explain this to her?" Alice whispered.

"I don't particularly care right now," I said. "We need to check on everyone first."

We headed up the stairs instead of down and found all the teachers and students in the old medieval kitchen, cowering in and around the enormous fireplace.

"Charlie!" Meredith sprang up and rushed to me. She threw her arms around me and squeezed so hard my ribs hurt. "Charlie, Alice, thank goodness you're both all right. We've been so worried."

"Is anyone hurt?" I asked.

"No injuries," she reported, stepping back. "Everyone's in here."

"Thank God," Alice murmured, passing her hand over her eyes. "Thank God."

They crowded around us, hugging and crying as we explained the danger was over, the soldiers all gone, and Mrs. Denk had returned and demanded our presence. No one rushed out to greet her, not even the teachers.

"What happened?" asked one of the senior teachers. "Where did all those soldiers come from? And what did they want with you, Alice?"

"I, er, that is..." Alice bit her lip and shrugged. "It's complicated."

"Her family is the violent, rambunctious sort," I answered for her. "They came to collect her but she didn't want to leave the school. She explained as much to them and they left." I doubted my explanation convinced more than the most gullible. It certainly didn't convince the girls I'd pegged as having supernatural powers. Like me, they'd seen enough strange phenomena in their lifetimes to know that inexplicable things happened from time to time. They alone would get a fuller account later. It was time we wayward girls got to know one another better.

"There you are!" Mrs. Denk stood in the kitchen doorway. She bore no signs of concern or confusion. Her face was as devoid of expression as always. "Why are you all in here, cowering as if your lives were in danger?"

Several women exchanged glances. I inched behind Alice, hoping Mrs. Denk wouldn't single me out and send me back to the dungeon.

"Our lives *were* in danger," one of the teachers said tentatively.

"Nonsense. It was all a show, put on by the villagers. Village idiots, I should say," she muttered. "I'm going to have a stern word with them about frightening my girls and staff like that." She stepped aside and clasped her hands. "Classes are canceled for today. There is much cleaning up to do. Alice, for goodness sake, put on some clothes. When you're decent, come to my office. We'll discuss your punishment for fraternizing with the villagers."

"I don't understand," Alice muttered.

Mrs. Denk's nostrils flared. "Don't pretend innocence. It was *you* they asked for. Who did you upset to cause all this?"

"I...I'm not sure." Alice glanced at me. "I've never met anyone from the village. Indeed, don't blame them. These events came about because of my family. They're quite dramatic when they want to be, and they have wanted me to come home for some time."

"And you refused?"

"Alice loves it here," I said. "She tells me she has learned so much under your tutelage. Haven't you, Alice?"

"Oh yes. I simply adore French and deportment classes. I can see a grand future awaits me now, where before...well, I was very wayward. My mother despaired of me."

Mrs. Denk's lips flattened. "I'm sure she did." She flicked her hand to hurry Alice on her way.

Alice left with a sigh of relief. It would seem she had escaped punishment, for now. I tried to follow her, but Mrs. Denk stepped in my way, blocking me. I braced myself for a fight. If she tried to send me back into the dungeon, I would employ every fighting skill Lincoln had taught me. If I went back down there, I risked never coming out again.

"I see you were released," she said, her tone wintry.

"I managed to escape during the chaos."

The lines above her lips deepened. "I won't ask for the name of your accomplice, but I will require your apology and a promise of good behavior."

"And if I don't?"

Her mouth twitched in what I suspected was an attempt at a smile. "Back in the dungeon you go."

Or I could escape. But it was far too cold outside for me to survive very long without shelter. I could sell the engagement ring and use the money for accommodation and travel, but I had to find a buyer first, and one willing to pay its worth. The nearby village of Inglemere was too small to have a jeweler with the funds to buy it. I must keep to my original plan of escaping in springtime, when the roads were better and I wouldn't freeze to death if I needed to spend the night outside.

I ignored the voice of protest whining in my head and gathered my resolve. "I apologize, Mrs. Denk."

"For your willful behavior." When I merely nodded, she said, "Go on, say it."

"I apologize for my willful behavior yesterday. It won't happen again. I promise not to disrupt class, counter your orders, or speak unless spoken to. I'll be on my best behavior and throw myself on your mercy. Please forgive me, Mrs. Denk." If I was going to commit, I might as well go all the way.

She glared down her nose at me. After several beats, she stepped aside. "You may go."

I hurried out of the kitchen to the room I shared with Alice. She smiled when she saw me. "She set you free!"

"After I groveled sufficiently."

She pulled a face and turned her back to me. "Lace me."

I concentrated on tying her corset laces. "Are you all right after your ordeal?"

"Perfectly fine, but I feel so responsible. The door is completely smashed and everyone was so terrified."

I didn't tell her about the damage done to the castle's towers. She felt awful enough as it was. "No one was harmed, that's the main thing." I finished tying her and turned her to face me. I caught her hands. "I'm going to tell you something that very few people know about me."

"That you see ghosts?"

I bit my lip. "More than that."

Instead of looking horrified, she seemed morbidly fascinated. "How thrilling. You have my utmost silence on the matter, Charlie. I promise I won't tell a soul."

"I'm a necromancer." I told her how I could raise dead bodies and control spirits, none of which caused her to shrink away, revolted. She listened intently as I told her about my real mother, my adoption, and my eventual arrival at Lichfield.

"He abducted you!"

"*That's* the part of my story that disturbs you?" I laughed. "Alice, you're wonderful. Yes, he abducted me but I became aware of another side to him. Perhaps. I think." I waved off the topic, having no wish to dredge it up at that moment. I'd spent an entire morning hardly thinking about Lincoln. It felt like progress.

"I've never met anyone who can see ghosts before," she said as she put on her dress. "And Meredith can too?"

I nodded. "There are others here with supernatural abilities too. And then there's you."

She plopped down on her bed. Our room was small, hardly wide enough to fit both our beds plus the washstand and a narrow chest of drawers we shared. There was no fireplace, and only an embrasure in the window in which to sit.

I sat beside her. "Tell me about yourself, Alice. Tell me why your dreams came to life."

She sighed. "I don't know why, and they haven't always come alive. That was only the second time. The first was just before my parents sent me here. I've always had vivid dreams, you see, even as a child, and always about the same world and creatures. I'd wake up, convinced I'd had tea with the Mad Hatter or met the Cheshire Cat. Mama told me I was being ridiculous and dismissed them as mere dreams. Everyone did. I believed that too, but then the queen became involved."

"The Queen of Hearts?"

She nodded. "Nasty woman, always wanting to cut off people's heads for every slight, no matter how small, and based on flimsy evidence. I pointed out the bias in one of her so-called trials and the next thing I knew, she ordered my arrest. I ran off, but she sent her soldiers after me. I had that dream several times until one day I woke up and my parents were in my room, screaming at me, trying to wake me. The soldiers had come to the house looking for me."

"Bloody hell. Sorry," I added with a wince. "Old habit. What did you do?"

"I didn't do anything, but the very next day, my parents sent me here. They called it a finishing school." She peered up at the ceiling and shook her head. "More like a prison."

"Did they explain why? Did they discuss the dreams with you?"

"No, but they must have connected the soldiers' presence to my dream, otherwise they wouldn't have been so desperate to wake me."

"You didn't ask them why you were that way?"

She shook her head. "My parents aren't people you discuss that sort of thing with. They're very conservative, and appearances are important to them. More important than me," she mumbled into her chin.

I closed my hand over hers. "I'm sure they love you."

"Do they?"

"Of course. You're their daughter."

"Am I?" She sniffed and peered at me through teary eyes. "I don't look like either of them. My mother has red hair and my father's dark. They're both quite short, too."

I put my arm around her. "Don't jump to conclusions until you know for certain."

She stared down at her hands. "I suppose they sent me here because they didn't know what else to do with me. At least they didn't lock me away in a real prison."

"Very true," I muttered, recalling my time in a police holding cell. The castle's dungeon was paradise by comparison.

"Charlie, what am I to do? What if the queen's soldiers return the next time I fall asleep?"

"It has only happened twice so far, the last time being...?"

"Two months ago."

"Did something trigger it then and this time too?"

Her mouth twisted to the side in thought. "I was anxious about you being sent to the dungeon. I pleaded with Mrs. Denk to free you, but she refused. In fact, she said you would be punished more for my impudence." She cringed. "She told me you would go without food for an entire day. I'm sorry, Charlie."

"It's hardly your fault." I hugged her. "I would have done the same thing in your situation. And the other time, two months ago?"

Her face colored. "A business associate of Papa's asked me to marry him. I've known him since I was young. He's older than me by about twenty years, and kindly enough, but I didn't want to marry him. My parents wouldn't listen to my protests and insisted I encourage him. It was awful. I contemplated running away, but then the next thing I knew, I had the dream where everyone came to life. I haven't been in communication with my parents or the gentleman since they sent me here."

"And those are the two worst situations you've found yourself in? You've never been more upset?"

"There was the time my little brother died. I was inconsolable for weeks. My dreams didn't come alive then."

I lay down on the bed and considered how I would feel, given the two situations that had triggered the living dreams. Upset, yes, but angry and frustrated too. As a young woman, few people listened to your opinion, let alone allowed you to make decisions. At least Lincoln, for all his faults, respected me.

I sat up. "Do you think you've ever been angrier?"

She leaned back on her hands. "No-o. Perhaps not."

"Or frustrated?"

"Not both together." Her features lifted and she sprang up. "Charlie, do you think that's it? Do you think it's a combination of anger and frustration that's making my dreams come to life?"

"I don't know. Perhaps."

She paced the room, which she managed in three strides. "You may be right." She turned and paced the other way. "My God, I think you are. I hated the powerlessness I felt both times. I was backed into a corner with no way out."

"A way out was provided by your dreams," I said quietly. "In a rather dramatic way."

She laughed and caught my hands. "You're right. I *know* you are."

"That makes you happy?"

"At least now I know the trigger. It's *such* a relief."

"I imagine it is." I smiled. "I don't suppose you have any food tucked away anywhere? I'm starving."

She gasped. "Of course you are! I'll sneak down to the kitchen and get you something." She gave me a quick hug then left.

I removed my clothes and washed then dressed in fresh linen and a green woolen dress. My hand still hurt so I wrapped some linen around the swelling. I tucked myself into bed, skirts and all, and considered Alice's strange affliction. I was glad she now knew her trigger, but it would be nearly impossible to never feel frustrated and angry again. This entire drama would likely reoccur. Poor Alice. Imagine having an entire army chase you and a powerful queen wanting to chop off your head! It made the killer who was after me and other supernaturals seem tame.

Despite the morning's turmoil, my thoughts wandered to the days before my departure from Lichfield, and the mystery surrounding the deaths of Reginald Drinkwater and Joan Brumley, as well as the attempts on my own life. The murderer had probably committed more crimes too. We'd been deeply suspicious of the untimely deaths of Captain Jasper and the men who'd helped him in his mad scheme to develop a serum to bring dead people back to life. What made it so much worse, however, was the likelihood of someone with access to ministry archives being involved, or perhaps even being the murderer. I wondered if Lincoln had unearthed the culprit yet.

Lincoln.

It was these quiet moments I hated most of all. They allowed me time to think, and I inevitably thought about him, about his change of heart, and what our lives might have been like together if we'd married. Tears burned my eyes and clogged my throat.

Dreaming about that future was pointless. *My* dreams never became real.

Alice returned carrying a covered plate. "I found some slices of cold meat, cheese and bread." She dug into her skirt pocket and pulled out a parcel wrapped in cloth. "And a small slice of fruit cake. Will that do? "

"It's the best meal I've had in an age," I said, accepting the plate. "Thank you, Alice."

***

Mrs. Denk had some local youths clear away the rubble from the turrets and patch up the worst of the damage until more permanent repairs could be undertaken. A carpenter and his apprentice came to fix the front door. With so many men around, we were ordered to resume classes out of sight. I suffered through needlepoint and watercolor painting with a cheery smile that was all show for Mrs. Denk's benefit. When it finally came time for a rest between classes, I gathered the girls whom I'd pegged as supernaturals and led a quiet but enlightening exchange.

I discovered that the two girls whose hands changed to furry paws could in fact change their entire person at will. Sometimes, however, it happened without them realizing. I'd noticed the fire starter lighting the fire in the grate once with her fingers, but there was little more to her trick than that. She conjured the fire and it came. She also never felt cold, a fortunate side effect. Then there were the two girls who could move objects simply by thinking about moving them. It was eerily similar to Reginald Drinkwater's magic, and that put them in direct danger if the killer ever learned of their existence. They were safer here than anywhere, even with Alice's occasional dream coming to life.

While the two body-shifting girls knew about the other, the rest all thought they'd been the lone freaks in the school—or in the world, in the cases of some. Most had been sent to Inglemere by guardians who were frightened of their magic, with Alice being the only one whose actual parents had sent her. The parents of the other girls were all deceased, although some were well informed about their magic and all had been urged to keep it a secret. Learning that there were other supernaturals in the world, aside from themselves, lifted their spirits enormously.

Meredith and I explained our abilities, and not a single girl screwed up her nose when I mentioned raising the dead. I went to bed feeling as if I'd accomplished something important, something that would change those girls' lives more than learning needlepoint or how to greet a duchess. For the first time since leaving Lichfield, I didn't feel so alone, or that my life had come to an end. My future was still uncertain, but I wouldn't be too upset to stay longer at the school. I could endure Mrs. Denk if I had friends.

She summoned me to her office the following afternoon. Dread settled like a lump in my stomach, as I traversed along the grey stone corridors. Had she heard us talking? Did she think us all mad? What if she isolated me from the other students?

I paused at a window. The sun's rays were weak, wintry, but I'd been kept away from windows since the workmen arrived, and I craved a glimpse of the sky. A carriage waited on the drive near the castle steps, a black clad driver huddled into his caped great coat. We had a visitor. How unusual.

It wasn't until I drew closer to Mrs. Denk's office that I realized the visitor must be inside, and that the visit must be on my account. Otherwise, why summon me?

I paused at the door, my heart in my throat. I didn't knock. My hand felt too heavy to lift.

As it turned out, I didn't need to knock. The door opened.

He opened it. Lincoln.

The sight of him sucked the breath from my chest. I couldn't tear my gaze away. I took in every inch of his face, from the tied back hair to the stubbled jaw and small grooves around his mouth. They were more pronounced than the last time I'd seen him, and I had to dig my nails into my palms to stop myself stroking them away. The shadows beneath his pitch black eyes were also deeper. He must have had little sleep. It should have felt like a victory, but it did not.

"Charlie." His flat voice gave nothing away, although the heavy swallow was a small sign that he wasn't entirely indifferent to seeing me. His gaze, too, darted across my face, as if he were comparing the sight to his memories.

I steeled myself against the sudden rush of blood through my veins, but to no avail. It warmed my face, pumped my heart faster, and set every part of me on edge. I certainly wasn't indifferent to seeing him, but I wasn't yet sure how I felt.

"What do you want, Lincoln?"

"I want to take you home."

CHAPTER 4

"We're going to miss you." Alice drew me into a fierce hug and sniffed.

"And I you," I said. "I'll write often."

"That would be wonderful. I never receive correspondence."

She passed me on to Meredith who also asked if I'd write. "Of course," I said. In her ear, I whispered, "Take care of one another. You never have to feel alone again."

She gave me a wobbly smile. "Thank you, Charlie. I'll never forget you and what you did for us."

I laughed. "I didn't do anything except point out some things you would have observed sooner or later." To the ghost hovering just behind her, I added, "Take care of them, Sir Geoffrey. Keep the French at bay."

He nodded solemnly. "You're a courageous lass. Safe journey."

I hugged each of the supernatural girls and once again told Alice that if living at the school became unbearable, she only needed to write. I'd first mentioned it when I'd returned to my room to pack and inform the other girls that I was leaving. Alice had sat in shock for a long time, her eyes full of unshed tears. It had taken some convincing before she believed she would be fine without me and that her dreams might not come alive again now that she knew her trigger. At least she no longer felt as alone as she had before. She had friends in the other supernaturals.

Our farewells were all too brief. Lincoln wanted to leave Inglemere immediately to catch the train out of York early the following morning. I was not looking forward to the journey back to London with him.

"Goodbye, Miss Holloway," Mrs. Denk said with a flare of her nostrils. "It was a pleasure having you at my school."

"If it was such a pleasure, why did you punish me at every opportunity?"

If I hadn't felt Lincoln move to stand at my back, I would have known by Mrs. Denk's gaze lifting and the flattening of her lips. "She exaggerates," she said.

"Charlie doesn't exaggerate," he said with ice-cold calm.

"Punish any of the other girls in such a manner, and we'll send the authorities here." I found it difficult to keep the triumph out of my voice. I'd wanted to experience this victory over her ever since my arrival.

Mrs. Denk's nose whistled with her heavy breaths, but she didn't say anything. I wondered if my threat or Lincoln's presence explained her stony silence. Behind her, several of the girls bit back smiles.

I climbed into the carriage with my reticule, Lincoln behind me. He closed the door, and I waved at my friends through the window until we passed through the gatehouse and I could no longer see them.

"How did she punish you?" he asked.

"It no longer matters."

"It matters to me."

I couldn't look at him, so continued to stare at the barren winter scenery out the window. "I didn't like deportment class. Or French. Or being told what to do all the time."

"Were you harmed?"

"Not really." His pause compelled me to glance at him. His intense dark stare was as fathomless as a deep winter lake. "What made you change your mind?"

"I thought your life was in danger."

"How did you—? Oh. Your senses." I spread my gloved hands over my reticule on my lap. My engagement ring was inside. Had he noticed that it wasn't on my finger earlier? He must have. He noticed everything. "The situation resolved itself without anyone getting hurt. So why are you still collecting me if I am no longer in danger here? I was under the impression my presence at the school would be a permanent arrangement."

Weighty silence filled the cabin for several beats. I thought he wouldn't answer, then he said, "I want you back at Lichfield."

I didn't suspect for a moment that he'd missed me or that he loved me. Perhaps he was capable of feeling guilt, however, or his strong sense of duty meant he felt obliged to keep me safe personally. He'd told me the murderer hadn't yet been found, and we both knew the killer would seek me out sooner or later, even here.

I broke my gaze and returned to looking out the window. Low stone walls clung to the barren hills in the distance, with the occasional tree standing sentinel near a barn. The muddy, pitted roads slowed our pace and made the cabin rock relentlessly. I had a devil of a time keeping my knees from bumping Lincoln's. The space was far too small.

"Tell me what happened to endanger you," he said in a rumbling, rich voice.

"No," I said to my reflection. "I don't feel like talking to you."

That ended any discussion between us all the way to York. I even managed not to meet his gaze again. If he was looking at me, I couldn't tell. The only time we acknowledged one another was when he drew out a blanket from the storage compartment beneath his seat. He handed it to me, and I laid it across my lap, politely thanking him.

He'd taken rooms in a hotel near a railway station. My room had its own small sitting room where I informed him I would eat supper. He didn't ask to join me and I didn't invite him.

"Goodnight, Charlie," he said stiffly at the door. The porter had gone inside with my luggage. "If there's anything you need, my room is next to yours."

"There is something, as it happens." I opened my reticule and felt inside. "I need to give this back to you."

I held out the ring. He kept his hands behind his back but his shoulders stiffened. "Keep it."

"No." When he didn't move, I went to slip the ring into his coat pocket.

His hand whipped out and caught my wrist. His grip was firm but not bruising. I could have pulled free but didn't. His gaze pinned me. "It's yours," he said quietly.

The porter emerged from my room. He cleared his throat and skirted around us. Lincoln let me go.

"I don't want the bloody ring," I said through gritted teeth, loud enough for the retreating porter to hear. "I don't even want to look it at. It was a symbol of our engagement, and we are no longer engaged." I slipped the ring into Lincoln's pocket. He didn't try to stop me. "Goodnight."

I stepped into my room and kicked the door closed. The fire in the sitting room burned low. I added more coals and stoked it up before flopping onto a chair with an enormous sigh. It had been a long, trying afternoon, and I felt exhausted. Keeping my emotions in check had been tiring, but now that I was alone, I let my tears out. When that didn't make me feel better, I threw a cushion at the wall. It did nothing to relieve my anger. I thought I'd set the hurt and anger behind me, but seeing him again had brought it all back to the surface again.

Yet overriding all that was sheer relief at the thought of going to London again, and Lichfield in particular. I couldn't wait to see Seth, Gus and Cook. I wanted to ride my horse, sleep in my own bed, roam the estate and see what changes appeared in the winter garden. Being near Lincoln once again was a large part of it, but not all. I doubted I could ever feel the blind adoration I'd felt for him before. His actions had cured me of that.

I was still a little exhausted from my dungeon ordeal and went to bed early. I slept better than I had in days. A porter came in the morning to help me with my luggage. Lincoln waited in the foyer, a small brown suitcase at his feet. He picked it up and took mine from the porter.

"Good morning," he said, eyeing me closely. I looked away. "Did you sleep well?"

"Yes."

We didn't speak as we headed to the station across the road. I carried my hat box, which he stored for me above my head in our train compartment. Our *private* compartment. It seemed I had to endure his presence for the entire journey.

"How long before we reach London?" I asked as the train rolled away from the station in a cloud of steam and soot.

"We'll be there early afternoon. Are you warm?"

"Warm enough."

Lincoln set his case on the seat beside him and opened it. Sitting atop his spare shirt was a fur muff that he handed to me. Beneath the muff was a book. I recognized it as the one I'd been reading before I left Lichfield. A blue ribbon marked my page. He gave me the muff then held out the book. A small crease appeared between his brows as he realized I couldn't turn pages with my hands inside a muff.

"I'll turn the pages for you," he said.

"That won't be necessary." I handed back the muff and took the book. "My gloves are adequate, thank you." I settled near the window and opened the book to the marked page. I read it twice and still didn't take in a single word.

I gave up after my third attempt at the same page. There would be no concentrating on this task or any other. I felt much too aware of Lincoln and my own reaction to him. My heart hadn't ceased its hammering all morning.

I hazarded a glance at him, only to find him looking at me.

"May I ask a question about the threat on your life?" he said.

"You may."

"Was it a result of something the headmistress did to you?"

I shook my head. "It was the Queen of Hearts' fault."

"And she is?"

"A figment of Alice's imagination. Or, rather, her dreams. They come alive, sometimes."

His brows lifted. It was the most movement of the hard planes of his face since greeting me. The old, stony-faced Lincoln Fitzroy certainly hadn't been set aside, even though he had changed his mind and collected me. "She's a supernatural," he said. It wasn't a question.

"She and some others at the school. Aside from Alice, there's a medium, two who can move objects with their minds, a fire starter, and two who change form. I gathered as much information as I could from them last night—about themselves, their families, and their abilities. The report is in my belongings. I was going to send it to you, but I can transfer the information to the ministry files myself when we get...back to Lichfield." I'd been about to say "home," but I couldn't allow myself to feel that way about the house yet. Not until I knew what my future held. "That's if we're going there."

"We are. You never have to leave again."

A weight I hadn't known had been there lifted from my shoulders. *Home.* I was going home—forever, if I wished. Or until he changed his mind again. "Nevertheless, I won't allow my hopes to rise this time," I muttered.

He went very still. Only his fingers moved, curling into the fur of the muff. "I won't send you away again, Charlie. You have my word."

I spluttered a harsh laugh as my temper rose. It hadn't been far from the surface since he'd walked back into my life, and I could no longer contain it. "Your word! And what is that worth? You promised that I would have a home at Lichfield, yet you sent me away. You promised to marry me, and yet you ended the engagement. Your word holds no weight with me."

I turned my shoulder to him and stared out the window. Hot tears burned my eyes but didn't shed.

Part of me wished I was back at the school, getting to know my new friends further. It wasn't lost on me that one of the reasons he'd given for sending me there had been so I could have a normal life and make friends, and I had done exactly that, in a way.

Our compartment door opened, and I turned just in time to see him walk out. He shut the door. Despite wanting to go after him, I remained seated. What I wanted and what I should do were two entirely different things. From this moment on, I would listen to my head more than my heart. Listening to my heart led to it breaking.

It was easier to concentrate on my book without him there, and I almost finished it by the time we reached London. Lincoln didn't rejoin me until the train slowed and chugged into the station. He did not meet my gaze.

He took down my luggage and indicated that I should go ahead of him. The platform was crowded and he remained close, his alert gaze darting around, looking for signs of danger. I would have to remain aware too, now that I was back in London. I would also have to remain at Lichfield until the murderer was caught. One prison had been swapped for another, but at least Lichfield housed the people I loved. And there were no deportment lessons.

The road outside King's Cross Station was just as busy as the platforms and concourse inside, despite the horrid weather. London had heralded my return with sleeting rain. It pelted from the sky and soaked through my clothing in the seconds it took to race from the station exit to the nearest waiting hack.

I climbed inside while Lincoln spoke to the driver and secured our luggage. He joined me moments later. Drips of water trickled from his hairline into his collar.

His hand left a wet patch on the seat when he lifted it to wipe his forehead.

"Sorry," he said, out of the blue.

"The weather is hardly your fault." I peered out the window because I liked looking at him too much, and looking at him played havoc with my emotions. "Are Seth and Gus too busy to collect us?"

"They left."

My head whipped round to face him. "Pardon?"

"They no longer wished to work for me."

I blinked. "Oh," was all I could manage.

"They might come back when they learn you're home."

Seth and Gus gone. Surely they had too much at stake simply to walk away. They both needed the work, and they both believed that unmasking the killer was important. Lincoln must be wrong. No doubt they'd expressed their anger with him over sending me away, so perhaps he'd interpreted that anger as something more.

"Or they might decide to stay away," he went on. "If that's so, I'm sure they'll visit you."

I removed my soggy hat and set it on my lap. "What about Cook?"

"He's still at Lichfield, as far as I know." He pulled his watch out of his pocket and flipped open the case. "I have to go out again after we get back. The supernaturals listed in the archives need to be warned that their life is in danger."

"Not all of them, surely. Only the ones whose magic could be used to bring back the dead."

"I'll start with them."

"You've made a list?"

"I don't need to."

Of course. Everything was safely stored in his perfect memory.

"You need Seth and Gus to come back and assist you. Fetch them first then split the list by three."

"It'll be faster if I work alone."

I doubted that but I was in no mood to argue with him over his stubbornness again. I wouldn't win.

It wasn't a long drive to Lichfield Towers, thank goodness. I couldn't decide what was worse—the tense silence or my wet clothes. The familiar high fences and hedges of the beautiful properties at the edge of Hampstead Heath made me forget both, however. Glimpses of the lovely homes through the gates shed my dreary mood and quickened my heart. Despite the awkwardness between Lincoln and me, despite the grim weather, and the prospect of Seth and Gus not returning, I didn't want to be anywhere else.

My breath caught in my throat as we drove through the heavy iron gates and along the winding drive. Lichfield loomed ahead, its wings spread in a welcome. I used to think it gloomy, its central tower forbidding, but no longer. There was nothing more homely than its gray stone walls and the smoke drifting from three of its chimneys. If Seth and Gus no longer lived there, why were there three fires? Had Lincoln told Doyle when to expect us?

The butler greeted us at the doorway with two umbrellas. He opened the carriage door and gasped upon seeing me. "Miss Holloway!"

"Good afternoon, Doyle. You weren't expecting us?"

He looked quite foolish with his mouth ajar and his eyes wide. "No. I, er, was given no warning." He glanced past my shoulder to Lincoln then handed me an umbrella. "Welcome home."

"Thank you, Doyle. It's wonderful to see you again. But I insist you call me Charlie."

He held out the other umbrella to Lincoln, emerging behind me, but he refused it, and once again got thoroughly wet as he took down the luggage. I hurried up the steps and glanced at my surroundings. Little had changed. The only difference was the calling cards in the salver on the table by the door. Visitors had called in Lincoln's absence. Five, in fact, all women, and very well to-do going by the thickness of the cards and the toff-sounding names. I stamped down on the pang of jealousy screwing into my chest. His callers were none of my affair, anymore.

I continued to the kitchen, stepping lightly so as not to alert Cook to my presence. He stood at the central table, his sleeves rolled to the elbows, his hands buried in dough. He did not look up.

"God, I missed these delicious smells," I said with a smile.

He glanced up. Without so much as a dusting off of his hands, he rounded the table and scooped me up. He was warm and soft, like one of his soufflés, and smelled like flour and butter and spices.

"It's so good to see you again," I said, pulling back to look at him. His eyes sparkled and a grin split his moon-like face.

"And you!" He glanced past me. "You escaped? Does he know?"

I laughed. "He fetched me. I don't know why."

"He missed you," he said with typical bluntness. "He ain't a machine; he just want folk to think he is." He laughed and hugged me again. "Thank God you be back. It be hell here since you left. Seth and Gus be gone."

"I heard. Do you think they'll come back?"

He nodded. "Once they hear of your return. Only I'm not sure where to find them."

"Then how will we inform them?"

"Seth will be in touch with his mother."

"His mother?"

He grinned. "The hoity toity Lady Vickers be living here now. You'll meet her, soon enough." He told me to wait and fetched something wrapped in a cloth from the pantry. He handed it to me. "I were saving this for Lady V, but you have it." I unwrapped three slices of cold beef and ate one while Cook watched. "Take it with you upstairs. Go have a bath. You be wet and cold." He nudged me with his elbow and returned to his dough. "These biscuits be ready by the time you get out."

I took the service stairs to the second floor and kept an eye open for Lady Vickers as I hurried to my old rooms. I wasn't ready to meet her yet. A warm bath was called for to fortify my nerves first.

Lincoln emerged from his rooms, already changed into dry clothes. His damp hair hung in tangled waves to the nape of his neck. He carried his jacket and tie and the top button of his shirt was undone. My heart skipped at the sight.

He spotted me before I could duck into my old rooms and pretend I hadn't seen him. His pace slowed, as if he was surprised to see me. Or perhaps he didn't want to get too close. "I know this is awkward for you," he said as he drew near, "but I hope you can bear it."

I squared my shoulders. "It's not awkward for you?"

His hand settled on the door handle, blocking my exit. "I...don't know."

"What do you mean, you don't know?"

His Adam's apple bobbed and his knuckles went white. "I feel a lot of things right now, but I can't separate them. They're jumbled together. Like the mixture for one of Cook's cakes." His gaze dipped, as if he could no longer meet mine. He opened the door. "I'll be scarce in the near future as I warn the supernaturals and continue with the investigation."

I wondered how hard it had been for him to tell me about his feelings. He wasn't a man who liked to discuss emotions. Sometimes, I wasn't sure he had the same emotional range as the rest of us. I was beginning to think that his regimented and lonely childhood didn't completely explain his lack of empathy, and it was more probable that he lacked a piece in his heart that the rest of us possessed.

"The committee won't be told of your return," he said. "Nor anyone else. That should give you some freedom for the time being."

"You're not ordering me to remain here?"

"Ordering you hasn't worked before; I see no reason why it'll work this time."

"If I do go out, I'll be careful."

He inclined his head in a nod and walked off.

"You're limping," I said before he'd gone too far.

His step changed to his normal one. "You're mistaken."

Liar. He'd definitely been limping. I resisted the urge to go after him and retreated to my rooms instead. I didn't care if he limped. I didn't care if his entire leg fell off. He could go to hell and stay there, for all I cared. I would never again worry about his wellbeing. He certainly didn't worry about mine.

***

I returned to the kitchen via the service stairs again. It was easier to avoid Lady Vickers that way. I had not, however, anticipated running into her maid.

"Who are you?" I blurted upon seeing the pretty woman carrying a tray up the stairs.

"Bella Briggs, miss." She bobbed an awkward curtsey that almost saw the covered plate slide off the tray. She caught it just in time, only to over correct the tray. "Bloody hell!"

I grasped the tray's edge and helped her right everything on it before a disaster occurred.

She giggled. "Sorry, miss. Forgot myself there. You won't tell her ladyship, will you?"

"I won't if you won't. You're Lady Vickers' maid?"

"At your service."

"Don't curtsey!"

She giggled again. There appeared to be no malice in her, but I was still wary. We'd been duped before. The last woman we'd employed had ended up kidnapping me. While Bella seemed utterly guileless, it was best to be cautious.

"Mr. Fitzroy oversaw your employment himself, did he?" I asked.

"Seth did." She thrust out a hip and her full lips curved into a seductive smile. No need to ask how she'd got the position. It was unlikely to be for her skill at balancing a full tray, and more likely to be her skill at pleasing Seth in bed. I wondered if his mother knew. "D'you know when he'll be back?"

"Hopefully soon." I nodded at the tray. "Can you manage that up the stairs?"

"Course." She headed past me without a backward glance, which was probably just as well.

I continued to the kitchen and tucked into the biscuits Cook had made. They were still warm. Doyle poured me a cup of tea from the pot by the stove.

"You still got your pet?" Cook whispered when Doyle went to fetch a bottle of wine from the cellar.

I touched the amber orb beneath my clothing. "Still got it, and I didn't have to use it once. Well, almost that one time when the Queen of Hearts' soldiers attacked."

If he'd had eyebrows they would have shot up his forehead. Doyle returned before I had a chance to explain. I wasn't yet sure what the butler knew, and since Cook didn't ask any questions about the soldiers,

I assumed Doyle was still in the dark about the ministry's true purpose. I couldn't imagine his ignorance would last much longer with the oddities we frequently encountered.

"Mr. Fitzroy is limping," I said to them both. "Did something happen to him while I was away?"

"A circus strongman were murdered," Cook said with a shake of his bald head. "Death investigated, but I don't recall him getting injured." He looked to Doyle.

Doyle spent a long time reading the wine bottle label.

"Doyle?" I prompted. "What is it? What happened?"

The butler cleared his throat. "It would be ill-advised for me to mention something that Mr. Fitzroy wouldn't want you to know." He didn't look entirely convinced by his own words, however, and I didn't think it would take much to get him to tell me.

"He won't punish you." I glared at Cook when he opened his mouth to protest. "Come now, Doyle, I only have Mr. Fitzroy's interests at heart. Does he need to see a doctor?"

Doyle sighed and plopped down on a stool positioned at the table. "I don't know. He hasn't confided in me, but I suspect his feet need tending to. There was a lot of blood."

"Blood!"

"On the carpet in his sitting room. He'd tried to clean it up, but it's a devil to get blood out."

"Amen," Cook muttered.

Doyle's lips parted and a small wheeze escaped.

Cook plucked at his apron. "Not human blood." He turned to me, his back to Doyle, and winked.

"I found bloodied glass, too," Doyle went on. "He'd thrown it out, but I saw it hidden amongst the other rubbish. I didn't go specifically looking, mind," he protested, despite no one accusing him of doing so.

"What sort of glass?" Cook asked.

"Again, I wasn't trying to pry into Mr. Fitzroy's business."

"But?"

Doyle sighed. "But it looked to be a tumbler. It smelled of brandy."

"He cut his foot on glass," I said, numbly. That must have been painful. No wonder he was limping. "How did he break a tumbler? And which foot?"

"Both, I'd say, and on the soles, going by the distance between the stains and their shape," he added.

"He *walked* over broken glass!" But Lincoln could avoid shards easily enough by stepping across furniture instead of the floor to his bedroom to get shoes. Was he drunk? "Did he go mad in my absence?"

Doyle and Cook didn't say anything, and neither met my gaze.

I set aside my teacup and leaned forward. "Tell me," I urged. "Tell me everything."

"There you are!" The powerful voice filled the kitchen as thoroughly as the speaker's tall, solid frame filled the doorway. A handsome woman with thick hair tumbling over her shoulders stood in the doorway, hands on hips. Her hair was the same color as Seth's with only a little gray here and there. "Briggs said I would find you here. What are you talking to the servants for? Come, Charlotte. I need to speak with you." She turned and strode away, not stopping to look back when I didn't follow. Clearly she expected me to catch up.

"Go on, Charlie," Cook said, thrusting his chin in the direction Lady Vickers had gone. "You go and tell her you won't be spoken to like that. You be the lady of the house, not her."

"You're right." I stood and tugged on my sleeves.

It wasn't until I had almost reached the drawing room that I wondered if Cook was over-stating my role. Was I still the lady of the house? Or had I lost that title after my engagement to Lincoln ended?

CHAPTER 5

From afar, it was difficult to reconcile the woman with the lovely fair tresses as having a grown son. Even dressed in deep mourning black, Lady Vickers was attractive, albeit with a rather forbidding air. Perhaps if she smiled she would appear softer, more approachable, but the stern set of her brow and stiff shoulders served as a reminder that she considered herself far above me. It wasn't until I drew closer to her, seated on the sofa, that I saw the whiteness of her knuckles and the worry in her eyes.

"Good afternoon, Lady Vickers," I said with a bob of my head. "I'm pleased to finally meet you."

"And I you, Miss Holloway."

"Please, call me Charlie."

"And you must refer to me as madam. Ma'am is acceptable too. Not my lady. You're not a servant."

I sighed and wished I'd stayed in the kitchen. She patted the sofa cushion, and I sat beside her, biting back a retort that I wasn't a dog. I didn't want to offend Seth's mother, particularly if we had to muddle along in one another's company. Lichfield Towers was large but not large enough that we could avoid the other. Just like I wouldn't be able to avoid Lincoln.

"Seth told me all about you." It sounded like a warning, and I expected her to list the numerous reasons why I wasn't fit to be friends with her son. "He admires you." My surprise must have shown on my face because she smiled. I was right; it did soften her appearance. "He tells me you're the only one who can handle Mr. Fitzroy. If it's true, that is quite a feat indeed."

"If it were true, he wouldn't have sent me away."

"He fetched you back, didn't he?"

"Even so, he's not someone who can be *handled*. Not by anyone."

"No need to be snippy with *me*, Charlie. It was Seth's observation, not mine."

I sucked air between my teeth and let it out slowly. "How long do you plan on staying at Lichfield, madam?"

"As long as necessary." Her gaze shifted to her hands in her lap. "My friends cannot accommodate me at the moment. I'm sure they will soon, however."

I felt horrible. The poor woman had created a scandal by running off to America with her footman, and now that he'd died and she'd returned to England, she would have found doors closed and the invitations non-existent. The calling cards would indicate otherwise, however. "You're most welcome to stay here as long as you like," I said.

"Mr. Fitzroy has already made that clear to me. I must say, I like it here, despite the house's size."

"It's too large for you?"

She laughed. "My dear girl, this drawing room is a *quarter* the size of my old one."

She must mean her grand estate in England, not her American house. From what Seth told me, her accommodations in New York had been unfortunate, to say the least. Her second husband hadn't been able to keep his new wife in the style she'd been accustomed to as Lady Vickers. She may have retained her title, but she'd lost her home, friends and reputation when she wed the footman. A heavy price for love. I hoped he'd made her happy.

"I hope you won't be too uncomfortable," I told her with as much sweetness as I could muster. "Or find our company too dull. I'm afraid we rarely have callers."

"That has already changed since my arrival. As much as I would like to say they've come to call upon me, it's my Seth and Mr. Fitzroy they've come to see. Since the ball, the young ladies are rather taken with them both."

"Ball? Lincoln went to a ball?" And here I thought he'd been busy chasing murderers. He'd been to a ball!

"Lady Harcourt's annual Christmas event last week. It was quite the sensation when we three turned up."

"I can imagine."

She patted my hand. "Now, my dear, I know you and Mr. Fitzroy were once engaged, so I do hope I haven't upset you by telling you about the ball and the callers, but I felt you ought to know. If I were in your position, I would appreciate the knowledge."

I nodded. It might seem odd, but I did appreciate her telling me, and hearing her put it like that, her gossiping didn't come across as malicious.

"I also want to assure you that Mr. Fitzroy behaved very properly and hasn't encouraged any particular girl," she went on. "He seems like the sort of man who respects your feelings and will try his utmost to protect your reputation. I'm sure he'll put it about that *you* ended the engagement, and he'll then wait a suitable period before pursuing another."

I laughed. "Madam, my reputation is hardly worth protecting. As to pursuing another, I'm quite sure he has no interest in marriage, either to me or anyone else."

"That may be so, but as to your reputation, I beg to differ."

I arched my brow. "Seth has told you that I lived on the streets for several years, dressed as a boy, has he not?"

She didn't bat an eyelid at my bluntness. "He did, but few know your past. If we put it about that you are my friend, or ward, and brush over the particulars, no one will think you're anything but a gently-bred girl."

"You wish to lie to your friends? To what purpose?"

"To catch you a suitable husband, of course." She blinked at me as if she thought my question utterly idiotic.

I blinked back, thinking *she* was the idiotic one.

"I'm sure I can snare you a gentleman far superior to Mr. Fitzroy. You're pretty and have a neat figure. You have spirit, too, which some men like. And those eyes! If you play your cards right, you'll have them falling to their knees in no time."

I held my hands up and shook my head. "Thank you for your kind words, but I'm not interested in finding a husband."

She took my hand in both of hers. Her gaze turned sympathetic. "Dear girl, I know you're feeling hurt right now, but you mustn't wait too long. You're almost nineteen."

And yet I'd hardly lived. Perhaps in her world, girls over the age of twenty were no better than the scraps left after a meal, but not in mine. I'd seen very little of the countryside, and only just learned to ride a horse. There suddenly seemed like a lot to do before I settled down and became a wife. It was odd how I'd only begun to feel that way now and not before going north.

I'd certainly been eager to be Lincoln's wife a mere two weeks ago.

"If I am to assist with your launch into society, then I want you to promise me one thing." Lady Vickers had become stiff and formal again, her chin thrust out in queenly arrogance.

It was more interesting to discover what her single condition was than argue with her over my "launch". "Go on."

"I want your assurance that you will not chase after my Seth."

"Pardon?" I spluttered.

"If I am to champion you to the right people, you must promise not to try to snare my son. It's nothing personal, my dear. While I'm sure you would be a fine wife for him, he cannot wed a poor girl. He requires a wealthy heiress to help restore us to our rightful position."

I burst into laughter, only to stop abruptly when she looked offended. "You have my word, madam. I will leave Seth for the heiresses to fight over. I'm sure he'll be very popular."

That seemed to appease her somewhat. She puffed out her considerable chest and a small smile lifted her face. "He already is. His attendance at the ball signaled his readiness to take a wife, hence all the callers of late."

That probably meant Lincoln's attendance had been taken the same way. It would explain Lady Vickers thinking he wanted to marry, in time. I wondered if he knew that his presence at the ball had been a signal of his availability to the better part of London.

"That's the problem, you see," Lady Vickers went on. "Seth's not here to receive his callers. It's becoming increasingly difficult to make excuses for his absence."

"Lincoln suggested that he and Gus might return now that I'm back."

"He did leave in something of a lather over Mr. Fitzroy's treatment of you." Her lips flattened, but I couldn't discern what she thought of that.

"It's settled then. Will you send word to Seth tonight or wait for tomorrow?"

She frowned. "Charlie, you don't seem to understand. I don't know where he is."

"He didn't tell you? His own mother?"

"He doesn't think our relationship requires me to know where he is all of the time," she said tightly.

"He ought to at least tell you where he's living."

"Quite." She sighed. "I was hoping you could find him for me. Perhaps the cook knows."

"You didn't ask him?"

She wrinkled her nose. "I thought you could."

"I've already asked, and he doesn't know, but I have an inkling. Gus is close to his great aunt. He probably told her his movements. I suspect if we find Gus, we'll find Seth. I'll send word to her in the morning."

"No, no, no. We must fetch him back tonight. Goodness knows where he's living. I hate to think of him spending a freezing night out there alone. He ought to be *here*."

I doubted Seth was either cold or alone. Most likely he was in the warm bed of one of his mistresses. I just hoped it wasn't Lady Harcourt. While he'd finally seen what a viper she could be, he was still vulnerable when a pretty face and lush figure were thrust in his face.

"You wish me to send word tonight? I suppose Doyle can take a message."

She shook her head. "Let's go in person. It'll be faster."

"You wish us *both* to go?" It wasn't safe out there for me with the murderer on the loose.

But no one knew I was back. The murderer wouldn't be waiting for me at the gate. Even Lincoln had given me permission to leave, in a way.

"I'll gather my coat and gloves," I said, rising. "And I'd best tell Cook to pass on a message to Lincoln in case he returns and we're not here." It wouldn't be wise to pull the dragon's tail by failing to keep him informed of my movements.

***

I made sure to lie as flat as I could across the coach's seat so that only Lady Vickers, sitting opposite, would be visible to anyone watching. I added "hiding in conveyances" to my list of reasons for not wearing corsets and waited for her to declare it safe to rise before sitting up. Dusk muted what little color the city could muster—the red and green of a holly bush, the blue of a woman's hat ribbon—but at least it wasn't raining. The versatile Doyle wouldn't get wet driving us to Gus's great-aunt's home on Broker Row near the Seven Dials district.

Bella Briggs had fixed Lady Vickers' hair and fastened a perky black hat on top, but the hat had already begun to slip and the hairstyle resembled sagging sails around her ears. Clearly hair wasn't one of Bella's talents. Lady Vickers remained vigilant, having taken it upon herself to keep watch for ne'er do wells as we approached the bleaker areas of the city. I wasn't sure if she was protecting me from the murderer or simply looking out for thieves. I didn't tell her that I used to live near Broker Row with a gang of boys when I'd been about fifteen. She looked horrified enough by the grimy faces and ragged children.

"Wait here," I said, as Doyle slowed the coach. "I'll see what I can learn from Mrs. Sullivan."

"You can't go out there alone!" Lady Vickers said.

I thrust my arm across the door, blocking her exit. "I'll be fine. It's best if you stay here and keep an eye on the coach."

She clasped her coat closed at her throat. "You're right. Doyle can't manage on his own. But will you be all right, my dear?"

"Of course. I'm used to places like this. Besides, it's not yet dark." Darkness brought out the real dangers. Few respectable people ventured outside on a cold night near Seven Dials, but many disreputable ones went in search of mischief.

The frosty air nipped at my nose and cheeks as I stepped down onto the pavement. I nodded at Doyle but he was too busy surveying the street for dangers to notice. Mrs. Sullivan lived in a narrow tenement lit by a hissing lamp that would fail to penetrate the darkness in another hour. I quickly knocked and was glad when the door was just as quickly opened by the broad-faced charwoman herself. She greeted me eagerly and asked me to join her and the girls—young, homeless women she took in from time to time—but I politely refused.

Moments later I recited an address to Doyle and climbed back into the coach. We lurched forward before I'd completely shut the door.

"Did she say if Seth is there too?" Lady Vickers asked.

"No. If he's not, Gus will know where to find him."

Gus had taken a room in an old house in Clerkenwell; it must have once been home to gentry but now looked out of place among the modern tenements on either side of it. Where they stood strong and upright, the house leaned to the right and seemed to cling to its patch through sheer luck. It took some moments for the door to be opened, and by Gus himself, no less.

"Charlie!" He blinked rapidly, as if he assumed his eyes were playing tricks, then drew me into a warm hug. "Bloody hell! You escaped! Blimey, you'd better come in. Once word gets out, he'll be after you."

I laughed. "I didn't escape. Lincoln fetched me. Apparently he changed his mind."

His eyes narrowed. The one with the scar became a mere slit among the muscular bulges of his face. It wasn't a handsome face, but it was wonderful to see it. I hugged him again. He chuckled and circled his big arms around me.

"So does Death have a heart?" he said, pulling away. "Or does he work better when you're here?"

I hadn't thought of it like that. I'd been wondering why Lincoln collected me when he didn't show any emotion toward me. It seemed unlikely that he wanted to resume our relationship...and yet he'd been worried about me. "Did he not work well while I was away?"

His thin lips thinned even more. "He was more reckless, careless and arrogant, but he talked to me and Seth more, too. Told us what his plans were, and such, like we was his equals, not his servants. He never used to do that."

"No," I said quietly, "he did not."

"Come in. Meet Miss Parkin, my landlady. She's a bit soft in the head and will prob'ly forget you in five minutes, but she brews good tea."

I glanced over my shoulder at the waiting carriage. Doyle touched the brim of his hat and Gus greeted him heartily. Then he spotted Lady Vickers inside. She did not acknowledge him but stared straight ahead.

"What'd you bring Lady Muck for?" he said with a sour twist of his mouth.

"I couldn't help it. She's looking for Seth. Is he here?"

"No."

"Do you know where he is?"

"Aye."

"Then we'd best go to him straight away. She's anxious to have him home again."

He grunted. "She'll be even more anxious when she sees what he's been doin' since he left Lichfield."

"Oh?"

The corner of his mouth lifted as if it had been hooked. "You'll find him at the Brickmaker's Arms about now. It ain't a place for ladies."

"Are you suggesting Lady Vickers doesn't come? We could try and take her back to Lichfield, but I doubt she'll like it. What happens at the Brickmaker's Arms that isn't fit for ladies to see?"

His grin widened, revealing jagged teeth. I used to think it a menacing smile, but now it made me grin in response. "Bare-knuckle fights."

My heart sank. "Seth's fighting again? But why? He's paid off his family debts."

He lifted one bulky shoulder. "Might be he just likes getting beat up."

"Nobody likes getting beat up, particularly Seth. He adores looking in the mirror too much."

He snorted a laugh. "Let me get my things."

"You'll come back to Lichfield tonight?"

"Course. Miss Parkin won't mind. She hardly remembers who I am, most of the time. Gets scared when I come round a corner, and I have to tell her all over again that I'm rentin' one of her rooms."

"Perhaps she should take in female boarders."

"Or ones whose faces won't frighten the hairnet off her."

He disappeared and reappeared at the coach window a few minutes later. He knocked and I lowered it. "Evenin', milady." He doffed his cap to Lady Vickers. "Charlie told you we're takin' you home first?"

I sat back and kept my mouth shut. I'd told her no such thing. Perhaps it was wicked of me, but I saw no reason why she shouldn't see the places her son had frequented in his quest to pay back the debts she'd left him with. To be fair, the debts had been run up by her first husband, Seth's father, but she could have stayed in London to help her son face their creditors.

"I will be coming with you," she said with a haughty lift of her chin. "I want to make sure Seth does as he's told and returns home—tonight."

Gus rolled his eyes and joined Doyle on the driver's seat. Perhaps I should have, too. Lady Vickers sat sullenly opposite me, muttering, "He's been away long enough. He made his point." I thought Seth's point had nothing to do with her, but perhaps I was wrong.

We drove along the near-empty streets, the darkness punctured only by the hazy glows of the street lamps and our own carriage lamps. Although it was early, few people were out, and those that were hurried with their heads bent and their collars pulled high. At least there was no fog, yet.

The carriage pulled up outside a tavern with dim light rimming the windows. The Brickmaker's Arms sign swung in the breeze, its hinges squeaking tunelessly. The door opened and a drunkard spilled out along with a blast of voices. The fellow stumbled then managed to continue on his way, stopping only once to prop himself against the tavern wall before heading off into the pitch black lane.

Gus opened the carriage door, and I hopped down. Lady Vickers hung back, a handkerchief over her nose and mouth.

"Stay here," I told her. "We'll fetch him."

"He's here?" she mumbled into her handkerchief. "He's in this filthy place?"

I walked ahead of Gus, only to have him grab my arm and pull me behind him.

"I'll go first, Charlie. Put your hood up. Don't let 'em see your pretty face. I ain't goin' to be able to make 'em all leave you alone, and we don't know what condition Seth'll be in to help."

I swallowed. If Seth was badly hurt...it didn't bear thinking about.

My arm was accosted again—this time by Lady Vickers. She marched in step with me, the handkerchief tucked away out of sight. She looked like a commanding officer about to step into a battle she knew she couldn't win, but was determined not to surrender anyway. It didn't fill me with much confidence.

I patted her hand. "I'm sure he'll agree to come home tonight."

She blinked hard. "Thank you, Charlie. If you will employ all your powers of persuasion, I would be most grateful."

I smothered a smile. "I'll do my best."

Lady Vickers emitted a small gasp as we entered the tavern and pulled out her handkerchief again. She coughed into it and muttered something I couldn't make out over the voices and laughter. I'd wager it had something to do with the stink of urine and sweat, a combination that reminded me all too much of the dens where I'd lived alongside the other boys in my gang.

"You get used to it," I told her.

"I think I'm going to be sick."

"Do it in the corner where no one will notice."

Gus forged a path through the patrons and the broad sweep of Lady Vickers' skirts widened it. I trailed behind and only had to hiss once at a man who tried to pinch my cheek. He snickered but didn't try again.

Gus asked the keep behind the bar if Seth was "down below." The keep nodded, then turned his squinty gaze onto Lady Vickers and myself.

"Who're they?" he asked.

"Seth's mother and my friend," Gus said. "They're all right. They know to keep their mouths shut."

The keep looked dubious, but a few coins passed across the counter by Gus's big paw changed his mind. The keep jerked his head and we followed him to a door that led to a storeroom lit by a single lamp. It stank of ale; a pleasant change from the rest of the tavern, although Lady Vickers didn't lower her handkerchief.

The keep lifted a trapdoor in the floor, hidden behind barrels, and Gus descended the steps without a word. I indicated Lady Vickers should go next. She peered through but didn't follow.

"Why is Seth in the cellar?" she asked, pocketing the handkerchief.

"Dancing lessons," the keep said with a chuckle.

"He's already an excellent dancer."

"Get a bloody move on," he growled. "I'm busy."

I urged her with a nod and a smile. She wrinkled nose, lifted her skirts, and stepped through the trapdoor. Not many women of her station would have. I admired her fortitude.

I followed them down the staircase into the room. It was a vast space and mostly empty, except for tables and broken chairs stacked along the walls. A shirt and waistcoat hung on the leg of an upturned chair. Four lengths of rope marked out a large central square in which Seth stood, his bare back to us. He spoke with another man dressed in a yellow cravat and a green and gold waistcoat. His dapper attire and oiled mustache were at odds with his protruding brow and thick neck. The men were alone.

"Seth!" Lady Vickers cried, her voice managing to be both shrill and trembling. "Seth! Come here, at once."

His shoulders slumped as if all the breath had suddenly left his body. "Gus, I'm going to kill you."

"She ain't the only one I brought, if you care to look, dolt," Gus said, grinning.

Seth turned and I drew in a gasp at the sight of his cut lip and bruised cheek. I suspected his knuckles would be in a worse state, but he'd tucked them behind his back so we couldn't see.

Lady Vickers whimpered. "Oh, my dear boy. Your beautiful face."

Seth didn't seem to have heard. He broke into a grin. "Charlie!"

He came toward us, but his mother intercepted him. She grasped his chin and twisted him this way and that. After a thorough inspection, she let him go. "What is the meaning of this? Why are you naked? Cover up at once. There's an innocent young woman here."

"And thank God that she is!" Seth bypassed his mother and scooped me up into a hug. "Avert your eyes, innocent young woman, before my nakedness corrupts you."

I laughed and hugged him back. "Put me down before your mother faints," I whispered.

"She never faints. Her constitution is much too strong, unfortunately. A fainting spell every once in while would give me peace." He put me down, still grinning from ear to ear. The cut on his lip opened and began to bleed, but he didn't seem to notice.

His mother swooped in with her handkerchief in one hand and Seth's shirt in the other, her lips pursed tight. She reserved her scowl for me, however. "Remember your promise," she whispered.

Seth was too busy dressing to hear. "You escaped!" he said, tucking in the shirt. He did not complete the task and left half of it out. His mother finished the job while he buttoned. "I knew you would. Good girl."

"What are you doing down here?" Lady Vickers asked before I could respond. "And don't tell me it's dancing lessons." She looked around, taking in the rope marking out the boxing ring, the thug who stood watching us with an impatient tap of his foot, and finally, the blood-stained floor.

Seth quickly tucked his hands behind his back again, but not before I noticed the cut and bruised knuckles. Poor Seth. Why had he taken up the brutal sport again? Not only was bare-knuckle fighting illegal, it was utterly inhumane. The toffs loved it as much as the low-lifes upstairs. It was one of the few activities that crossed the class divide. That and whoring.

"I'm, er..." Seth swallowed and stared at his mother.

I tried to think of something to tell her but couldn't. Gus came to his rescue. "Meeting his tailor." He nodded at the brute. "Who else would dress like that but a man of fashion?"

I pressed my lips together to suppress my grin. Gus winked at me.

The brute suddenly stood straight and drew back his round shoulders. He fidgeted with his cravat and stepped forward. "I was just fittin' the mister here for a new suit, ma'am." He shot a smug grin at Seth, pleased to be included in the lie.

Lady Vickers sniffed. "Does no one use your title anymore?" she said to Seth. "It's Lord Vickers," she said loudly to the brute, as if he were hard of hearing. "And you will address him as such or he'll take his custom elsewhere."

The brute's top lip curled up like a dog ready to attack. "I'll return for another fitting later," Seth told him quickly. He ushered us toward the steps, shooting wary glances back at the thug.

"What about *tonight's* fitting?" the man growled. "We had an agreement."

"You'll have to find another...client. Surely you must see that I can't stay now."

The brute hurtled toward us like an out of control boulder rolling down a hill, his yellow teeth bared. "Come back here, you fucking cock-licker!"

Lady Vickers' jaw dropped. Then it became hard and her eyes harder. She planted her feet and turned. Definitely not a fainter.

"Mother!" Seth shouted. "Move!"

She thrust her hands on her hips. "How *dare* you call my son such *vile* things!"

"Move, lady," the thug snarled. "I ain't got no quarrel with you." When she didn't budge, he shoved her aside with a sweep of his arm.

She stumbled and would have fallen if Gus hadn't caught her.

"Go! All of you!" Seth settled his feet in much the same way as his mother had done. He closed his hands into fists and hunched into a fighting stance. "Gus, see that they get to safety."

"Seth!" Lady Vickers screamed. "No!"

CHAPTER 6

"He'll be all right," I assured Lady Vickers, taking her hand and dragging her with me to the steps. "He's very capable with his fists."

She allowed us to usher her up the stairs, only stopping when the smack of skin against skin signaled the start of a fight. She turned in time to see Seth duck beneath the thug's fist and land his first punch. The brute reeled back, but Seth didn't leave it there. He went after him.

Lady Vickers whimpered and pressed her handkerchief to her nose again.

"Don't watch," I said, taking her arm. "We'll wait for him in the carriage."

We hurried through the storeroom and the tavern, then outside to the carriage. "That man..." she murmured once inside the coach cabin, "he's not a tailor, is he?"

"No," Gus said, taking the seat beside her. He laid the blanket across her knee and tucked it around her. "Nor a dancing instructor, neither."

We didn't have to wait long before Seth tumbled into the carriage. "Go!" he shouted to Doyle. His clothing was in disarray, his hair hung in sweaty tangles, and blood smeared his nose. He grinned. "Bloody hell, it's good to see you, Charlie."

"And you too," I said, smiling at the absurdity of our situation. "You're getting blood on your shirt."

He wiped his shirtsleeve across his nose then inspected it. "Damn. Blood's hard to get out."

"I'm sure Bella will try for you."

His mother's flinty glare told me she knew precisely what Bella would try to do with Seth.

"God, we missed you, Charlie." He still grinned, his perfect white teeth flashing in the light from the lamp hanging by the door. "How did you escape? Where are you hiding? Are we heading there now?"

"Slow down." I laughed. "I didn't escape. Lincoln retrieved me."

His smile wilted. His lips parted. "Who knocked some sense into him, then? Mother?" He laughed. I covered my mouth to hide my smile.

"Seth!" Lady Vickers barked. "Explain yourself. Have you been *fighting*? For *money*?"

"What gave it away? The blood? The fight promoter with the thick neck and no fashion sense? His outfit is a crime but try telling him that. He thinks he's the modern day Beau Brummel."

Beside me, Gus snorted. "Did you get hit in the head? You're talkin' like somethin' came loose in there."

Lady Vickers leaned closer to Seth and inspected his cuts and bruises. Aside from his bloody nose and cut lip, one of his eyes sported a yellow bruise that must have happened previously. Perhaps he *had* been hit in the head too many times in recent days. No one ought to be as cheerful as Seth after being battered black and blue.

"Look at your beautiful face." Lady Vickers clicked her tongue as she turned his chin this way and that. "And at such a crucial time too, when you need to be looking your best. What will the girls think now?"

He jerked out of her grip. "You'd be surprised at how excited a few bruises gets them," he growled. "If this doesn't elicit more callers, I don't know what will. I'm sure you'll be satisfied with their newfound enthusiasm once word gets out."

"Once word gets out that you've been prize fighting, we'll be fortunate to be invited anywhere ever again." She sniffed and dabbed at the corner of her eye with her handkerchief, but it was already dry. While she had certainly been worried about him when the fight broke out, she showed no signs of concern for her son's wellbeing now.

"Never fear, Mama. All will be well now Charlie's back. You'll see."

Lady Vickers scowled. I suspected I would once again have to reassure her that I had no intentions of trapping her son into marriage.

Seth grinned at me. "And just in time for her birthday too."

***

Lady Vickers shadowed Seth all the way to the kitchen, her handkerchief fluttering and her black skirts rippling. "Let me at least wipe the blood off."

"I'm fine!" he snapped over his shoulder. "Nothing a hearty meal can't cure. What's for supper, Cook?"

Cook looked up from the pot he was stirring on the stove and greeted Seth with a grunt. "Supper's for them that live here."

"I live here again, as of tonight." Seth clapped him on the shoulder and peered into the pot. "I'm half starved. Look at me! I'm fading away." He picked up the wooden spoon Cook had rested on the pot rim, dipped it in and slurped off the contents.

"Oi!" Cook snatched back the spoon. "Lost your manners as well as your common sense, I see."

"It's been a trying evening," Lady Vickers said from the doorway. "Bella can bring me supper in my room. Will you dine with me tonight, son?" She didn't seem to want to venture in any further. It was as if we stood in the sea and she on the shore, not willing to get her skirts wet.

"I need to speak with Charlie. I'll join you for breakfast." Seth strode back to his mother, kissed her forehead and told her he loved her dearly. Always the charmer.

It worked too. She smiled and patted his cheek. "Goodnight, dear boy." She left but not before shooting a warning glare my way.

I fetched bowls and Cook ladled soup into them then removed bread from the oven. Gus and Doyle joined us, after seeing to the horses, and we four sat at the table like a family, albeit an odd one. Yet it wasn't complete. Lincoln's absence left a hole that I, for one, felt keenly. Gus was the first to mention him, soon after his first slurp of soup.

"When's Death gettin' back?" he asked Doyle.

"He didn't say," the butler said.

"You know what he be like," Cook said. "He could be gone for days."

"Or he could wander in at any moment," Seth added.

We all looked to the door.

I sighed. "Apparently he's warning all the..." I glanced at Doyle and searched for another way to tell them without giving too much away.

"Supernaturals." Doyle patted the corner of his mouth with his napkin then continued consuming his soup as if he'd not said anything significant. "Mr.

Fitzroy informed me of the ministry's true purpose before he left."

Seth and Gus exchanged looks. "And you don't think it...odd?" Seth asked.

"I'm not employed to have an opinion on my employer's affairs."

"Bet it don't stop you from havin' 'em," Gus muttered into his bowl which he'd brought to his lips. He tipped the final dregs of soup into his mouth and set the bowl down with a satisfied thunk on the table. "There enough for seconds?"

"Just leave some for the others," Cook told him.

"Why did Fitzroy collect you?" Seth asked me. "Did he say?"

"He thought I might be in danger," I said without meeting their gazes.

"He must have seen it," Gus said, concentrating on not spilling any soup from his very full bowl as he made his way back to the table.

"He told us about his seeing power," Seth clarified. "Before we left."

"He didn't tell me," Cook muttered.

Doyle had a stunned look on his face. It would seem this was news to him too.

"He doesn't know what you're doing all the time," I assured him. "And he can't read your mind. He only knows when someone is here or not."

"And when Charlie's in danger," Seth said, watching me. "It's strongest where she's concerned. So what happened? Or did he overreact?"

"Lincoln, overreact? The word isn't in his vocabulary. There was a situation at the school, but it resolved peacefully when Alice woke up." I gave them a brief version of events, which led into a discussion about Alice's powers and that of the other girls. "It seems we witches are considered wayward by our parents and guardians."

"Wayward?" Cook asked.

"The school's name."

They gave me blank looks.

"It's the School for Wayward Girls, up near York. Didn't he tell you?"

"He told us nothing," Seth muttered, tearing off a chunk of bread. "Not the name of the school, where you went, how far away it was. Nothing."

"Oh. I see. Well, that's its name, and so-called difficult girls are sent there to be polished and primped into young ladies. There were several supernatural students."

"So you be a young lady, now?" Cook asked with a lopsided grin.

I laughed. "Two weeks wasn't nearly long enough. The teachers gave up in despair and the headmistress..." *Sent me to the dungeon.* "The headmistress saw me as a personal challenge." There was no point in telling them what she'd really said and done. Besides, Mrs. Denk and I had come to a truce, of sorts.

"You didn't climb trees, did you?" Gus asked, humor brightening his eyes.

"I may have, but so would you, if you had to sit in a room and sew all day. I was more in danger from the boredom than anything Alice could dream up."

Doyle wiped his bowl with his bread. "Was it wise to leave her there?"

"I don't know. I hope so. Now that she knows what makes her dreams come to life, she should be able to control it."

They fell silent. Perhaps, like me, they were considering the horrors that could befall Alice and the others if she didn't keep calm. I was beginning to wish

I'd brought her back to Lichfield, but it was much too dangerous for her at the moment with the killer not yet caught.

"So Fitzroy collected you, even though you weren't in danger by the time he arrived," Seth said. "That's quite a change of heart. Last time I saw him, he was as bloody-minded as ever. I was ready to thump him when he wouldn't tell us where you went."

"Why didn't you?" Gus growled. "Because he would have pummeled you into the ground, maybe?"

Seth merely grunted.

"So you don't know why he changed his mind?" I asked.

"He missed you," Cook said with shrug.

"Or needed you," Gus added.

"Same thing," Seth said.

"No, it ain't," both Gus and Cook said.

"Whatever his reasons, thank God you're back." Doyle's conviction surprised me. I thought that he would have cared the least for my return, not knowing me particularly well. "He was...difficult in your absence. Perhaps that will change now."

"Difficult how?"

"He was volatile, erratic. He acted dangerously, on occasion, without a care for his own wellbeing."

He must have been referring to Lincoln's cut feet. Did he think Lincoln had broken the glass himself, then walked over the shards on purpose?

"He were like he used to be," Gus added. "Before you came to live here, Charlie."

I swallowed heavily. Lincoln never cared much for the lives of others, hence the moniker the men had given him—Death. I liked to think he'd changed, that his feelings for me had helped re-shape him, but perhaps I'd been a fool to hope. The more I thought about it, the more I suspected that was the case.

Lincoln had stopped pretending, in my absence, and reverted back to his true self without the blinkers of love keeping him on the straight path. The blinkers had come off me too, so I shouldn't judge him too harshly.

I stood and collected the bowls. When I reached Seth, he caught my wrist and inspected my hand. "Where's your engagement ring?"

"I gave it back to him."

Someone sucked in a breath. Seth let me go with a frown. "Are you mad? Why would you end it? Don't you want to be mistress of all this? Don't you want to be his wife anymore?"

"I...I no longer know what I want. My future is uncertain. I do know that things are different between Lincoln and me now. They have to be. We cannot go on as we were. I'd be a fool to pretend all is well again."

"You don't have to pretend, but you can talk to him, tell him how you feel."

"I told him on the journey back. Believe me, Seth, if he didn't understand how I felt after that, then he truly does lack empathy."

His frown deepened. "He didn't try to talk you around?"

"Why would he?"

"He fetched you back, Charlie. Doesn't that say something? Doesn't that imply he missed you and still loves you?"

"If he wanted to resume our relationship, he would have said as much when I tried to hand back the ring. He has been cool to me."

"Cool or wary? Perhaps he's trying to gauge your feelings first before he recommits."

I picked up his bowl and headed into the scullery. Seth may be right, but it didn't matter. Lincoln had betrayed me, and I would not forgive him for it.

Without forgiveness there could be no returning to what we had.

"You should have sold the ring," Gus called out. "A stone like that would fetch a pretty sum. Ow! What was that for?" he snapped.

"For being an fool," Seth growled.

"I'll do the dishes," Doyle said. I hadn't realized he'd followed me into the scullery. "You should take care of your hand."

I curled my fingers up into a fist to hide the welt still visible there. "You saw."

"A good butler sees everything. Including how tired his mistress looks."

I gave him a weak smile. "I'd rather be your friend. But thank you, Doyle. I think I'll retire early. It's been a long day. A good day, but a long one."

He picked up an empty pail by the door. "Everyone is glad you're back, Charlie. Everyone."

***

Lincoln requested my presence for a meeting in the library after breakfast, along with Seth and Gus. I had expected him to be out, but he claimed that all the London-based supernaturals had now been warned, and it was up to them whether they heeded his warning or not.

"It's time to set our minds to catching the murderer," he said.

Our minds, not his alone. It was a good sign that he wanted all of us involved in the endeavor. Perhaps.

"How?" Seth asked. His cuts didn't look so bad after cleaning away the blood, but his mother had still fussed over his "roughened" appearance at breakfast. She'd made him wrap bandages soaked in a foul-smelling liquid around his bruised knuckles. The bandages were now steaming in the fireplace where he'd thrown them.

"The only way I can see to move forward is to question Thomas Rampling." Seth gave me a dark look.

"Who is Thomas Rampling?" I asked.

"A dead man who may know the identity of the killer. Didn't you tell her, Fitzroy?"

"There hasn't been time." Lincoln stood by the fire while Seth, Gus and I sat in the armchairs arranged around the hearth. He looked tired. It didn't detract from his handsomeness.

I studied my clasped hands in my lap to keep my gaze averted from the distraction and to hide my sore palm.

"You had the entire journey from York!"

"Seth," Gus hissed. "Shut it."

I could feel their gazes on me, so I looked up and mustered some defiance. "Our compartment was full," I lied. "We had no opportunity to talk at length about the murders. And when we did...we had other things to discuss."

Lincoln shifted his stance from one foot to the other. I glanced at his face and caught him looking at me. A small crease connected his brows.

"Then you best get comfortable, Charlie," Gus said. "We've got quite a tale."

They told me about the circus strongman's murder, and how Lincoln's informant led them to a gunman named Jack Daley who'd pulled the trigger. Somehow they managed to get Daley to divulge the name of the man who'd hired *him*—Thomas Rampling. I suspected Lincoln had employed his usual method of coercion to force Daley to talk, since he avoided answering my question about it. Unfortunately, Rampling had drowned before they could speak with him, and it was his spirit they wished me to raise. Hopefully he could identify the mysterious man who'd hired *him*. All they knew was that he was a toff and had sent Rampling to pay gunmen to kill supernaturals whose powers could potentially be developed to bring the dead back to life, something that Victor Frankenstein had tried, and failed, to do with my necromancy.

Seth leaned forward and rested his elbows on his knees. "Rampling's spirit is our only hope of finding the truth."

"What about Gillingham?" Gus said with a shrug. "You goin' to investigate him, sir?"

"It's unlikely that he's guilty," Lincoln said.

"What about Gillingham?" I asked. "Is he a suspect for any particular reason, or simply because he's a turd not fit to grace the bottom of anyone's shoe?"

Seth smirked and Gus chuckled. I could swear the corners of Lincoln's lips twitched too. "Lady Gillingham is a shape-shifter," he said.

I sat back in the chair, the breath knocked out of me. "Bloody hell. You mean like the two girls I met at the school?"

"I suspect so. She turns into a...creature."

"Did she tell you this? Or her husband?"

"I overheard them talking and became suspicious enough to investigate. I climbed in through her bedroom window and watched her sleeping."

My fingers curled into the leather armrest. "I see."

"She was covered in fur and resembled a wolf, of sorts. Her heightened senses allowed her to hear and smell me. She attacked, stopping only when she recognized me. We talked and she told me that she was born with the ability to change at will between her human form and this other, but she's mostly the other creature during sleep. Her husband discovered this fact last summer." Around the time Lincoln kidnapped me because of my necromancy. It was soon after that the killings began.

I let the armrest go. Small half-circles from my fingernails dented the brown leather. "You said you don't consider him to be a suspect. Why not?"

"His wife disgusts him, yet he hasn't killed her."

"She can't bring the dead back to life though, or in any way reanimate body parts or raise spirits. If he's only killing those types of supernaturals, then he might still be the murderer."

Lincoln nodded, and I suspected he had kept that fact in mind but still didn't think Gillingham was the murderer.

Gus snorted. "He hates his wife."

"He's terrified of her," Seth added. "He doesn't like to be near her. He doesn't want their children tainted."

"Some people would consider a supernatural trait to be an enhancement," I said huffily.

"Not Gillingham." Seth sat back, crossed his legs, and flashed his white teeth in a smile. "That's why there's no fear that he'll want to marry you, if his own marriage ends. My apologies if that disappoints you, Charlie."

I rolled my eyes, catching Lincoln once again watching me intently. "I'll cope with the disappointment."

"I still reckon Gilly's guilty," Gus said. "I don't like him."

"If we killed everyone we didn't like, there'd be no one left on the committee," Seth said.

"I weren't talkin' about killin' him."

"How naive you are."

"No one will kill anyone without good reason," Lincoln cut in. "Not even Gillingham, if he proves guilty."

"Spoil sport."

It would seem there was only one option available to us then. Raise the spirit of Thomas Rampling. At least now I knew why Lincoln had fetched me back. He did need me, but not for his own happiness. He needed me to use my necromancy, just like he'd needed me in the beginning of our acquaintance. I wasn't surprised. Lincoln had very few needs for himself, either emotional or physical.

I may not have been surprised but disappointment pierced my chest like a needle.

"Does Rampling have a middle name?" I asked.

"James." Lincoln once again shifted his stance, this time drawing a little closer. "Charlie, if you don't want to do it, you don't have to."

"Of course I want to," I snapped. "It's what I'm here for, isn't it?"

Seth and Gus looked to Lincoln. He shook his head but said nothing. I blew out a breath and began. "Thomas James Rampling, I summon you here to me. Thomas James Rampling, please come to me in spirit form for...a conversation."

White mist coalesced in the corner of the library in the form of a man. Like a charcoal sketch, he didn't look real or alive, but he did nevertheless have form that drifted through the room toward me. His face was bloated from his drowning, and I found it difficult to look at him. After surveying his surroundings, taking in each of the men in turn, he settled near Lincoln on the other side of the enormous mantelpiece.

"Mr. Thomas Rampling?" I asked.

"Who're you?"

"My name is Charlie. I've summoned you here to ask you some questions."

"How'd you do that?"

"It's an inherited skill. Will you willingly answer some questions for me about the man who hired you to hire Jack Daley?"

The mist dispersed, as if a strong breeze had caught it, then quickly reformed into the shape of Thomas Rampling again. "What d'you want to know?" he asked, looking to Lincoln.

"Only I can hear you," I told him. "We are the Ministry of Curiosities, a group formed to keep account of all supernaturals, such as myself. Daley killed a supernatural and we'd like to know why and who ordered the murder. He told us you hired him. Did you?"

The mist shimmered. "What are the consequences if I did? Not confessing, mind, just asking."

"There are no consequences. Since you're already dead, there is nothing anyone in this realm can do to you and we're not interested in laying blame posthumously. In the realm where you exist now, they already know your earthly deeds and have judged you. Confessing to us makes no difference."

His eyes narrowed. "Why should I tell you anything?"

I sighed. "Because I'm asking you nicely, and because I believe you are not a cruel man, but one forced to do cruelty because of your circumstances."

"I have no craft, no skill, and I couldn't find work," the ghost explained. "I needed the money."

"Your cousin believed you to be a good man," Lincoln said. He must have guessed that Rampling was being obstinate. "Honor his memory of you by helping us catch the man behind these murders."

"Very well." Rampling passed a hand across his swollen face. "I was paid to hire Daley, sure enough. I gave him the directions to the victims, and passed on his fee. But I didn't see the face of the man who hired me. I can't tell you his name or describe him."

"Bollocks," I muttered before I could stop myself.

Rampling's eyes widened, and I apologized for my language and repeated what the spirit had said for the benefit of the others. Gus and Seth both swore too. Lincoln's chest rose with his deep breath.

"He must know something that can identify the man," Lincoln said. "Otherwise why was he killed?"

A good point. I looked to the spirit whose brow had crinkled into a frown in thought.

"Is there something other than his appearance you would know him by?" I asked. "Something on or in his coach perhaps? A monogramed letter? A distinctive ring?" I had a thought that made my breath hitch. "A distinctive walking stick?" Like the one Lord Gillingham used.

Rampling shook his head. "Not that I can recall."

"Think!"

The mist drifted around me, leaving a chill in its wake. I watched him float to the ceiling then dip under the table and sweep up the ladder to the highest bookshelves. Finally, he resettled in the same spot, his frown cleared.

"I think I know why," he said. "I followed him that first night I met him. My cousin drives for a lord and lady and he happened to pass me by soon after I met the man who hired me. My cousin was just filling in time, driving around, waiting for his mistress to finish her shopping. I asked him to follow the toff's growler at a distance with me as his passenger. Thought I could squeeze some money out of him later, to keep his identity quiet, if I knew where he lived. But he didn't go home, so it was pointless. We followed him all the way to Brooks's on St. James. His growler was just pulling away from the curb when we drew closer, and a footman greeted someone at the front door. I didn't see his face," he added before I could ask. "He had his back to me. The footman knew him, though, so I'd wager he was a member of the club. If you want to find him, try there."

It wasn't much, but it was something. I relayed the information to the others. "What about his build?" Seth asked. "Tall, short, fat, thin?"

"Taller than most, but his build was impossible to determine beneath all the capes on his great coat. His collar was turned up and with his hat on, I couldn't see his hair."

"Did he walk like an old man?" I asked. "Or a young one?"

Rampling shrugged. "Can't recall. Nothing so as I noticed."

Damnation. It wasn't much at all.

"If he had his back to Ramplin'," Gus said, frowning in thought, "then the toff wouldn't have seen him and wouldn't know he was bein' followed. So why kill him?"

"He was tying up loose ends," Lincoln said. "Just in case. Once we found Daley, he must have been worried that we'd find a thread linking Daley to him."

"Is Daley still alive?" I asked. Others who'd been linked to the murders had died in police custody after we discovered their guilt.

"As far as I am aware," Lincoln said, "but I haven't been near the police station recently."

"No great loss if he's dead," Gus muttered. "The man were a monster, Charlie. You don't want to meet the likes of him in a dark alley."

I'd met men who prayed on the vulnerable in my time living on the streets. They were capable of the utmost cruelties, although thankfully I'd been spared the worst. I quickly learned to identify the type and kept well away from them. Nevertheless, Gus's words sent a shiver down my spine.

"Rampling," Lincoln said to the spirit, "when did you follow your employer's conveyance?"

"A month or more ago."

"Can you be more specific?" I pressed.

Rampling's spirit shimmered. "I don't recall the date, but it were two days before Daley made his first kill."

"Two days before Drinkwater's death," I told Lincoln.

"The sixteenth of November," Lincoln said.

"Can I go?" Rampling asked.

"He wants to leave," I said to Lincoln. "Do you have any more questions for him?"

"Just one," Lincoln said. "Tell me about your murder."

"He sent me a note to meet him at the river," Rampling said. "I recognized his handwriting. I waited but he didn't come. I was about to leave when something hit the back of my head. I remember falling into the water. After that, nothing."

I repeated this for Lincoln. He gave a single nod. "That's all. He may leave."

"Thank you," I said to the spirit. "You've been most helpful. I wish you peace in your afterlife. You may go."

The mist dispersed and floated away. I leaned back in the chair and rubbed my forehead. While it didn't tax me to speak with spirits, I nevertheless found it upsetting if they'd died before reaching old age. They were so real to me and yet they were gone from this world. Sometimes, it was hard to fathom.

"Does Gillingham belong to that club?" Gus asked.

Lincoln nodded. "As do Eastbrooke, Marchbank, Andrew Buchanan and almost every aristocrat in London. I'm a member."

"I used to be," Seth said, "when I could afford the fee. It was a terribly dull place, without women."

"We'll both attend today," Lincoln said. "Gus will drive us."

"How will we find this fellow? It's a needle in a haystack situation."

"By sifting through the hay. Prepare the horses," Lincoln said to Gus. "We'll leave shortly."

Gus left with Seth behind him. I stood to go too.

"A moment, Charlie." Lincoln waited until the men were out of sight before suddenly taking my hand. He turned it palm up, revealing the welt from Mrs. Denk's cane. So he'd noticed.

His thumb gently stroked alongside the wound. A lump welled in my throat at the unexpected tenderness. Damnation. Why couldn't I remain indifferent?

I snatched my hand away.

CHAPTER 7

"How did you get that?" Lincoln asked with a nod at my hand.

"From a run-in with the headmistress. Don't concern yourself."

"And if I want to concern myself with your wellbeing?" he asked quietly.

"Why now?" I bit back. "You didn't two weeks ago."

"I thought you'd be well cared for at the school. If I'd known the headmistress did that to you, I would have collected you sooner."

"Forgive me for not writing, then. I didn't think my letters would be welcome." I picked up my skirts and marched for the door.

I didn't realize Lincoln had followed until he grasped my arm. He spun me round and pulled me close. Not so close that our bodies touched but near enough that I felt his warmth and saw his pupils dilate.

I steeled myself for a confrontation, but he quickly let me go and stepped back. "You're right. Letters wouldn't have been welcome. I wouldn't have read them."

His honesty stung, even though I appreciated it. Lincoln had never been one for spouting sweet yet false words to get his way with me. It was one of the things I'd liked about him.

"I didn't want to be reminded of you," he said. "I avoided everything here that I associate with you."

I crossed my arms, determined to ward off his words and any kindness he might show me now. I refused to be affected by them. "How unfortunate that your seer's sense didn't sever when I left, or you might have succeeded in never thinking about me again."

"I didn't succeed before I sensed your life was in danger either. It seems I don't need to be near the things I associate with you to think of you."

I swallowed heavily again. This conversation wasn't going at all as I expected. "That passes in time, so I'm told."

"I was told the same thing."

I huffed out a bitter laugh. "Since we are speaking to one another about injuries incurred during my absence, tell me about your feet."

His features settled into a blank expression. "There is nothing to tell. You saw me at a weak moment."

"A moment when you forgot to walk without a limp." Speaking with him was a battle in itself where neither of us got the upper hand. I felt like I had to be on my guard the entire time, and yet I neither advanced nor retreated. "I know about the broken glass and the blood on your floor. Before you get angry with Doyle for telling me, you should know that he's only concerned for your welfare."

A beat passed. Two. His eyelids lowered and he watched me through his lashes. "Does your asking mean that you are concerned too?"

I bristled. "I'm curious as to why you broke a glass then deliberately walked over it."

He watched me. I bore it with what I hoped was a defiant stance and a lack of emotion, but it wasn't easy. His scrutiny made it difficult to maintain a façade of indifference.

After a few moments, he stepped around me. He waited, a hand on the door handle. It would seem I was dismissed. With my chin tilted up and my gaze on the door, not him, I strode out of the library.

"I'm glad you're home," he said while I was still within earshot. "I know you think I'm not, but I am. Immeasurably."

"Is that so?" I tossed over my shoulder without stopping. "I suppose my return will help assuage some of your guilt."

When I reached the landing on the main staircase, out of sight of him downstairs, I ran the rest of the way to my rooms. Once inside, I sat on the floor, my head on my knees, and cried. Not from sorrow, but from sheer, utter relief at being home and for the frustration of being so near Lincoln again. I thought I'd be able to bear seeing him every day, but I was no longer sure that I could. He wasn't someone I could remain indifferent to.

***

I was never very good at waiting. It felt like an eternity watching for Lincoln, Seth and Gus to return from Brooks's Club through the parlor window. Surely it shouldn't take long, but two hours after their departure, they still hadn't returned.

Lady Vickers tried to convince me to join her on the sofa and sew, but even that mundane task proved a trial. I started at every creak of the house, every breath of wind rattling the window panes. Doyle's arrival with tea provided some relief, not because of the tea or his presence, but because he brought the newspaper with him. He passed it to Lady Vickers and then left. She flipped to the society pages. I scanned the front page for some news, but it was mostly of a political nature and not interesting to me.

Lady Vickers gasped. "Good lord. My my. She'll be upset at seeing this."

I knew she was goading me into asking her, but I didn't care. I needed the distraction. "What is it?"

"Listen to this." She snapped the paper open and cleared her throat. "'This newspaper has learned of the scandalous past of one of London's most illustrious dames. Never one to shy away from a party, H's low birth did not hinder her rise after marrying a peer, but this as-yet unverified information may well do so. It has come to our attention that the celebrated beauty danced at The Alhambra in her youth. The proprietor of that establishment, Mr. Golightly, refrained from commenting, but our source tells us that H was a popular performer with the audience.'"

An audience that consisted mostly of gentlemen eager to associate with the dancers during the long interval and afterward. I'd been there and learned of Lady Harcourt's past as a dancer from Golightly's assistant, Miss Redding, a dancer herself. Lady Harcourt met her future husband at The Al and had managed to keep her past a secret. Until now, it seemed. Her reputation had been clinging to respectability by the barest margin in recent times. Miss Redding seemed to want to reveal the secret, and another former dancer, Mrs. Drinkwater, had threatened to do so too. Only by divulging information about me to her blackmailer had Lady Harcourt avoided her scandalous past being aired. I'd been tempted to air it myself, on occasion.

Lady Vickers couldn't possibly know any of that, however. "H?" I asked innocently.

"Julia—Lady Harcourt—of course. All the clues are right here." She pointed to the article, the first and most prominent on the tattler page. "'Low birth,' 'marrying a peer,' 'beauty.' The extra clue of 'H' is hardly even needed." She smiled at me. "Oh, how the mighty fall."

"You don't like her?"

She sniffed. "She was among the first to snub me after my husband's debts became known. She pretended to be sympathetic, of course, but I saw through her act."

"Why would she snub you?"

"Nobody likes to be on the lower rungs, and at the time, she was still firmly attempting to climb out of the mire of her birth. By being the first to ostracize me, she made herself more popular with that waspish set. They simply love to dip their forked tongues into malicious gossip. She proved to have the cruelest tongue of all and quickly became their leader. I have no sympathy for women of that ilk. None at all. Sadly, society is riddled with them, from top to bottom."

"Does Seth know how she treated you?" Surely not, considering Lady Harcourt had been one of his mistresses up until very recently. He'd even seemed fond of her before he'd learned how cruel she'd been to me.

"I doubt it. He's a man, and men have no use for gossip. Their world doesn't revolve around it like ours, my dear." She gave me a severe look over the newspaper. "Society madams are like sharks in the water, just waiting for their prey to swim past. They can smell vulnerability, and when they do, they attack. You must remember that, Charlie. Remember to never show fear or weakness to them, even if you feel like curling into a ball in the corner of the room." She suddenly patted my knee and grinned. "That's why Julia hates me still. She loathes my defiance, my unwillingness to play her games. If you follow my guidance, I'll steer you through the treacherous waters safely. I don't particularly care for myself. My dash is done, and I will lie in the bed I made for myself, but I still know which way the sharks are swimming, and I can help you."

"I don't particularly care for swimming in their ocean," I said. "But thank you."

"You may not care for it, but you will find yourself there."

"Why would I?"

"You want a good husband, don't you? Your first marriage is very important, and has nothing at all do with love. Set yourself up first, and worry about finding love elsewhere later."

I stared at her, not quite able to believe what I was hearing. Her thoughts on marriage couldn't be further from mine. "I have no interest in marriage at the moment."

She scoffed. "You will."

"And when I am interested, I won't be hiding my past from my husband or from those around me." I could have said more but there seemed no point explaining it to her. Her opinion was unlikely to change.

She lowered the newspaper altogether and took my hands in both of hers. Her look of sympathy forced me to sway back and dread what she might say. "If you're waiting for Mr. Fitzroy, then I must warn you not to get your hopes up. He will be quickly snapped up now, mark my words."

"I'm sure he will be," I said tightly. "If he makes it known that he wants a wife, they'll beat down his door to be first in line. He's handsome and rich." But not at all good marriage material. I'd known that all along, and yet I'd wanted to marry him anyway.

Before.

"Good." She let my hands go. "I'm pleased to see you accepting the situation. You're an understanding girl with a good head on your shoulders. You'll make an excellent wife, one day. When you're ready," she added with a wink. "But it doesn't mean we can't scope out potential candidates in the meantime."

I groaned.

"You'll thank me, one day," she said. "This is my gift to you, Charlie, for your birthday tomorrow. I cannot afford more."

"Oh. I don't expect anything from you."

"Nevertheless, I'm offering it. Please, accept it."

I nodded, not at all sure what I had just accepted.

She picked up the newspaper again but did not read. Her jaw set hard. "Now, just to remind you again, Seth is not an option for you."

I laughed. "So you've stated several times already. To repeat my answer—I'm not interested in your son."

"So you say, but I've seen the two of you together. You get along well."

"Like a brother and sister, not paramours."

She considered this a moment. "Seth always wanted siblings. I suppose you and Gus have taken on that role for him in a way." She returned to her newspaper, and I headed back to the chair by the window. "The interesting question is," she said from behind the paper, "who informed the newspaper of Julia's past at The Alhambra?"

I'd wager it was Miss Redding. Her jealousy of Lady Harcourt had been obvious.

The crunch of wheels on gravel had me leaping off the chair. "They're back!"

"Good. I need to speak with Seth. There are a number of invitations to consider. I must write a list of the ones he and Mr. Fitzroy plan to attend."

It was going to be a very short list.

I left her in the parlor and made my way to the kitchen to greet them and have a discussion out of Lady Vickers' hearing. Lincoln and Seth came in through the door that led to the courtyard. Gus must have remained in the coach house to tend to the carriage and horses, but with Seth wearing a clean, well-cut gentleman's suit, he didn't have to help.

"Well?" I said, stretching my fingers over the warm stove. Cook and Doyle were enjoying their own cup of tea at the table. Upon seeing his master, Doyle scrambled to his feet and stood awkwardly. Cook slurped his tea. "What did you learn?" I pressed.

"Marchbank was the only one of the three male committee members not at the club that day," Lincoln said. "Buchanan was also there, as was his brother."

"His brother! Lord Harcourt!" We'd met Lady Harcourt's eldest stepson when his brother, Andrew, disappeared. I'd thought he and his wife were living peacefully in the country. "The staff remembered?"

"The manager's memory is good but not infallible. I asked to see the wagers' ledger for that day. Every day, wagers between members are recorded by the club manager. Between questioning him, the footmen, and reviewing the ledger, we ascertained who was there and who was not. Both Buchanans like to gamble, and General Eastbrooke and Lord Gillingham are well known at the club."

"So it seems Marchbank is not a suspect."

"It would seem so."

"What if the killer be someone else?" Cook asked. "Someone we don't know."

"That's a possibility," Lincoln said. "I have the names of everyone recorded in the wagers' ledger."

"Can we see the list?" I asked.

Lincoln tapped his temple. "It's in here. I'll write them down for you."

Seth poured two cups of tea from the teapot on the stove and handed one to Lincoln. Lincoln hesitated then took it.

"Sit," he ordered Doyle as he himself sat.

Doyle expelled a breath and resumed his seat, albeit with a rigid back and shoulders. An awkward silence simmered among our little group. It was inevitable, I suppose, but I didn't like it. I knew just the way to break it, although I didn't expect the situation to explode the way it did.

"We need to draw the killer out," I said.

Lincoln looked up sharply. "No."

"How?" Seth asked.

"No," Lincoln said again, louder.

"I agree with him," Cook said. "It ain't a good idea."

"How?" Seth repeated. "Will someone answer me?"

"We'll announce my return to Lichfield and draw the killer to me," I said.

"No!" the three of them shouted.

"I agree." Doyle surprised me by voicing his opinion too. He seemed a little embarrassed to have contributed to the conversation and quickly sipped his tea, his gaze averted once again.

"It's too dangerous," Seth added.

Cook crossed his arms and glared at me. "It be a foolish idea, Charlie."

I crossed my arms too and matched his glare. "But—"

"No," Lincoln cut in with cold, calm finality. "And that's final."

I blew out a breath. "Overbearing men," I muttered. "Very well. We'll keep my return to ourselves for now, but I refuse to cower in here for more than a week. If the murderer hasn't been exposed in that time, I'll make my return known. Surely that will draw him out."

"We'll renegotiate in a week," Lincoln said. It wasn't an agreement, but I doubted I'd ever get one from him—or the others. I hoped a week would be long enough, if only to avoid a confrontation between us. I was still exhausted from the last one.

"One more thing," I said when he got up to leave. "You should know that Lady Harcourt's past has been exposed in the newspapers. We read the article just now. She'll be upset."

"Bloody hell." Seth dragged a hand over his face and down his chin. "How did they find out?"

"Through an anonymous source."

"She's going to be more than upset. She'll be on a rampage to find out who did it. Let's hope she has no reason to come here in the next little while. I, for one, don't wish to face her."

Lincoln simply nodded and went to leave, but Lady Vickers blocked his exit.

"It seems I have to come to the kitchen every time I wish to speak to one of the men in this household, including my own son," she said with a pointed glare at Seth.

He lowered his head and sipped his tea with great concentration.

"I've asked you both, time and again, to review the invitations received in your absences, but neither of you told me which events you will be attending."

"I won't attend any," Lincoln said. "Excuse me, madam, I have work to do."

Lady Vickers did not move. I held my breath. If I had blocked his exit, he would have simply picked me up and moved me out of the way. I couldn't imagine him doing that to her, but it would have been amusing to watch. My lips curved into a small smile as I waited to see what he'd do.

"You ought to attend something," she said. "Dinner at the Mosely's will be a lively affair. It's tomorrow night so I must reply today."

"Send my apologies."

"And mine," Seth said cheerfully.

His mother entered the kitchen, allowing Lincoln to slip past. She marched over to stand by her son, drawing herself up to her full height and peering down her nose at him. "Mr. Fitzroy is making a mistake. I won't allow you to make it too, Seth. I'll accept the invitation on your behalf."

He stood. He was taller than his mother, but she somehow seemed the more formidable of the two. "If Fitzroy's not going, then neither am I." He walked out.

She picked up her skirts and stormed after him. "You *will* go! Do you wish to make your mother a laughing stock?"

"You're quite capable of doing that without my help," he shot back.

Her shocked gasp echoed along the corridor. Cook chuckled. "I'll wager a shilling she'll win."

***

I spent the afternoon in the attic, adding new files for each of the supernatural girls from the school. From the attic window I could see the drive and the three callers Lady Vickers received. None stayed long, and I suspected they'd come to see either Seth or Lincoln, perhaps both, rather than the baroness herself. Considering she did not leave the house all day to make her own calls, I'd wager she was still somewhat excluded from society. Going by her cheerful mood when I rejoined her in the drawing room, after the third visitor left, I suspected she was telling the truth when she said she didn't care for the society set. She was going through the motions of receiving them entirely for Seth's benefit.

Not that *he* cared. He hardly spoke to his mother upon his return with Gus and Lincoln. They reported that Lord Harcourt had indeed been in London recently but had since returned to his country estate.

"He was here about the time Rampling was contacted by the mysterious man," Lincoln said, "as well as when Rampling was killed."

We four sat in his study as dusk darkened the room. I'd spotted the bloodstained rug as I entered and tended to agree with Doyle. The stains were a stride's length apart.

"But if it were Harcourt," I said, "why would he want to kill supernaturals who may or may not be used to reanimate the dead?"

"Why would anyone?" Gus muttered.

No one had an answer to that.

"So what now?" I asked with a shrug. "What will you do tomorrow?"

"Celebrate your birthday, of course!" Seth grinned. "Nineteen, eh? I remember that age. So young, so innocent."

Gus snorted. "You were not innocent at nineteen."

"Nor were you."

Lincoln seemed not to hear their banter. He sat at his desk, his focus on his hand resting on the papers there. Just beyond the papers sat a small ring box with my engagement ring nestled in the deep blue velvet. Why would he keep it on his desk and open like that?

"Is something wrong?" I asked him.

He glanced up. Blinked. "No."

"If there's nothing more," Seth said, rising, "I'm going to the kitchen to see what Cook's preparing for dinner."

"And to avoid your mother."

"The kitchen is no longer a safe-haven for me," Seth said on a sigh. "Nowhere is."

They nodded at Lincoln and left. I followed. "I'll have Doyle order a new rug," I said to him when I reached the doorway. "This one is ruined."

***

"Charlie! Wait!" Gus bounded down the stairs the following morning, one hand behind his back. When he reached the bottom, he thrust out a large parcel wrapped in brown paper and tied with a string. "Happy birthday."

"You got me something?" I said, accepting it.

"Of course."

"Should I open it now?"

"If you don't, I'll open it for you."

I laughed and untied the string. "You're so sweet. I wasn't expecting gifts. I've hardly been home long enough for you to shop."

"I got it before you left. If I knew you were goin' to be sent away and might not come back, I would've given it to you. Your leavin' caught me unawares."

"It caught everyone unawares." I handed him the string and opened the paper to reveal a black velvet hat sporting a frothy blue feather at the front and a matching ribbon around the crown. "It's lovely, Gus. Thank you." I pecked his cheek. "Are you heading in for breakfast?"

He offered me his elbow and we entered the dining room together. Lincoln and Seth were already seated, but both stood upon seeing me.

"Happy birthday, Charlie!" Seth drew me into a hug without a care for the new hat which I managed to thrust out of the way before it was crushed.

"Thank you," I said.

"Happy birthday," Lincoln said and sat down again. He resumed eating his bacon and reading the newspaper spread out on the table beside him.

Seth took my hand. "You can eat after you've unwrapped my gift."

"I'm so fortunate," I said, accepting the package. Tears quickly welled as I opened the wrapping to reveal a new pair of black leather gloves. I'd not celebrated my birthday since my mother died. I'd never told the boys in my gang the date of my birthday for fear it would lead to questions about my age. No one had wished me a happy birthday for five years, or given me a gift. Now I had two.

"Thank you," I said to Seth. "They'll go marvelously with the hat."

"You mean the hat will go with the gloves. They're made from the best kid leather." He picked them up and stroked them against my cheek. "See how soft they are?"

Gus snorted and headed to the sideboard, where Doyle had laid out the usual breakfast of toast, eggs and bacon. A separate covered dish occupied the center with one of Lincoln's cards leaning against it. The card had been reversed to show the blank side with my name scrawled on it in a hand I recognized from Cook's marketing lists. I lifted the lid and gasped. Three pastries, all different shapes and sizes, were arranged on a white plate. The thick triangular one with the lattice top appeared to be filled with fruit, a flatter rectangle had creamy custard spilling from the ends, and the square one dusted in sugar hid its secrets beneath golden flakey pastry.

I smiled. They were Cook's gift to me. I'd told him all about the delicious French pastries I'd tried on my journey to Paris with Lincoln, giving him as many details as I could remember. He must have recreated these based on my descriptions.

Gus dropped a piece of bacon onto his toast. "He never cooked me nothin' like that for my birthday."

The pastries were a delight. The square one turned out to be filled with chocolate that oozed into my mouth when I bit into it. It took me back to the wonderful, peaceful mornings Lincoln and I spent in Paris, sampling the most delicious food and enjoying one another's company. No one tried to kill or kidnap me there, and he'd treated me with respect and kindness. It seemed like a lifetime ago.

I thanked Cook after breakfast in the kitchen.

"My pleasure," he said. "It were a challenge to make them, and they not be exact, most like, but I liked doing it." He chucked me under the chin. "Have a good birthday, Charlie."

"It's off to a wonderful start so far."

Doyle shyly handed me something he'd been holding behind his back. Like the other gifts, it was wrapped in brown paper but was tied with a green ribbon, not string. "Oh, Doyle, you didn't have to," I said, unwrapping the book of short stories. "Thank you. I love reading."

His cheeks pinked but his chin didn't drop from its lofty height. "Since you have to remain at Lichfield for the next little while, I thought you might like something to occupy your time."

"I certainly will."

Lincoln suddenly appeared in the doorway. "Charlie, may I see you in my study for a moment." He didn't wait for me, but strode off.

"Has he given you anything yet?" Cook whispered.

"No, but I don't expect him to. I'd be surprised if he even remembered it was my birthday."

Cook snorted. "You'd best go."

I hurried up the stairs but slowed down as I passed my door and headed toward his. I suspected he was going to give me a gift, and I didn't know if I wanted to accept anything from him. Not only that, but being alone with Lincoln played havoc with my nerves.

The door was open and he stood waiting for me, the knuckles of one hand resting on the desk. "Happy birthday," he said again.

"Thank you." I swallowed. Should I sit? Remain standing?

Light from the window caught the diamond in my engagement ring, still sitting in its box on his desk. If that was my gift... No, it couldn't be. He hadn't wrapped it. Indeed, there were no parcels on his desk. I blew out a breath.

"I wanted to give you your gift in private." He opened his desk drawer.

I closed my eyes and willed my heart to cease its hammering.

"Charlie?"

I opened my eyes and blinked. He stood holding a document several pages thick. "What's this?" I said, accepting it.

"The deeds to a house in—"

"You're giving me a house!" I shook my head and shoved the document into his chest. "Don't be absurd."

He swallowed heavily and stared down at the papers. "It's in Harringay, not far from here. The area is close enough to the city for commuting yet retains much of its rural nature."

"Are you not listening, Lincoln? I don't want it. It's too much."

"It's not very large."

A bubble of laughter escaped. I threw my hands in the air. "It's a bloody house! Even a stinking rat-infested room in Whitechapel is too much to give your ex-fiancée on her birthday. I won't accept it."

"It's already yours. I paid for it yesterday and had your name put on the deed." He pointed to a spot on the top-most page. My name was clearly written in the space.

I fell back and placed a hand to my throbbing heart. "You're throwing me out of Lichfield again, aren't you?"

His eyes widened. "No!"

"Why else would you give me a house, for God's sake? You want me to leave Lichfield but you don't want to feel guilt for forcing me to live on the streets or for sending me to a school, so you bought me a bloody house to move into."

He stepped toward me. "Charlie—"

I stepped back. "I'm glad you're able to put a price on your guilt, Lincoln. Glad you can buy your way to feeling better about yourself." I picked up my skirts and spun around.

He caught me before I'd taken a single step. I tried to pull free, but his grip was too strong. "That's not why I bought it for you." His voice shook, but whether from rage or another emotion, I couldn't tell. He turned me to face him, but I refused to look at him and instead focused on his shoulder. "I wanted to give you something special for your birthday. Something that will make a difference to your life."

"Forcing me to leave Lichfield made a rather large difference to my life. What else am I to think, when you buy me a house, except that you want me to live there, away from my—" I suddenly choked and tears welled again. "Away from my home," I managed to finish on a whisper.

His deep breath rustled my hair. I was very aware that he still held me and that we stood very close. "It's not a house for you to live in, unless you wish to, but a house for you to *have*. The area is a growing one, and rents will rise. The property is a good size for a couple or small family."

I blinked away my tears but still could not look at him. He let me go. I shook my head, unable to speak for fear of choking on my emotions again. It was all too much, too confusing. Why was he doing this for me when he'd been so cruel only weeks before? Out of guilt?

Or was it because he knew I would one day be on my own again, gone from Lichfield, and in need of shelter?

I couldn't think through my tumultuous thoughts. I felt like I was floating adrift, unable to steer my boat. I turned and ran from the room. He didn't follow.

I ran outside and across the lawn. The wind nipped at my face and teased my hair from its pins. It whipped my cheeks and stung my eyes. By the time I reached the bare trees in the orchard, I was out of breath, yet my mind was a little clearer. I climbed my favorite apple tree, even though it gave me no shelter, barren as it was. When I reached the topmost limbs, I sat in the fork of two branches and wiped away my tears.

The estate of Lichfield spread before me, draped in what remained of the morning frost. Smoke from four of the chimneys curled up to the insipid blue sky, but otherwise, the house was quiet, dormant. Lincoln hadn't followed me out. I shivered, suddenly cold. *This* was my home. If Lincoln was telling the truth, and he didn't plan on sending me away again, why give me a house that I wasn't going to live in?

'I wanted to give you something that will make a difference to your life,' he'd said.

I suddenly understood. Aside from a home, which I already had in Lichfield, the one thing I desired most of all was freedom to do as I pleased, to not be a victim of others' whims, even his. As an unmarried woman with no money and no experience working in a trade, I was entirely at his mercy, something that had been driven home to me all too well. By giving me the house, Lincoln was giving me a means to earn money through the rental income, or to keep the capital if I chose to sell it. The house gave me freedom and independence that few women possessed, and even fewer unwed ones.

It certainly would make a difference to my life, and not merely in a financial way. It bought me time to choose my own future. I didn't need to rush into marriage; I could wait. It meant I would never have to rely on Lincoln—or anyone—rescuing me, as I'd had to do at the school. If I ever found myself in that situation again, I could just leave and live off the money from the rent. I would never again be homeless.

I laid my cheek against the cool, rough branch and breathed. Just breathed. My thudding heartbeats were loud in the stillness, echoing through my body, between my ears. Was this real? Was I now truly safe and in command of my own life?

Or would my security be once again ripped from me when I least expected it?

The rumble of wheels on the drive made me sit up straight and peer over the treetops toward the gate. Two carriages approached. If the occupants looked toward the orchard at the side of the house, I would be seen in the bare tree.

I climbed down, snagging my hem on a twig. "Damn." I picked up my skirts and ran toward the back of the house. I peeked round the wall, just as the carriages stopped at the front steps. General Eastbrooke alighted from the foremost coach, followed by Lord Gillingham. Lady Harcourt and Lord Marchbank stepped out of the second one. Hell. The committee had arrived.

CHAPTER 8

"Have you gone mad?" Lord Gillingham's voice could be heard from where I stood in the depths of the service area at the back of the house.

I bit my lip and slipped past Bella, arranging tea things on a tray, to join Gus and Cook in the corridor just outside the kitchen. "He sounds angry," I whispered. There was no need to whisper. The committee members wouldn't have heard us speaking in our normal voices, but it came naturally.

"Bloody furious," Gus said. "Sounds like they just learned Fitzroy's been warnin' the supernaturals. That were quick."

They all had spies—some in government organizations where they even set triggers on certain files to alert them of anyone requesting the records. It wouldn't surprise me if they also had people watching the supernaturals here in the city too.

"You haven't thought this through." General Eastbrooke's voice boomed in response to something someone, probably Lincoln, had said.

"What will it take for Death to hit one of 'em?" Gus asked with a snicker.

"Or kill 'em," Cook added. "My money's on Gilly going first."

"Is Seth with him?" I asked.

Gus nodded just as Doyle appeared up ahead. His brisk footsteps were at odds with his usual steady pace. "Tea! And quickly!"

"Bella be doing it now," Cook told him.

"Which room are they going into?" I asked, following Doyle into the kitchen.

"Library," he said, shooing Bella out of the way. She clicked her tongue and thrust her hands on her hips. He ignored her. "Out of Lady Vickers' hearing."

"But not out of mine."

"You're going to listen at the door?" Cook said.

"Of course."

He grunted. "Don't get caught."

"I'll go in now," Gus told me. "I'll stand by the door and tap it if someone is about to leave."

"You're a marvel," I said.

He walked in front of me and signaled with a nod when he reached the end of the service corridor that it was clear to move forward. Muffled voices grew louder as I approached the library, but I couldn't make out their words. Gus opened the library door enough to slip through and I heard Lord Marchbank chastise Lincoln for taking matters into his own hands. I wished I could see Lincoln's reaction.

Gus winked at me then closed the door. I crept across the tiles and put my ear to it. Not for the first time, I wished the house had secret passages and rooms to make sneaking about easier.

"You're a fool," said Gillingham. "You overreacted, as usual."

"Lincoln never overreacts," Lady Harcourt snapped. How curious that she was now defending Lincoln. The last time I'd seen her, they'd argued. Perhaps my departure from Lichfield had rekindled her hopes of renewing a romantic liaison with him.

"In this case, he has," Gillingham went on. "We won't know where to find them now. What's the point of the ministry at all if we don't know where the curiosities we're supposed to be monitoring are located?"

"Agreed," Eastbrooke intoned.

Doyle joined me and I stepped to the side, out of sight. With the tea tray balanced on one hand, he opened the door with the other. All chatter ceased.

"I'll serve, thank you, Doyle," Lady Harcourt said.

A moment later Doyle reappeared and returned to the service area. I resumed my position by the door.

"It was a foolish move, Lincoln," Eastbrooke went on. "Particularly when they could have acted as bait to draw the killer out."

"No one will be used as bait," Lincoln growled. "They're not pieces of meat."

"Don't pretend they're normal humans either," Gillingham shot back.

For a man whose wife was "inhuman" too, his words were cruel indeed. I, however, felt quite unaffected by them. I'd ceased to care what Gillingham thought of me very soon after meeting him.

"While I don't blame you for taking such drastic action, you should have consulted us," Lady Harcourt said. "We are the committee, after all."

"And I am the ministry's leader," Lincoln said with perfect calm. "I don't work *for* the committee."

"You don't have to be alone, either."

I rolled my eyes. Could she be any more overt? He was discussing work, and she was making suggestive remarks about his private life. That wasn't the way to

Lincoln's heart. Not that I knew the way either—or even if he had one—but innuendo certainly wasn't the answer.

"I don't *work* alone," he countered. "I work with Seth and Gus."

"Thank you," Seth said. "And I want it known that I agree with your decision. Those people have a right to know their lives are in danger."

"No one cares what you think, Vickers." Gillingham sounded bored. "You're not on the committee and you're not the leader. You and your gorilla shouldn't even be involved, if you ask my opinion."

"I didn't ask it," Seth said with a laconic airiness. "No one did."

"Gentlemen," Marchbank intoned. "Let's keep to the facts. And the main fact is, we don't know where these people are now."

"They could wreak all sorts of havoc," Eastbrooke said.

"They haven't done so to date," Lincoln said.

"They may not have caused us trouble in the past, but you shouldn't have divulged the situation to them. It's ministry business. Highly confidential."

"Now they know we exist," Marchbank added. "You gave away our secret."

"They think I work for the police," Lincoln said.

"It doesn't matter what they think," Gillingham shot back. "They're aware they're being monitored."

"I fail to see how that is a problem."

Gillingham's snort came clear through the closed door. "Then you're a fool."

"Enough, Gilly," Lord Marchbank said. "There's no need for name calling."

I couldn't quite hear Gillingham's grumbled response.

"The problem remains," Lady Harcourt said, "that we don't know where these people are now. Please tell us you had them followed, Lincoln. It would ease our minds greatly."

"They've been instructed to report their movements to me," he said.

"Good."

"Voluntarily?" Eastbrooke asked. Lincoln must have nodded, because he added, "Why would they do so?"

"You've put a lot of trust in them," Marchbank said.

"Most realize the dangers of their own powers," Lincoln told them. "They understand that a monitoring system is necessary and of long term benefit to the nation."

Someone made a scoffing sound. I'd wager it was Gillingham.

"Will you keep their whereabouts to yourself?" Marchbank asked.

"I will. I made them a promise that no one else would be told."

"That doesn't include us," Gillingham said.

"*No one* will be told. Is that clear?"

A pause then, "Are you implying you don't trust us?" Gillingham spluttered.

"I don't trust anyone."

A more weighty statement could not have fallen from Lincoln's lips. It was followed by complete silence, but it lasted mere seconds, before all four committee members voiced their opposition. It was difficult to distinguish one from the other, but the angry tones couldn't be clearer.

"He's mad," Gillingham said once the other voices ceased. "You've gone soft, Fitzroy. It's that necromancer girl's influence. First you send her away without telling us where, and now everyone else who poses a threat to London."

I sucked in a breath and pressed my ear firmly to the door, wishing I could hear Lincoln's reaction. But if he did react, it wasn't loud enough. The truth was, Lincoln *had* softened compared to when I'd first met him. Back in the summer, he wouldn't have warned the supernaturals. He would not have seen them as people to protect; they would have simply been names in a file to be monitored. Had *I* softened him?

"Do be quiet, Gilly," Marchbank snapped. He sounded more irritated than I'd ever heard him. The man's feathers were rarely ruffled. Perhaps he simply didn't like being told he was untrustworthy. I wondered if Lincoln would tell him later that he was the only one not under suspicion, thanks to the fact he'd not been at Brooks's Club the day the murderer employed Rampling.

"You're letting him get away with this?" Gillingham cried. "My God, March, it's not on. Not on at all, I tell you. There's no place for autonomous behavior in the ministry. He is supposed to act under our direction, not outside it. We should have known he'd end up this way, raised as he was, alone in your household, General. He wasn't trained to consider others."

It was the most insightful thing to ever come out of Gillingham's mouth. Lincoln had indeed been brought up alone to be an unemotional leader. Although saying Lincoln had been *trained* to think that way, like a dog, was putting it coldly.

"Are you accusing me of raising him improperly?" Eastbrooke bellowed.

"Stop it!" Lady Harcourt's high-pitched command cut through me like broken glass. "Enough bickering. I cannot cope with this at the moment. It's trying my nerves."

"Your private life and its effect on your nerves is hardly our problem, Julia," Gillingham shot back. "Do not bring it into ministry meetings."

Lady Harcourt's response could not be heard.

"The fact remains, you think one of us is the murderer," the general challenged.

"I haven't formed any opinions," Lincoln said. "It may be one of you, or it may not be."

"Outrageous." Gillingham's mutter didn't sound too far from the door. I hoped Gus still stood there, ready to knock in warning if anyone wanted to leave. "I've never been so insulted."

He ought to hear the insults we hurled at him. They got quite colorful at times. I'm sure Seth and Gus were both biting their lips to stop their smiles.

"We can't force him to tell us," Eastbrooke said.

"No, but we can force him out of the ministry," Gillingham said. "He's only the leader because of us."

"Don't be absurd," Eastbrooke said. "The prophecy made him the leader. We can't break it."

"The prophecy said he became leader. It didn't mention for how long."

"I'm not leaving the ministry," Lincoln said. "And that is final. Is there anything else? I'm a busy man."

"You're walking on a thin edge, Fitzroy," Gillingham warned. "A very thin edge."

A quick, light tap sounded on the door. I spun round, only to trip on my torn hem. I scrambled to my feet, but tripped again. The door opened. I lay utterly exposed on the tiled floor.

I glanced back over my shoulder and swallowed my gasp. Lord Gillingham appeared in the widening gap of the open door, his head bowed. He had not seen me, thank God.

"Gillingham, a word before you leave," Lincoln said.

Gillingham turned. "What is it now?"

I half crawled, half slithered across the tiles to the large urn and hid behind it. I pulled my knees up and gathered my skirts around my feet just in time. Lady Harcourt strode out of the library ahead of Lord Marchbank and General Eastbrooke.

"A private matter," I heard Lincoln tell Gillingham. "Regarding your wife."

Lady Harcourt stopped and glanced back as Seth and Gus emerged from the library. "What's that about?" she asked as the library door closed.

"No idea," Eastbrooke said, while Gus collected coats from the stand by the main door.

"Perhaps he's taken umbrage to the way Gilly treats his wife in public," Marchbank said with a disinterested air.

"How does he treat his wife?" Eastbrooke asked.

"With disrespect." Marchbank accepted his coat and gloves from Gus as Doyle joined us.

Eastbrooke grunted. "Gilly treats everyone that way. And anyway, why would Lincoln care?"

"Perhaps he feels sorry for her. Perhaps he likes her."

Lady Harcourt bristled. She snatched her gloves from Seth as he handed them to her. With his back to me, I couldn't see his expression. He helped her on with her fur coat then caught her arm so she couldn't leave. She glared at him but didn't demand he unhand her.

"You two go on," she said to the general and Marchbank. "Gilly can take me home."

The two men bowed and left. Doyle shut the door behind them, then he and Gus passed me to go to the service area. Gus's jaw dropped when he saw me but his pace didn't slow. Doyle must have seen me hiding too, but he gave no indication. I kept myself as small and tight as possible.

"Julia, are you all right?" Seth's rich, warm tones sounded genuine. He must still care for her wellbeing or he wouldn't be asking.

The bitter taste of disappointment filled my mouth like bile. He knew what she was like, knew how she resented me and had orchestrated my kidnapping by Mrs. Drinkwater, yet here he was being kind to her. All over a little gossip, too.

Lady Harcourt glanced at the library door. It remained shut. "I'll manage."

He removed his hand, but she caught it. She stepped closer to him, pressing her considerable chest against his. She peered up at him, all fluttering lashes and pouting lips. I wanted to choke. "That's very sweet of you, Darling, thank you. I feel better already knowing you're in my corner."

I wished I could see Seth's reaction. He didn't move, and his unemotional question gave nothing away. "Do you know who spoke to the papers?"

She shook her head and dabbed the corner of her eye with her little finger. Seth handed her his handkerchief and she accepted it with a weak smile. "I'm so glad we're friends again, dearest Seth. Look at you." She lifted a hand to his face. "My poor Seth. Have you been fighting again?" She gasped. "Not with Lincoln, I hope?"

"No."

"Then who?"

"Husbands, Julia. Always the damned husbands."

She threw her head back and laughed. "Oh, Seth, thank you. I needed that." She stood on her toes and kissed him. I heard his intake of breath and wondered if she'd made the cut on his lip sting or if he'd been taken aback. "My darling Seth. It was silly of us to fight, and over such a small matter as... Well, she's gone now, and we should set our disagreement aside too. I miss you terribly." Her voice turned throaty. "Why not visit me tonight?"

He extracted himself from her grip and stepped back. "I must decline the offer. My mother is trying to find me a wife, and it would be a blow to my prospects if I was caught sneaking out of an eligible widow's house in the early hours."

She blinked at him, her face a picture of dawning horror. It was the moment she realized Seth had no interest in reacquainting himself with her delights. "That sort of thing has never bothered you before," she said, voice harsh. "And you told me that marriage didn't interest you."

"It bothers me now. As to marriage, I am undecided. I'll assess each candidate on her merits and make a decision in due course."

She pulled her fur cloak closed over her chest and looked away. "I see."

"I'm sure your other lovers will fill the void." He laughed at his crude innuendo. "I saw Andrew yesterday at Brooks's, by the by."

Lady Harcourt went rigid. "Stop it, Seth. Cruelty doesn't suit you."

The library door opened and Gillingham emerged. The sickly pall of his face was starkly white beneath his rust colored hair. With his walking stick under his arm, he snatched up his own hat, gloves and cloak and strode past Seth and Lady Harcourt to the front door.

"What did you say to affect him so?" she asked Lincoln.

"Ask him," he said, strolling out of the library.

"I dare not. I might get my head bitten off." She hurried after Gillingham without so much as a goodbye.

Seth closed the front door and blew out a breath. "Meeting?"

Lincoln nodded. "Fetch Gus."

I stood to reveal myself. Seth drew in a breath, but Lincoln's brow merely lifted.

"Bloody hell, Charlie!" Seth threw his hands in the air. "Can't a man have a private conversation around here without someone listening in?"

"If you wanted a private conversation, you should have gone somewhere private," I said, passing him. "So are you really going to give your mother's candidates serious consideration?"

"Are you mad?"

I laughed and followed Lincoln into the library. He collected half-empty teacups and placed them on the tray. I knelt by the fireplace and added more coal from the scuttle. The warmth and glow mesmerized me, and I stared at the coals until I heard footsteps approach. He sat on the armchair near me.

"Have you considered my gift?" he asked quietly.

I stared down at my hands on my lap. I nodded.

"And?"

The entry of Seth and Gus stopped me from answering, which was just as well since I didn't know how I wanted to answer. I had considered his gift, but I hadn't yet come to a conclusion. There was a rather important question that needed answering first—what strings came attached to it?

"Did you ask Gillingham about his wife?" Seth asked, sprawling in the large armchair on the other side of the fire.

Lincoln nodded. To me, he said, "I take it you don't need to be informed of what took place in the meeting?"

"I heard most of it," I said, sitting on the rug and tucking my feet beneath my spread skirts. "I expected Marchbank to be on your side, but he was just as angry with you for sending those people away."

"Marchbank may not be innocent."

Seth sat forward. "Why do you say that?"

"It's something Gillingham just told me."

"Interestin'," Gus said. "A guilty man throwin' suspicion onto someone else, maybe?"

"Perhaps," Lincoln said with a nod. "It requires further investigation before any conclusions are drawn."

"Well?" Seth urged. "What did Gilly say?"

"I told him I knew about his wife's ability to change her form. He was shocked that the secret was out."

"He certainly looked shocked," Seth said with a tilt of his lips. "He was white as a ghost, and his hands were shaking."

"Perhaps he was ashamed, too," I said. "Ashamed that you know who—rather, what—he's been...intimate with."

"She wasn't in that form during intimacy," Seth protested.

"How do you know?" Gus said with a wicked gleam in his eye.

"She wasn't," Lincoln answered for him. "She told me as much."

"Even so," I said, "Lord Gillingham strikes me as someone who wouldn't want others thinking him a lesser man because of his wife's other form. Other more dominant form."

"True." Seth nodded knowingly. "Go on, Fitzroy. What did he tell you?"

"I asked him if his distaste for his wife colored his perceptions of supernaturals in general. I suggested to him that he hated her animal form, and he took that hatred out on others who are different."

"You accused him of being the killer?" Gus blew out a breath. "That's bold."

Lincoln merely lifted one shoulder. "While I don't expect him to tell me outright if he is, I wanted to gauge his reaction."

He should have asked one of us to remain with him then. Lincoln wasn't very good at reading people's expressions. "How did he react?" I asked.

"He went pale, as you saw, and he stutters when he's anxious. He told me that he doesn't hate his wife, but she does disgust him, and he's not sure how to react to her anymore. As his wife, her place is beneath him, so he told me. He considered her the inferior half of their marriage."

"Good lord," I muttered. "His thinking is positively barbaric."

"And yet not unusual among men, in my experience," Lincoln said quietly. I looked up sharply to see him watching me, his dark gaze heating my skin.

"Don't look at me," Seth said, hands in the air. "I happily put women on a pedestal. All the better to—"

"Shut your hole," Gus said with a roll of his eyes. "No one was talkin' about you, anyway."

I cleared my throat. "Go on, Lincoln. What else did he say?"

"He made a very clear case for not being the killer," he said. We all sat forward. "He claimed that if he was going to kill a non-human, as he calls supernaturals, he would have started with his wife."

I pressed my hand to my chest. "I suppose."

"I don't necessarily agree with that logic," Lincoln went on. "He used to care for his wife. He has been intimate with her before he learned of her true form. The memory of that affection could stop him from hurting her. He has no such connection to the other supernaturals.

"I tend to agree," Seth said with a nod. "The heart plays odd tricks. While I don't doubt that her true form disgusts him, it takes quite a monster to kill a woman you've been intimate with. Not that I'm speaking from experience, mind. I adore all my previous lovers. Except for one or two," he added with a glance at the door.

"So we are none the wiser," I said on a sigh. "He's still a suspect."

"As is Marchbank."

"Ah, yes. What did you learn about him?"

"In his anxiety, Gillingham tried to throw suspicion onto others. He told me that Marchbank has very good reason to hate people with supernatural powers. One of them killed his father."

CHAPTER 9

"He wasn't killed by a supernatural," Seth said with smug certainty, as if he'd caught Gillingham out in a lie. "Marchbank's father tossed himself off a bridge one night, in front of witnesses. The river police fished the body out of the Thames the next day. The key here is the word witnesses—plural."

"According to Gillingham, Marchbank was hypnotized into killing himself," Lincoln said.

"Hypnotized!" Gus snorted. "Gillingham's a tosspot if he thinks we'll believe that. Mesmerizers are all quacks."

"I've never met a true hypnotist, but there is an account of mind control in the ministry records. It's vague, and the mesmerist died before Marchbank so it couldn't have been him."

Seth rubbed his chin, no longer so cocky. "Are you telling us that Marchbank's father was *talked* into ending it all?"

"Hypnotized," Gus said with a roll of his eyes. "Not talked. It ain't the same."

"I thought you said they were all quacks."

"They are."

"Do you think Gillingham was lying?" I asked Lincoln.

"I couldn't tell."

"No, I don't suppose you could. You're not very good at that sort of thing."

He arched his brows ever so slightly.

I'd gone this far; I saw no reason not to continue. "Empathy is not your strong suit. I believe Gillingham pointed that out to you earlier."

His brows rose even further. Gus and Seth studied the fireplace with intensity.

"Do stop looking so surprised, Lincoln. It's true and you know it. So, the question now is, how will we determine if Gillingham is speaking the truth?"

"I'll ask Marchbank," Lincoln said. "I need to know more about the hypnotist, whether he was involved in the death of Old Marchbank or not. He must be recorded in our files."

"I don't understand," I said. "If Gillingham knew about the hypnotist—and Marchbank too, presumably—why is the fellow not in our records already?"

"The hypnotist ordered Old Marchbank to erase his ministry file. The current Lord Marchbank only knew about him because he found references in his father's diary, but no name or description. Gillingham doesn't know how Marchbank the younger knew the hypnotist killed his father, however."

"Diabolical," Seth murmured.

Gus threw up his hands. "They ain't real. You're too gubbillil, Seth."

Seth pulled a face. "And you're an idiot if you think that's a word."

"Let's not dismiss the possibility that hypnotists exist," I said. "Real ones. But are we to believe the hypnotist had Marchbank kill himself all because he didn't want his name listed in our records?"

"There must be more to it," Lincoln said with a nod. "For now, the key question is, why wasn't I informed?"

"It's also important to know if this is enough for Lord Marchbank to be angry with all supernaturals. Enough to kill."

Doyle entered and collected the dishes. None of us spoke; not because we didn't want Doyle to hear our conversation, but because we were still digesting Gillingham's news. If he was right, then we had an entirely new and dangerous type of supernatural on our hands. One capable of doing great harm. If a past committee member had succumbed to a hypnotist's powers, even after knowing what he was capable of, then the general public could be in even greater danger.

"So what now?" Seth asked. "Are we taking the day off to celebrate Charlie's birthday?"

I laughed. "I'm sure you can find something better to do than spend the day here with me. What about the other names from the Brooks's ledger? Did you write them down, Lincoln?"

He nodded. "I'd like to start with Andrew Buchanan and his brother, Lord Harcourt. Considering our prior associations with them, their knowledge of the supernatural, and access to our archives, they're our most likely suspects."

"Want us to travel to Harcourt's estate?" Gus asked. "A bit o' fresh air will do us all good."

Lincoln shook his head. "Not yet. See what Buchanan has to say, first."

"I know you prefer the direct approach," I said, "but I think we should tread softly."

"I can tread softly." Was he offended? It was difficult to tell.

"Is there some way you can question him about his movements without raising his suspicions?"

"I could interrogate his valet."

I winced. Lincoln's interrogation methods were not at all soft.

Seth shook his head. "Valets are usually loyal to their masters."

"I'll pay him for his silence," Lincoln said.

"There's always the risk he'll tell Buchanan."

"I think this would be better left to Seth," I said. "He's very good at casual conversation."

Seth nodded thoughtfully. "I am, aren't I?"

"And not quite as threatening as you, Lincoln."

Lincoln bristled. I don't think I'd ever seen his spine straighten like that or his lips purse quite so much. I'd not thought it possible to offend him, but perhaps I had. "I'm not always threatening."

The loaded silence was broken by approaching footsteps on the tiles outside the library. Doyle must be returning to see if we required anything.

"We need to learn Buchanan's movements," I said, "then make it seem as if Seth just happens to be in the same place at the same time by coincidence. They can strike up a conversation, and Seth can casually weave in questions about Buchanan's whereabouts on the dates we know Rampling met with his mysterious employer."

"Right," Gus said. "So how do we know where Buchanan's going to be so Seth can come across him?"

"I can arrange it," Lady Vickers announced, sweeping into the room in a cloud of black. Oh no. Doyle had left the door open.

"Mother!" Seth shot to his feet. "How much of that did you hear?"

137

"Only enough to know that you wish to speak with Mr. Buchanan."

"Nothing before that?"

She waved a hand. "I assume Mr. Fitzroy conducts...private business. It's all far too vulgar for my liking, although I understand the necessity of these secret meetings and discussions." She gave Lincoln a firm nod, as if she knew precisely what he was up to and had decided it was a little underhanded but not enough to be concerned. I wondered how she'd react if she knew the truth.

"You know where Mr. Buchanan will be?" Lincoln prompted.

"I know where he'll be tomorrow night." She turned a triumphant smile onto her son. "At the dinner party I asked you to attend."

Seth fell onto the chair with a groan. "I'll dust off my dinner suit."

***

I returned to the attic to resume adding to the ministry records, and I took the opportunity to check for hypnotists. There was only the one whom Lincoln mentioned, but he'd died over a hundred years ago.

The attic was a pleasant room with its grand views over the estate and neatly arranged files stored in a cabinet of small wooden drawers. There was little dust, despite our lack of maids, and part of it was arranged like a small study with a desk and chair in a nook by the window. Old furniture and boxes containing pieces left behind by the previous owner were stored in the deeper recesses at the back. I had little need to venture down there.

"You don't have to do this." Lincoln's voice startled me. I swallowed my gasp but couldn't hide my jump. "It's your birthday."

I returned to the files I'd been flicking through but took in none of the information. "Do you stop working on your birthday?"

"You're not me." His voice sounded closer.

I slammed the drawer shut, drew in a fortifying breath, and turned to face him. He stood only a few feet away, his collar undone and white shirtsleeves rolled to his elbows, revealing strong, tanned forearms. His eyes seemed blacker, but that could have been due to the poor light in the attic. His face, with its noble cheekbones and hard planes, gave nothing away. The pointer finger on his right hand stroked the thumbnail, but he was otherwise still. He simply watched me with that unreadable expression, as if he expected me to guess what he wanted.

"I've been thinking about the murderer," I said to fill the awkward silence.

He looked away. His right hand curled into a fist.

"I feel as if we're examining this case in pieces, but not seeing the whole. No, that's not quite right either." I drew in a steadying breath and let it out slowly. His presence addled my brain.

"Go on," he said, drawing the chair out for me.

I sat and he perched on the desk, his hands holding onto the edge. "We need to go back to the beginning, back to the basic elements. We've been trying to find out who hired Rampling and Daley, but there's another path we can take. We were going down that path before..." I swallowed. "Before I went away."

"The link between Frankenstein, Jasper, Brumley and Drinkwater. I've been thinking about that too, but I fail to see how we can progress without investigating Rampling's story. It's not impossible," he added quickly. "I don't doubt you. You have a way of seeing things differently to me. It's...good. We work well together because of it."

I had never known Lincoln to ramble, and I wasn't sure if his rushed speech could be considered such. It was out of character, however. "I assume you came to that conclusion in my absence." And fetched me home because of it. If there was one thing that would make Lincoln retrieve me, it would be that. The ministry was, after all, everything to him.

He simply nodded and continued to watch me.

"We know that someone hired Captain Jasper to produce a serum to bring the dead back to life," I said. "Jasper never did make the serum. The man who commissioned him most likely killed him, in the holding cell, to keep him from talking to us."

He lowered his head, breaking off his unnerving stare. "Agreed."

"The same man contacted both Frankenstein and Drinkwater, after hearing they were also trying to reanimate bodies, although his information was incorrect in Drinkwater's case as that wasn't what he was attempting to do. Once he learned that they used magical means, he ended his correspondence. In Frankenstein's case, he left him in peace, presumably because he's not magical, yet he killed Drinkwater, presumably because he is. He also killed Joan Brumley, because he heard through Frankenstein that she was a necromancer. He's been trying to kill me too, almost from the moment I revealed myself to be Charlotte Holloway, necromancer."

"He doesn't want to use magic to reanimate the dead," Lincoln went on, looking up again but not with the same intensity in his gaze. "But he does want to reanimate them in some other way."

"And he doesn't want anyone to use supernatural methods to do the same. Because he's afraid of us, perhaps, or dislikes us intensely and is simply murdering out of spite."

"The former reason is more likely than the last," he said. "The fact that the murders only happened *after* Frankenstein used you would indicate as such."

"My thoughts exactly. He's afraid because he knows what we can do, yet it's the same thing he wants to do. He's afraid we'll do it first and reap the rewards of such a discovery." I extended my hands, palms up, presenting my theory to him. "What do you think?"

"It's possible." He crossed his arms and ankles. "Or he's afraid of not being able to control the reanimations if someone else develops a way of doing it. A magical way."

I nodded slowly, warming to the idea. "That's clever, Lincoln. I think you may be right."

"Financial gain is a very real possibility too."

"Perhaps it's a combination of both." I smiled and his face lifted.

"Charlie," he said quietly.

I held up my hand. I did not want to take the conversation into unchartered and treacherous waters. "The reasons why don't matter yet. What does matter is the who. And that brings us to my next point, and something I've been considering. What if the murderer succeeded in commissioning another doctor after Jasper's death? Perhaps even another military doctor? The military component throws suspicion onto General Eastbrooke."

Lincoln's fingers tapped. "Jasper was dismissed from the army's medical corps by the time he was commissioned, but I agree that a link to Eastbrooke exists there. However, we shouldn't limit ourselves to medical corps doctors."

It would seem he'd followed my train of thought without me having to voice it. Because of his seer's link to me or a more personal one? "So you think we ought to investigate other doctors."

He nodded. "One specializing in hematology and serums, as Jasper went on to do. We'll start at the major hospitals."

"We? Are you suggesting I join you?"

He opened his mouth but paused before saying, "If you'd like."

I got the distinct impression he'd been referring to himself, Seth and Gus in the "we," but I wasn't about to admit that. "I'll be careful, of course," I said, anticipating his response. "I won't allow myself to be seen leaving Lichfield. At the hospitals, you can pretend to be a doctor and I'll be your assistant. Or a journalist, perhaps. Yes, I think that's a better disguise. Blood research is most likely a small field. All the doctors would know one another. They're unlikely to know any journalists."

He inclined his head in an unconvincing nod.

"I can't be cooped up in here forever," I said. "At least this way I'm not being exposed to any of our suspects."

Another incline of his head.

"Shall we start this afternoon?" I asked.

"We'll visit one or two hospitals after lunch." I waited for him to leave, but he merely sat on the edge of the desk as if he were waiting for me to say something. About the case? His birthday gift? Or about his banishment of me?

I got to my feet and he quickly stood too. "I'm finished in here. I'll speak with you after lunch." I turned to go, but his long strides meant he easily beat me to the door.

"I came up here to talk to you," he said, his voice as smoky as his eyes. His hair was pulled back at the nape, but a few strands escaped and dripped over his forehead in black twists.

"We are talking."

"Not about work."

My pulse quickened. "I need more time to think about your gift."

"Not about that either."

"As far as I'm concerned, there's nothing else to talk about." I went to move around him, but he blocked my exit. "Don't," I growled, low and harsh.

He swallowed hard then stepped aside.

"Let's make one thing clear." I heard the steel in my voice, felt the fervent beat of my blood through my veins. It felt good to square up to him, to show him that I wasn't the same girl who'd fallen blindly in love with him. "What's happened between us is in the past. It's in both our interests not to dwell on it. I know you must have had reasons for sending me away, but..." I closed my eyes so that I didn't have to see his handsome face. "But I'm not ready to hear them. I'm not ready to forgive you."

I opened my eyes and turned away, my heart sore. It felt as if the wound he'd inflicted on it was still fresh, raw. Perhaps it would never heal. It was certainly going to take much longer than a few days.

"Will you ever be?" he asked quietly.

"It's too soon to know." I marched out and headed to my room without looking back. I ate luncheon in there, seated in the deep armchair by the fire, a book in my lap.

The soft knock on my door roused me some time later. I opened it to a scowling Seth. "I was sent to tell you that you're leaving soon. Gus will pick you up at the front of the house in fifteen minutes. It's raining. Take a coat and umbrella."

"You sound upset." I stepped aside and beckoned him in.

He hesitated, then with a sigh, entered. "I'm not at all happy that you're heading out this afternoon. It's too dangerous. What if you're recognized? I said as much to Fitzroy, but he simply responded with 'I know.' Either he's lost his mind or you coerced him into taking you."

"I didn't coerce him. Will you tell him he's lost his mind or shall I?"

He grunted. "I don't like it."

"So you noted. Are you coming?"

"Apparently I'm not needed. I have to follow up some of Brooks's members."

"You're disappointed."

"I'm bloody annoyed, Charlie. For one thing, you shouldn't be out for all the world to see you. You gave us a week, remember?" He threw his hands in the hair. "I can't believe he's allowing this! After going to all that trouble to send you away to keep you safe, too. He might as well parade you in front of the committee members."

I folded my arms over my chest. "First of all, I'll be careful. Secondly, are you sure that's why he sent me away? To keep me safe? Is that what he told you?"

"Not in so many words, but I'll wager my life savings that it is."

"You don't have any life savings."

"That's beside the point."

I sighed. "Seth, if that was his reason, he wouldn't have fetched me back after discovering I was perfectly all right at the school. He would have turned around and left me there."

His lips puckered in thought. "I see your point."

"I've had time to think about his reasons, and now I believe he saw me as a distraction. Perhaps I simply took up too much of his time, or he couldn't concentrate when I was around. Or perhaps he felt himself changing into a person who couldn't be the ruthless leader he'd always been. Perhaps he didn't like that change."

He sagged against the wall near the doorframe. "You may be right. Yet it still beggars the question, why did he fetch you back if that were the case? If you were a distraction then, aren't you still a distraction now?"

"I don't know. I suppose, except now we are not a couple. We're back to the way we were before everything became complicated."

He huffed out a breath. "Are you? I don't see it that way, Charlie. It's not the same at all."

I merely shrugged. He was right in that Lincoln and I could never return to how we'd been with one another. "You've remained friends with many of your paramours. Do you think Lincoln and I can one day be friends, of sorts?"

He shrugged. "The thing is, my lovers know from the outset that I'm not going to marry them. They understand our arrangement, and most want the same thing I do without the complications of courting. Your situation is entirely different."

I hugged my arms, feeling a little cold despite the warmth of the room.

He kissed the top of my head. "Now get ready. I want you to wear the largest hat you have, preferably with a veil, and something with a high collar."

"Would you like to choose something from my wardrobe yourself?"

"A capital idea."

Fifteen minutes later, I lowered the veil I'd hurriedly sewn to my hat brim. It only fell to my nose but it was dark enough to hide my eye color. I changed into my dark gray dress with the high lace collar that skimmed the underside of my chin. If I angled my face just so, very little of me could be seen.

I met Lincoln in the entrance hall. A hat covered most of his hair so that its length wasn't obvious, and he sported a false black mustache. I pressed my lips together to stifle my laugh.

"This arrived for you earlier." He handed me a letter from Alice.

"Wonderful! I've been worried about her." I tucked it into my reticule to read later.

Gus pulled up in the coach near the steps and Doyle saw us out. He handed Lincoln two umbrellas, one of which Lincoln held over my head and the other over his own. We climbed into the cabin. The space suddenly felt very tight, his knees too close to mine.

"Don't ever grow a mustache," I said as the coach drove off.

He stroked it. "I thought I looked distinguished."

I smiled. "If by distinguished you mean older, then yes. It ages you by ten years, at least."

"That's what I hoped. If I had one with gray in it, I would have worn that."

"You keep false mustaches in your room?"

"I purchased some from a wigmaker recently. I decided that if I am to do less...interrogating, I'll need more disguises."

"Sometimes interrogating is necessary. It's also something you do very well."

A gleam appeared in his eyes that I hadn't seen since my return to Lichfield. "You sound as if you doubt my ability to act."

Good acting required a certain degree of empathy. I didn't believe Lincoln had sufficient, but I wouldn't tell him that. I didn't want to destroy his lighter mood. "I'll assess you based on today's performance. Are you to be a journalist, then, and I your assistant?"

He nodded and reached into his inside coat pocket. "You'll need these." He handed me a pencil and notepad. "We'll try University College Hospital. It's closest, and they have a strong medical research department."

"I hope this garners results," I said quietly. "Otherwise we must rely on Seth's efforts today and his questioning of Andrew Buchanan. Speaking of Buchanan, how did Lady Harcourt seem to you earlier?"

"It's difficult to tell. She's good at keeping her feelings to herself."

Unlike me. I tended to wear my heart on my sleeve where it was exposed for the world to see. "It must be a difficult time for her."

"She has Buchanan for comfort."

"I doubt he'd be very comforting. That man has a nasty streak."

"That makes them a good match." He eyed me closely. "It's kind of you to worry about Julia, Charlie. It's not necessary, however. She's capable of looking after herself."

"I know. I was simply curious." I fished out Alice's letter from my reticule. "Do you mind if I read it now? I'm desperate to know how she fares."

"Go ahead. I admit that I'm curious too. Leaving her behind may not have been wise. Her power is too unpredictable for my liking."

I nodded and opened the letter, careful not to tear the flimsy paper. Her small, neat writing covered the entire page, leaving only the narrowest gap between the lines. I scanned it quickly then re-read it from the beginning. "All is well," I said on a breath. "There have been no further 'incidents', as she calls them, although she still has the dreams. She has become good friends with the other supernaturals, too, and they all have a better understanding of one another." I laughed softly at the next paragraph.

"What is it?"

"Mrs. Denk found herself locked in the dungeon overnight before one of the teachers realized and let her out. Apparently the spirit of Sir Geoffrey lured her in there. I shouldn't laugh. That dungeon was an awful place. A few hours down there feels like days."

He leaned forward, his eyes hooded. "How do you know?"

I folded up the letter and tucked it back into my reticule.

"Charlie?"

CHAPTER 10

"Mrs. Denk put me down there."

A muscle in his jaw tensed. He held my gaze until I could no longer stand it and looked away.

He touched my knee. "Why didn't you tell me?"

I shifted my knees away. "There was no point, since you came for me."

He leaned back and turned to the window. Rain splattered the glass, blurring the cityscape outside. It was difficult to tell where we were precisely, thanks to the monotony of grayness.

"Did you buy wigs too?" I asked to fill the silence.

"Just mustaches. I thought I might cut my hair to—"

"Don't do that.

He blinked. My vehemence surprised me too.

"Your hair suits you," I said with a shrug.

We arrived at the Gower Street hospital and headed inside to see the governor. We only got as far as his assistant in the outer office, a needle-faced man who peered at us over his spectacles. Lincoln must have decided he would do. He asked to see the head of the hematology research facility to interview him about his latest discoveries.

"For the article my editor asked me to write," he finished, indicating me holding my pencil and notepad.

"You've made a mistake," the assistant said with a frown. "We don't have any doctors specializing in hematology here."

"Oh." Lincoln sounded disappointed, if somewhat wooden. "Do you know which hospital I should try?"

"Why do you want to know?"

"My editor got wind of great strides being made in that area of medical science and wanted our paper to be the first to report on it."

The assistant clasped his hands on the top of his desk in front of him. "I don't know of any laboratories making great strides in hematology. Are you sure you don't mean infectious diseases?"

"The two are linked, are they not?"

"I suppose."

When the assistant said nothing further, Lincoln leaned forward. I held my breath and waited for the interrogation to begin. "I'm not supposed to tell anyone this," he said, "but the editor informed me that the paper's owner is considering donating a large sum to further the research." Then he did the oddest thing. He winked.

"Oh!" The assistant beamed. "How exciting!" He winked back. "I won't tell a soul."

"Thank you. The name of the hospital involved in hematology research?"

"I wish it were us now, but alas it's not. You need to speak to Dr. Bell from St. Bart's."

Lincoln thanked him and we returned to the coach. "Bart's," Lincoln directed Gus before closing the door.

"Well done," I said, settling on the seat. "You played your part well. My skepticism was misplaced."

He stroked his mustache. "I could get used to one of these if it means I'm taken more seriously."

"Believe me, people usually take you *very* seriously. You only have to give them one of your looks and they cower."

"Perhaps I don't want people to cower."

It was impossible to know if he was merely spouting what he thought I wanted to hear or whether he meant it. "Lincoln, you are who you are. You shouldn't try to change for other people."

He turned to the window.

"That goes doubly for growing a mustache and cutting your hair."

One corner of his mouth lifted. "Noted."

St. Bartholomew's Hospital had the grand distinction of being London's oldest hospital still operating on its original site. It was made up of a cluster of buildings accessed via the Henry VIII gate where a heavy-lidded porter eyed us.

"If it ain't an emergency," he said, "general admission day is Thursdays at eleven."

"We're here on another matter." Lincoln introduced himself as William Humphrey, journalist from *The Times*, and repeated his story about interviewing Dr. Bell for the newspaper.

The heavy lids briefly lifted before plunging to half-mast again. "Bell's laboratory can be found on the second floor in the north wing. He's always there." He waved at the multi-level building behind him. "Go through the archway. Staircase is on the right."

Lincoln thanked him and we headed from the gatehouse to the north wing, but not before a stiff wind almost ripped Lincoln's mustache off. He flipped up his collar, as if to ward off the cold, and pressed the false hair against his upper lip.

A nurse dressed all in white greeted us on the second floor. "Dr. Bell is very busy," she hedged with a glance along the corridor. "Would you care to wait?"

"Not particularly." Lincoln repeated his story about a financial grant. "Where can we find him?"

A gentleman walked past and the nurse hailed him. "Dr. Fawkner will assist you. He's Dr. Bell's assistant."

Dr. Fawkner looked far too young to be given any authority, let alone be a doctor. His curly blond hair ended high up his forehead and his childlike face sported rosy cheeks and cherubic lips. The cheeks grew even rosier as Lincoln repeated his story.

"Marvelous!" Dr. Fawkner declared. "It's about time Dr. Bell's work was taken seriously. He's a genius. His research is ahead of its time, but so few in the medical profession will acknowledge it. All the money's in infectious diseases, you know, and surgical equipment. Hematology is very much the beggar's specialty, around here. Come with me. I'll introduce you."

He led us down a long corridor, past dozens of doors, one of which was open to reveal two long tables against the side walls. Two gentlemen in white coats peered through microscopes and another took notes.

Dr. Fawkner knocked on the next door along, and a voice ordered us to enter. A bald gentleman with a neatly trimmed white beard looked up from the paperwork covering most of his expansive desk. His blue-gray eyes pierced his assistant, pinning him to the spot so that he didn't enter beyond the doorway.

"What is it, Fawkner?" Dr. Bell snapped. "I'm busy."

Fawkner cleared his throat. "Dr. Bell, this is Mr. Humphrey and his assistant. They're from *The Times* and have some rather exciting news for you." He was so enthusiastic that I felt a little sorry to be misleading him.

"I'll be the judge of that." Dr. Bell turned his sharp gaze onto Lincoln. I did not receive an acknowledgement of any kind. It was probably best that Dr. Bell not really see me. Even with the veil covering much of my face, it was safer to remain somewhat invisible.

Lincoln held out his hand, but Dr. Bell didn't take it. "I don't shake hands when I'm not wearing gloves," he said.

Dr. Fawkner shifted behind us. "My apologies," he muttered. "I failed to mention that."

Lincoln held a chair out for me and I went to sit.

"I didn't offer you a seat." Dr. Bell flicked his fingers and Fawkner left us. "What is it you want?"

"My editor wants me to interview you," Lincoln said.

"I fail to see how that is of benefit to me. Bloody typical of Fawkner to get excited over something as banal as an interview. I don't read the papers, Mr. Humphrey. I'd rather spend my valuable time perusing medical journals."

"The article will coincide with an announcement of a grant awarded to your department, funded by the paper's owner."

"How much is the grant worth?"

"Two thousand pounds."

Bell's white brows shot up. He leaned forward and steepled his hands on his desk. "Why my department?"

"Personal reasons, so I'm told."

Bell leaned back again. "I see."

Lincoln signaled to me to begin my note taking. I hoped my handwriting was up to the task if Mr. Bell asked to inspect my notes. My education had been stunted when my father threw me out at thirteen, and although I'd read a great deal since going to live at Lichfield, my writing lacked speed and grace.

"What developments are you currently working on?" Lincoln asked.

"I won't be answering any of your questions until I've spoken to your editor. What did you say his name was?"

"Mr. Marshall," Lincoln said without missing a beat. "I wish you luck getting an appointment with him. He's a busy man."

"Aren't we all? Nevertheless, I will speak with him first. Come back next week."

"It's a simple question, Dr. Bell. I'm not asking for any secrets, just some information about your current work. Do you have any private commissions, for example?"

Dr. Bell stood. "Please see yourselves out."

"The grant may be awarded to another if you don't cooperate."

"Fawkner!" Bell bellowed. His assistant appeared at the door. "See that Mr. Humphrey and his assistant find the exit. We wouldn't want them getting lost and stumbling into the laboratory by mistake."

Lincoln tensed. "We'll tell Mr. Marshall to expect you."

"This way, if you please," said Dr. Fawkner with forced cheerfulness.

Lincoln followed me out. Even though he showed no outward signs, I knew he was quietly seething, and probably wishing he hadn't gone to the trouble of disguises and stories. I wished the same, but as Dr. Fawkner led us down the staircase, I realized not all was yet lost.

"I am sorry for Dr. Bell," he said quietly when we reached the ground floor. He glanced back up the stairs and leaned toward Lincoln. "He's a meticulous man, very thorough, and doesn't take people at face value. Once he's verified that you are who you are, he'll be keen to speak to you. About most of his work, anyway." He laughed nervously and glanced once again up the staircase.

Most? "That's quite all right," I said. "We understand completely. Mr. Humphrey is very much like your Dr. Bell in that regard."

Lincoln gave a short, sharp nod. Dr. Fawkner smiled at me. "How charming to see a woman in a man's role. I'm all for women's rights. I have sisters," he said with a hearty smile. "One even wishes to become a doctor, but will probably have to settle for nursing."

"An equally marvelous profession." His smile widened at my enthusiastic response. Beside me, Lincoln shifted his weight. I ignored him. Dr. Fawkner was ripe for picking. "Your work here is fascinating," I said, injecting a hint of awe into my voice, "and so important."

"Life saving, you might say." He chuckled. "Life giving too, in a way."

Giving? Could he mean resurrection? "How intriguing," I said, breathily. "Whatever do you mean?"

"Just something Bell once said, Miss..."

"Filmott." I smiled and held out my hand.

"Miss Filmott." He took my hand and smiled back when I gently squeezed. "Charming."

"You were saying?"

"Ah, yes." He frowned as he gathered his thoughts again. "You'd be amazed at the types of things we're working on in our laboratories, but unfortunately I'm not privy to everything Dr. Bell does. Some of his work is very private. So much so that he won't even divulge its nature to me. Can't have rival doctors stealing our research, can we?" He laughed. "That's Dr. Bell's greatest fear. That and germs."

"Of course. It explains his reluctance to accept us without checking our authenticity first. I, for one, don't blame him at all. We have no problem with returning another day."

"You're very understanding." He chuckled and once again looked up the stairs. "You wouldn't believe it, but Dr. Bell has been sleeping in the laboratory lately. He's worried someone will attempt to steal his work if he's not there."

"Is that so?" That would make it difficult to peek at his paperwork. "It would help Mr. Humphrey if he has something to go on with while we wait for Dr. Bell to speak with Mr. Marshall. We'd like to interview the benefactors, and learn their reasons for funding such important work. Are you funded entirely by the hospital or do you also take on private work?"

"Both," he said.

"And the secret experiments are for the hospital or those private benefactors?"

"Private, but that's all I can tell you. They won't want to talk to the newspapers, but I'm sure the hospital will. The administrators are always looking for ways to increase funding, and a grant will get them very excited. Your article would also go a long way in advertising our research to more private benefactors— not to mention the fame, of course. Imagine being mentioned in a feature article in *The Times*!"

"We'll be sure to spell your name correctly," I assured him. "Thank you for your time, Dr. Fawkner. It's been a pleasure to meet you."

He sketched a bow. "The pleasure is all mine, Miss Filmott. Mr. Humphrey."

Lincoln and I walked back through the Henry VIII gate and out to Gus, waiting nearby with the carriage. "Home," Lincoln told him, and we climbed in.

"That was enlightening," I said.

He grunted. "If any of my employees blabbed like Fawkner did, I'd dismiss them."

"Good to know."

"You're not an employee."

"It's a pity Bell wouldn't talk," I said before I found myself sinking into his warm gaze, unable to get out.

He ripped off his mustache and stuffed it into his pocket. "Perhaps next time you should do all the talking. You're better at it. You and Seth."

"Don't be disheartened. You were very good. I don't think the soft, subtle approach would ever work on Bell, no matter who spoke with him. Fortunately we had Fawkner. The question now is, was he implying that their research was the same as the serum Captain Jasper had been working on?"

"It's impossible to know without seeing the experiments and results."

"How would you know what you were looking at? Oh, wait, don't tell me. Your scientific knowledge is as thorough as every other aspect of your education. Of *course* you can read blood test results."

His eyes narrowed. "My education wasn't thorough in all aspects. Science and medicine were particular interests of mine. If I hadn't been destined to be the ministry leader I would have liked to become a doctor."

"Is that so?"

"What about you? What would you have become if things had been different?"

"You mean if I hadn't been a necromancer, abandoned at thirteen, and oh, a woman, what vocation would I have chosen?"

"Yes."

I thought about it a moment. "Medicine certainly seems like a noble profession, but I did enjoy myself today, asking Dr. Fawkner those questions. So perhaps a journalist."

"Or a detective inspector?"

I shrugged. "Is being the ministry's leader such a terrible thing?"

"Not always. Not in the last few months."

I felt my face heat and looked away. I wished he wouldn't be so...nice. "Being a necromancer isn't all that awful, either. Now that I'm used to it, I like speaking to the dead, on the whole. I've met some interesting characters. It would be even better if I didn't have to hide what I am, or if someone wasn't trying to kill me."

He suddenly leaned forward and captured my hand in his. With gloves on, it should have lacked intimacy, but it did not. It felt very real and earnest. A lump clogged my throat. "It will be over soon. I promise you, Charlie. We'll capture the killer, and you'll be free to do as you please."

I smiled weakly and nodded. It was all I could manage. Then I pulled my hand away.

His hands hovered in mid-air for a moment before he settled back in the seat. "I'll return tonight and see what paperwork I can find linking Bell to a serum to reanimate bodies."

"You're going to break in?"

He nodded.

"But you can't! Dr. Fawkner said Dr. Bell sleeps in the laboratory."

"I can handle Bell."

"I know that," I snapped. "The point is, you'll risk exposure and arrest, or worse, if he keeps a gun in his drawer like Dr. Merton at the Lying In hospital."

He was silent a moment, his face impassive. "You sound worried."

"Of course I am! If you die..." I swallowed. "What will happen to me?" I regretted it as soon as I said it. It wasn't at all what had been on my mind, but I couldn't tell him that I cared about his wellbeing. I just couldn't. It was painful enough admitting it to myself.

"You'll have the cottage in Harringay," he said to the window. "There'll also be provisions for you in my will."

"Stop, Lincoln, please. Stop all of the kindness, the sympathetic looks, and the life-changing gifts." I fanned out my fingers on my lap, but the stretch did nothing to ease the tension coursing through me. "It's impossible to remain angry with you when you're like that, and I *need* to remain angry with you. It's easier than... It's just easier." I turned to the window, yet I couldn't get his wide-eyed stare out of my mind or the twitch of his lips. Something in my outburst had amused him. I couldn't think what. I'd sounded childishly petulant.

He didn't respond, and neither of us spoke the rest of the way home.

CHAPTER 11

"No success," Seth said as we sat in the drawing room after dinner. His mother sat with us, reading the newspaper, apparently oblivious to our conversation. We still had to be careful, however, although sometimes I wasn't sure why. If anyone could withstand the shock of learning about magic and supernaturals, it would be Lady Vickers. "The first five gentlemen on the list can all be accounted for on November sixteenth. Three weren't even in London, one had a business meeting, and the fifth was with his mistress all day."

"Did he tell you that?" I asked.

"His mistress did. The mistresses of the other men informed me of their whereabouts too."

"They *all* have mistresses?"

"It's entirely normal," Lady Vickers said from behind her newspaper. "And all the ladies have *affairs de coeur* too, albeit discreetly and after they've finished breeding, of course. Everyone does it. If one doesn't do it, one feels left out."

"That's not true, Mother."

She lowered the corner of her newspaper. "It is true, and Charlie needs to know. If she sets her sights on a good marriage, she ought to go in with her eyes open."

"A good marriage!" Gus echoed. "She ain't gettin' married to anyone but—" He looked to Lincoln.

Lincoln merely stood by the sideboard, his brandy glass dangling by his fingertips. He studied the swirling liquid as if he could see the future in it.

"Charlie?" Seth prompted. "What is my mother talking about?"

"Charlie has agreed to accompany me on social engagements. I think we'll make quite a formidable team, with her pretty looks and my knowledge of the right people."

Seth groaned and scrubbed his hand over his face. "You can back out of the agreement," he told me.

"It was your mother's gift to me." I hoped he understood that I couldn't back out without hurting her feelings.

"So you're goin' to balls and such?" Gus asked.

"It depends on what invitations I receive," I said.

"I'll put it about that she's available," Lady Vickers said. "Beginning with tomorrow night at the dinner party. I think she'll be quite the sensation, once people get wind of her mysterious background."

Lincoln set down his glass and walked out. I half-rose, out of instinct, but forced myself to remain seated. "Marriage is a long way off," I told Seth and Gus. "A very long way. I need some time just to be me and not someone's wife."

Seth drained his brandy glass. "You need a husband who won't treat you merely as a wife, but as a person with a mind of her own." He got up and strode to the sideboard.

"That's very sweet," I said. "It's no wonder all the ladies are charmed by you."

He beamed back at me. "They are, aren't they?"

Gus groaned and rolled his eyes.

"Did you say you went to Bart's today, Charlie?" Lady Vickers asked, once again studying the newspaper. "There's an obituary here for a Mr. Mannering. He was an administrator there, up until his death a few days ago."

"May I see that?"

She folded it and passed it to me. "I like to browse the obituaries and see who's fallen off their perch," she said. "It's one of the few pleasures left to me."

Gus and Seth peered over my shoulder. "Mr. Ira Hartley Mannering," Gus read. He tapped my shoulder. "An administrator will know his way around the hospital."

I handed the newspaper back to Lady Vickers and sprang to my feet. Without speaking, Seth and Gus followed me out.

"Who is he?" Lady Vickers called after us. "Why is he important?"

We hurried up to Lincoln's rooms, where he sat at his desk. There were no papers in front of him, however, and no books or other work. Just my engagement ring in its box.

"I know of another way into the laboratory," I said, focusing on my idea. "A way that is less dangerous than you breaking in."

"Go on."

We told him about the obituary. He listened with his arms crossed and his legs outstretched. "His spirit eyes can see in the dark, even from inside his dead body, and he will know where to go."

He shook his head. "If Bell is sleeping in the laboratory, he'll see him."

"Yes, but what does it matter? Mannering will be too strong to be stopped, and he can't be hurt or killed. Bell will be powerless to do anything. And he'll be none the wiser as to our involvement."

"I suppose this means you think you ought to come to control him."

"It'll be just like Bedlam."

"I seem to recall that almost ended in disaster."

"Almost but not quite. Lincoln, I don't think there's a safer alternative. You going in alone not only risks you but also Dr. Bell. At least if I direct Mannering not to harm anyone, he must do as I say."

"You don't trust me not to hurt Bell?"

Either Seth or Gus cleared his throat.

"I think you'll fight if you get cornered," I said. "If Mannering is cornered, it doesn't matter."

"She has a point, sir," Gus said.

"And this way we can all come along," Seth added.

"It's not a party," Lincoln said.

"It's better."

"Mannering's funeral is tomorrow. Morgan Brothers are the undertakers. They're not far from here."

Lincoln blew out a breath and shook his head. "Everyone should get some sleep. We'll leave at two."

***

Ira Hartley Mannering's spirit did not want to re-enter his dead body. I could hardly blame him. I wouldn't like to have my eternal rest interrupted by someone ordering me to occupy a bloated body that was beginning to go off. Thank goodness he was due to be buried in the morning.

I'd summoned Mannering then wasted no time directing his spirit into the funeral parlor to sink back into his body. Once he eventually agreed, he unlocked the door from the inside and lurched across the road with a lumbering, awkward gait, to where we waited in the carriage. He now sat beside Lincoln, his dead eyes unfocused and his arms hanging limply at his sides. He reminded me of a ventriloquist's doll, albeit an oversized, smelly one.

"What is the meaning of this?" he demanded. It would have been more authoritative if his false teeth hadn't come loose as he spoke and made it difficult to understand him. "Why have I been disturbed?"

"I'm sorry," I said. "You have my word that no harm will come to you."

He made a strange noise that I suspected would have been a snort if he were capable of drawing breath. In the light of the lamp hanging near the door, I could clearly make out the deathly pallor of his face, almost the same shade of gray as his beard.

"We need your help in combatting a great danger to the country, if not the world," I went on. "If we don't stop this menace, we could be overrun with undead corpses."

Lincoln lifted his brows. Perhaps I was being melodramatic, but there was no time and no point beating around the bush. Besides, it was all entirely true. If our killer succeeded in developing a serum, all of that could come to pass—and more.

"I fail to see what that has to do with me," Mannering said, attempting to lift his arms, one at a time.

"You used to work at Bart's, and we believe Dr. Bell, currently of that establishment, is working on a serum to bring the dead back to life."

His lower jaw flopped open and his teeth almost fell out. He slowly managed to lift his hand to push them back in. "Bell? Why would he do such a thing?"

"Someone is paying him."

"Who?"

"That's what we're trying to find out," Lincoln said. "You will go to the hospital and search his papers. Look for evidence of private benefactors in ledgers, letters, anything you can find in either his office or his laboratory."

Mannering tilted his head to the side to regard Lincoln. "Why would I do this for you?"

"Because I can make you," I said. "I don't want to, but if it comes to it, I *will* force you. Please, Mr. Mannering, this is important and urgent. People are dying because of this secret serum, and you are our best hope. It's dangerous for us to gather this information. Someone may get hurt, and we wish to avoid that at all costs. You, however, cannot be harmed, and you know the hospital layout well, don't you? You worked there for many years, according to your obituary."

"You saw my obituary? How detailed was it? How much space did it occupy?"

"A good several inches of one column. It was the largest listed for the day. Very eye-catching."

His lips inched up at the corners.

"So you're willing to do as we ask?" I said.

"It seems I have no choice in the matter."

Lincoln spent the rest of the journey telling him precisely the sort of paperwork to look for. Mannering spent much of the time attempting to lift both his arms together and by the time we reached the hospital gate, he'd succeeded.

"You will get used to moving your body soon," I told him.

"You've done this before?" he asked.

"A few times, yes."

"What an odd little woman you are."

I gave him a grim smile. Lincoln opened the door. "Good luck," I said.

"Wait." Mannering paused, half out of the carriage. "The gate will be locked, as will the north wing and the laboratory door."

"I'll pick the locks of the gate and north wing," Lincoln said. "As to the laboratory door, break it down. You have the strength."

"Or you could try knocking first," I said. "If Dr. Bell is inside, he'll unlock it. Overpower him without hurting him, then search his laboratory and office."

Lincoln opened the compartment beneath the seat and pulled out a length of coiled rope. He handed it to Mannering. "Tie him up with this."

Mannering's facial muscles jumped and twitched. It reminded me of the convulsive movements of Frankenstein's creations after he electrified them. The cold, damp foggy air drifted through the open door. I shivered and pulled my fur coat closed at my throat.

Mannering took the rope and lumbered toward the gate. Lincoln fetched the blanket from the compartment and laid it across my lap, then he followed the dead man. We'd covered the external coach lamps before leaving Lichfield, but I kept the internal lamp on with the curtains closed. I didn't even dare peek out for fear the light would be seen, and I didn't want to extinguish it altogether.

I heard Lincoln's voice mere minutes later. "Be prepared to leave quickly," he told Seth and Gus, both sitting on the coachman's seat.

Seth responded but I couldn't hear his words, and soon after, Lincoln rejoined me inside. I blew out a long, ragged breath, and released my hands. I'd been clutching them so tightly my fingers ached. My relief didn't surprise me, but it did irritate me somewhat. I didn't want to care for his wellbeing as much as I did.

We waited in silence. No sounds came from the direction of the hospital. Occasionally one of the horses snorted or moved, rattling the harness, but even those noises were muffled through the thick fog.

I'd never been very good at waiting. Doing nothing while others worked was an excruciating exercise in patience. It must have been even more difficult for Lincoln, however. Being a man of action meant he rarely had to sit and wait, yet he managed it without fidgeting, sighing or shivering. I failed miserably.

He leaned over and lifted the blanket on my lap higher. "Don't get cold," he said before sitting back again.

I inched the blanket to my chin. It didn't help. The longer I sat, the colder I became. My toes and fingers turned numb and my face felt as if frowning or smiling might crack it. How did Lincoln manage to remain so warm? He looked so...inviting. Mere weeks ago I would have curled up on his lap and nuzzled his throat. He would have wrapped his warm arms around me and—

The coach rocked as the horses moved. Gus said something to soothe them, but his voice was cut off by a shout.

"Go!" The door opened and Mannering burst in. He smacked into the other side of the cabin and fell onto the seat beside me. He spoke but I could hardly understand a word. He'd lost his teeth. "He'th coming!" he repeated.

"Stop! Thief!" came the cry from outside as the coach lurched forward. I recognized Dr. Bell's voice.

"You didn't tie him up," Lincoln said, more accusation than question.

"I did. Had to releath him, though. Couldn't leave him like that all night to be found in the morning by hith underlings. How ignoble for the poor fellow." He opened his jacket pocket and pulled out some papers. "Thith ith what I found. It may or may not be of uthe to you, but it wath all I could find of relevanth."

167

"Thank you," Lincoln said, placing them inside his jacket.

The coach suddenly swerved and we all lurched to the side. Mannering's body acted as a cushion for me, and Lincoln managed to put out a hand to stop himself slamming into the wall. He righted himself, shaking out his hand.

"What the bloody hell are you doing?" came Seth's shout. Gus echoed the question, with more colorful language. Who were they talking to?

"Get down!" ordered a stranger.

"Charlie," Lincoln said, helping me to sit up, "are you—"

The door was flung open and two uniformed policemen scowled at us. Both held truncheons and the one at the back carried a lamp. "Get out," said the front one. "You're under arrest."

CHAPTER 12

"Hands on your head," the policeman said. "You two, miss."

"What is this?" I asked before Lincoln took control in his, er, unique way. If we could talk our way of the situation, we must try to do so first. "We're just minding our business."

"Without lamps? And when something's amiss up at Bart's?" He jerked his head back the way we'd come.

I looked through the rear coach window to see a glowing arc of light, swinging back and forth. A moment later, another two policemen emerged through the fog, trailed by Bell. They must have been near the hospital and heard Dr. Bell's shouts and then signaled to the other constables using their lamp.

"Miss, set the blanket aside slowly and step outside," one of the policemen said.

I got up but Lincoln caught my hand. He gave a small shake of his head. Did he want to overpower them and escape? We could do it quite easily. We outnumbered them, and we had a corpse with incredible strength on our side. But I couldn't stop thinking about the dangers, not only to us but to the policemen. While I had no love for their kind, I didn't want to be responsible for any harm befalling them. Overriding that concern was my worry about Mannering. If something happened to me, who would send him back?

"You two!" Dr. Bell gasped, as much from surprise at seeing us, I suspect, as from his exertions. "I should have known you weren't journalists. Give back my papers this instant!"

"What are you talking about?" I asked, stepping out of the carriage. I glanced over my shoulder and winked. Then, to Mannering, I mouthed "Run." To the policemen and Bell, I said, "Thank goodness you came when you did." My voice shook and I clutched the constable's lapels with trembling fingers. "This horrid man has been forcing us to do his bidding. He made us lie to you earlier today, then forced us to drive to the hospital tonight."

"What utter rot," Bell snapped. He glanced behind me and swallowed hard. "My God," he whispered. "It *is* you. Mannering...tell me...how? I must know. Who did this to you? Who succeeded where I have failed? *Tell me*!"

I was suddenly shoved in the back so hard that the policeman and I fell to the ground. He landed with an *oomph*, and I on top of him. I looked up in time to see two other policemen racing after the retreating figure of Mannering. They would not catch him.

I breathed a sigh of relief, but perhaps it was too soon. We were still under arrest.

Lincoln helped me to my feet and the policeman dusted himself off. Seth jumped down from the coachman's bench.

"No further," the constable said, raising his truncheon and backing up toward his fellow policeman, a sergeant, going by his epaulettes. "Don't move."

"They have nothing to do with this," Lincoln said. His fingers wrapped around my arm as if he were reluctant to let me go. "That man hired them today to drive us around."

"It's true," I said. "Can they go?"

The policemen glanced at one another. The sergeant nodded.

Seth's gaze swept over us then he tugged on his hat and climbed up beside Gus. They drove off just as the two policemen who'd chased Mannering returned, alone.

"Go back to your afterlife," I quickly whispered into my coat collar. "I release you."

"Pardon, miss?" the sergeant asked.

I coughed. "You didn't catch that horrible man? Did you see his face? We can describe him, if you like."

"Come down to the station and we'll sort it out there. You too, Mr. Bell."

"*Dr.* Bell. That man..." He squinted into the white haze of fog. "That was Mannering."

"You know him?"

Bell's gaze flicked to Lincoln. "I...don't know."

The policemen directed Lincoln and me to walk between them. I lifted my collar to my nose, but it didn't keep the chill at bay. It felt like I was drowning in fog, so much like the airy stuff spirits were made of.

"Whatever that man stole from you, he took with him," Lincoln said to Bell. "I'm sorry, but we're victims too." If anyone could look at Lincoln and think him a victim, they weren't looking very hard. Even captured as he was, he showed no signs of worry. It was as if he were having a stroll on a pleasant evening.

"I doubt it," Bell growled. "But I won't press charges if you tell me how you did...*that.*"

"Ain't up to you," the sergeant said.

Bell, however, didn't seem to hear him. He grabbed Lincoln's sleeve. Even in the weak light of the street lamps, I could see the glimmer of something in his wide eyes. Madness? "Please, you *must* tell me. I'll give you my entire commission if you'll share your process with me."

The sergeant pulled him off Lincoln. Dr. Bell growled in frustration but meekly walked the rest of the way to the station. I no longer felt so cold, or so anxious about our fate, because now I knew it wasn't all for naught—Dr. Bell *had* been commissioned to bring the dead back to life. His reaction proved it.

***

"Let her go," Lincoln said after we arrived at the Snow Hill Police Station. "She's done nothing wrong."

"Neither of us has," I said. "That man, Mannering, forced us."

"We've only got your word on that," said the sergeant. "Wait 'till morning. The detective will sort it out. If he thinks you're telling the truth, he'll let you go."

"The morning!" I cried. "But that's hours away. What will you do with us until then?"

"Put you in the holding cells."

Bile surged up my throat. I put my hand out to steady myself. Lincoln stepped toward me, but a policeman held him back while another caught me.

He laughed. "The cells aren't too bad, miss. There's worse in the city, believe me. We keep ours clean and check 'em regular to make sure there ain't no misbehavin'."

I nodded numbly and blinked at Lincoln. He stared back, his eyes as black as London's starless winter night and just as grim.

"There's only two others in the women's cell," the constable went on cheerfully. "It's always quiet this time of year. Too cold to be out sinning."

Had it really only been six months ago that I'd sat in a cell in the heat of summer? That time, I'd been thrown in with the men. Men who'd seen me as a toy to pass around and then fight over. Men who wanted my body, even though they thought I was a boy. The spirit of a dead man had come to my aid then, and he had helped me escape. I had him to thank for being alive, and for changing my life, too.

"Charlie?" Lincoln said softly. "Are you all right?"

I forced a smile. "It's only for a few hours. I can manage until then, and when the inspector hears our story, he'll let us go." I hoped he understood that I was asking him not to make a scene, that I had faith in other—legal—methods.

"Let her go," he said again to the sergeant now steering Dr. Bell to one of the desks. "She's a young lady who doesn't belong in a place like this."

The sergeant sighed. "I agree, but I can't let her go until the inspector has spoken to her. I am sorry, miss." He offered me a smile. "Just a few hours."

It was a good sign that he was treating me gently. It meant he believed our story. I just hoped the detective inspector was as gullible.

Lincoln and I were separated, searched and placed in holding cells next to one another. They might as well have been on opposite sides of the city. We couldn't communicate in any way.

Lincoln had probably disposed of the paperwork in the coach before getting out, so I wasn't concerned about the police finding it. I was more concerned with staying warm in the freezing cell.

My two fellow prisoners were both whores, going by their painted faces and low-cut bodices. One, a scrawny figure whose age I couldn't determine in the poor light, sat with her chin resting on drawn-up knees. The other's snores were in danger of waking all of London. She did not rouse when the door slammed shut behind me.

The sleeping prisoner occupied the only bed so I sat on the floor nearby because it was as far from the other woman as possible. It soon became apparent why she'd moved to the opposite side of the cell. The sleeping princess on the bed reeked of gin and vomit.

"I don't smell much better," she said, as if she could read my thoughts. "But I don't have lice." She nodded at the woman scratching her head in her sleep.

I shuffled away from her and closer to the scrawny woman on the floor. She looked to be about my age. Her oily black hair hung around a face marked by the pox, and her shawl was so thin I could see through it in patches.

"You in for stealing too?" she asked.

"Yes, but there's been a mistake."

She snorted. "I tried tellin' 'em that too, but it didn't work."

I hugged my knees as she was doing, but I didn't dare close my eyes. I needed to keep my wits about me in case she wanted to attack me and steal my coat. The policemen had left it with me after they'd searched it.

"What'll happen to us, you fink?" she asked after a while.

"I don't know."

"I knew a bloke what was hanged once. A cove in my bruvver's gang, he were. Stole a gold watch off a toff, but he weren't quick enough and got caught. They said his body twitched and jumped 'round in the noose afore it went still. I reckon that's the spirit leavin', goin' up to heaven. What d'you reckon?"

"I think you're right."

She looked satisfied with my response. "My bruvver tried tellin' me there ain't no such thing as spirits and heaven. He says that bein' dead's just like bein' asleep, but I don't fink he's right. He's an idiot. Can't even write his name. I can write me letters, see. I got educated more 'an him."

"Tell your brother when you see him again that I know for a fact that spirits are real."

She raised her head. "How?"

"I've seen them and spoken to them."

She sat up straight. "You one of them mediums?"

I nodded. "Tell your brother there is a heaven, and good people go there in their afterlife. I know it for certain." I don't know why I felt compelled to tell her. Perhaps because she had nothing to look forward to in life, and I wanted her to know something else awaited her after death.

"What's it like?" she asked softly. "Heaven?"

I shrugged. "I don't know."

She scooted across the floor and clasped my arm in both hands. She looked so young and vulnerable with her hollow cheeks, scrawny frame and big eyes, full of wonder. "Tell me about the spirits you seen. What do they look like?"

I described the mists, the lack of color, and some of the conversations I'd had, without giving away too much. I didn't tell her about raising the dead, or the murderers I'd encountered. The more I spoke, the more she curled into my side, clinging to my arm as if she was afraid I'd float away if she let go. After a good while, her eyes began to droop heavily and her yawns grew more frequent.

"Go to sleep," I said quietly. "It'll be morning soon and you'll need your strength for the day ahead." I removed my coat and wrapped it around us both.

She snuggled into me, and her body relaxed into sleep.

I leaned my head against the wall and closed my eyes too. I didn't feel as if I slept a wink, but when I reopened my eyes it was lighter. A lackluster beam of sunlight struggled through the barred window, brightening more of the cell than the gas lamp. I remained still for a long time so as not to wake the sleeping girl. I could make out scratch marks on the walls, made by bored or scared prisoners. Some of them even formed names. I read as many as I could decipher to pass the time and to keep my mind off our investigation, off Lincoln, and off the memories of the last time I'd been locked in a holding cell. I wasn't very successful on any count.

The woman on the bed rolled over and broke wind. She then proceeded to snort and hawk up snot at regular intervals. When I'd lived with boys' gangs, I'd learned to ignore their disgusting habits. After a few months of living a mannered and clean life, my tolerance for bodily noises had diminished.

The scraping of the lock drawing back and the door opening acted like an alarm bell. The woman on the bed sat bolt upright, mumbling something into her chins that I couldn't make out. The girl leaning against me also sat up and rubbed her eyes. Upon sight of the constable, she once again curled into me, clinging to my arm.

"Miss Charlotte Holloway, come with me, please," he said. "Inspector will speak to you now."

The girl's fingers gripped harder. She blinked back at me.

"My name's Charlie," I told her.

"Betty."

"It's been a pleasure meeting you, Betty. Here." I removed the coat from my shoulders and wrapped it around her. "Keep this. I have another." And she was going to need it more than me.

"You're released too, Betty," the constable said. "Since this is your first time and the goods weren't found on you, you've been let off with a warning. Come with me, both of you."

Betty choked back a cry. "Thank God," she muttered. "Thank God." She hugged me and I hugged her back. "You're my lucky charm, Miss Charlie."

I smiled with genuine happiness. Not only for her but also for me. The constable had said she was being released "too." Did that mean I wasn't being charged? "Take care, Betty."

"What about me?" the woman on the bed cried with an indignant scowl.

"You get to enjoy the peace and quiet in here a while longer, Jenny," the constable said with a chuckle.

She lay down again with the loudest snort yet. "Pigs."

Betty and I followed the constable down the corridor to the front of the station. Betty was handed over to another constable who led her to one office while I was led to another. Lincoln met me at the door. His seer's senses must have anticipated my approach.

His burning gaze washed over my face, twice. "Charlie." He cupped my jaw in his hands and stroked my cheeks with his thumbs. He opened his mouth but said nothing. He didn't have to. It was all there in his eyes and touch. He'd been worried all night, and now sheer relief rendered him speechless.

He still cared. I was sure of it now.

I placed my hands over his and gently pulled them away. "You look tired."

"Miss Holloway, sit," the inspector said, indicating a chair. He was a middle-aged fellow with a sagging face and unhurried movements. His eyes, however, darted over me. I got the feeling he missed nothing. "I just have a few questions and then you may go."

Lincoln squeezed my hand. I hoped my answers matched his. I sat at the desk with the little wooden name plate telling me that the saggy faced policeman was Detective Inspector Donald.

"Tell me about that fellow you met, Mannering," the inspector said.

"Is that his name?" I asked in my most innocent voice. "Dr. Bell said it was, but he didn't introduce himself to me. Mr. Fitzroy and I were minding our own business walking past Bart's and that ghastly fellow approached us. He said he'd harm us if we didn't go to Dr. Bell's office and question him about his work. We did, but Dr. Bell told us nothing. That man was furious and demanded we help him break in during the night. Very reluctantly, Mr. Fitzroy hired a coach and drivers, then we returned to the hospital. He made us wait for him." The story was so weak, it barely held together. I hoped Inspector Donald was a dull-witted fellow easily intimidated by Lincoln's scowls.

"Can you describe him to me?"

I did, but in vague terms so that the description would most likely match Bell's but could be attributed to many men.

"The thing is," Inspector Donald said, "Mannering's dead."

"Then it couldn't have been him, could it? Dr. Bell must have been mistaken."

"The other thing is, I don't believe you." He turned to Lincoln. "Either of you."

Lincoln went very still. I wanted to reach for his hand again, but I dared not move. The inspector might see it as a sign of guilt.

Inspector Donald stood and buttoned up his waistcoat. "However, I've been ordered by my superiors to release you. I don't really care why. It's one less thing on my plate. Good day to you both. You may collect your things from the constable on your way out."

I was too stunned to move until Lincoln stood. "Good day, Inspector. Thank you for your time."

Inspector Donald's face sagged even further, but he didn't say another word as we left. Neither of us spoke as the constable handed over my reticule, gloves and Lincoln's belongings. I didn't want to say something that might give the inspector reason to revoke his decision.

Lincoln stopped at the door and wordlessly handed me his coat. He didn't ask where mine had gone.

"Miss Charlie! Miss Charlie!" Betty waved at me as we exited the police station. She stood in my coat, clutching a dirty hessian sack to her chest as if she were afraid someone would snatch it. "Ain't it grand to be free," she said, smiling.

"It is," I said, smiling back. "I hope we both manage to stay that way."

Her smile faded. She nodded and went to walk off.

"Betty, wait." I opened my reticule, then thought better of it, and handed her the entire thing. There was nothing in it of personal value, only some coins, a handkerchief and the bag itself. "Take this, and do be careful."

Her eyes brightened. "Are you sure?"

I nodded.

"Thank you, Miss Charlie. Thank you, thank you." She grasped my hand and kissed the back of it. Her fingers were freezing. I gave her my gloves and was about to tell her of a place to go when Lincoln got in before me.

"There's a woman on Broker Row near Seven Dials named Mrs. Sullivan," he said. "If you need a place to stay or some food, find her and tell her Charlie sent you. She'll take care of you."

Betty nodded eagerly. "Thank you, sir. I'll go there now. I don't want to go back to me old digs. The only thing waiting for me is my pa, and he'll just have me doing more of the same as got me in here."

I fared her well then fell into step beside Lincoln. Despite the cold morning and his lack of coat, he didn't shiver. "We need to send more money Mrs. Sullivan's way," I said. "Her house must be full to bursting."

"I plan to talk to her about getting bigger lodgings," he said. "If she's amenable to the idea, she can take in more girls and get some help too, if she wants it."

Sometimes, he surprised me into utter speechlessness.

"Are you all right?" he asked.

"Yes. You?"

"Fine."

"Good."

We headed away from the station and into the swell of morning traffic. Lincoln walked very close to me, our arms touching, his face a picture of sharp concentration.

That's when it finally sank in. We'd been released because Inspector Donald's superiors had ordered him to do so. But who'd ordered them?

"The committee members knew we were in there, didn't they?" I said, scanning the vicinity. If the committee knew, and one of the members was our murderer, then my life was once again in danger.

"It would seem so."

I pulled out my necklace with the imp enclosed inside the amber orb and clasped it hard.

"I'll keep you safe," Lincoln said, without looking at me. His little finger touched mine. He wasn't wearing gloves, and I no longer had mine, so the feel of skin on skin came as a shock. I moved my hand away.

"It's not just me, is it? Dr. Bell is also in danger now. Our killer doesn't like loose ends. Loose ends tend to talk."

Lincoln said nothing. No doubt he'd already come to the same conclusion.

"We'll go to the hospital now and warn him," I said.

He shook his head. "I'm taking you home first."

"That'll waste valuable time. No, Lincoln, we'll go to Bart's. Besides," I said, when he began to protest, "I'm safer with you. If the killer is someone on the committee, they'll be expecting me to return to Lichfield now while you continue to investigate. Won't they?"

I took his grunt as agreement. "Keep close to the buildings," he said. "Stay on my left away from the road, and stay alert."

A moment later, a man with his hat pulled low walked toward us. Lincoln steered me to the wall of the bank building. With my back pressed to the bricks and Lincoln's body so close that I could feel his warmth, we waited until the man passed.

Lincoln should have stepped back to release me but he did not. He moved even closer and I felt a small tremble ripple through him. It echoed through my body. I hadn't been this close to him in so long. Every night I'd lain in my bed in the castle I'd been assaulted with memories of him kissing me. I'd wanted him near me with every fiber of my being, wanted his kisses, his touches, his heated looks.

Yet I'd shoved them away just as hard when I regained my wits. I'd told myself it would never happen again, and if it did, I would not be swept up and sucked into his whirlwind again. I would resist.

Yet now...now I felt too confused to do anything but stand there and watch, looking for any small sign of how he truly felt.

He swallowed. His lips parted. He leaned in and the breath left my body, taking all common sense with it. Lincoln's lips skimmed lightly across mine. "Charlie," he whispered so softly that the breeze almost took it.

And then he clasped my face in both his hands and kissed me.

CHAPTER 13

I placed my palms against Lincoln's chest and shoved. He stopped kissing me. "Don't," I growled, punching him in the shoulder. "Don't do that. Don't, don't, don't." I punctuated each word with a punch and ended with another shove.

He stepped back. I strode past him and continued toward Bart's.

He fell into step beside me. "Sorry. I..." He dragged his hand through his hair. "I'm sorry."

"I don't want your apology," I spat. "I want..." What did I want? I didn't have a clue so merely shook my head.

"I couldn't help myself." Oh, wonderful. He chose *now* to be talkative. "I was relieved to see you unscathed this morning and couldn't control the urge."

"Ha! You are the most disciplined, self-controlled person I know. You could have resisted."

"Perhaps I didn't want to." He stopped suddenly and caught my arm, pulling me to a halt. The hospital gate with the statue of Henry VIII above it loomed ahead.

I followed his gaze to see Gus sitting on the driver's seat of one of Lincoln's coaches. Lincoln scanned the vicinity then headed over.

"Charlie! Fitzroy!" Gus beamed upon seeing us. "Thank Christ you got out. But how?"

"The committee have spies everywhere," Lincoln said, eyeing the porter at the gate from beneath his thick lashes. "I believe the hospital is being watched. Whether our visit to Bell yesterday triggered the spy to alert their master or mistress, or whether last night's scuffle did, remains to be seen. Either way, Bell is being commissioned to find a way to bring the dead back to life. He admitted as much."

"Thought so," Gus said. "Found the papers you left behind. They don't say much, and there ain't no names or signatures we can read, but it's as clear as a bell that he's got a secret commission that he ain't allowed to talk about." He chuckled. "Clear as a bell. Get it?"

I rolled my eyes. "So where's Seth?"

"Inside, tryin' to convince Bell to get out of the city. It ain't safe for him."

Lincoln took my hand and placed it on his arm. "Come with me. Hold onto your orb and keep watch. Gus, wait here."

"I was doin' that anyway," he muttered as we walked off.

"Clutch your stomach as if you're in pain," Lincoln muttered as we approached the porter.

I did and moaned for effect. The porter was a different fellow to the one from yesterday, fortunately. It didn't mean he hadn't been given our descriptions by Dr. Bell or the other porter. He could well be one of many spies watching the hospital.

Lincoln strode straight up to him. "My wife needs a doctor," he said. "Where do I go?"

The porter inspected me with a keen eye. He probably saw dozens of ill people a day, many of them ragged and poor, unable to afford a doctor to visit them at home. While we wouldn't look that desperate, perhaps having only one coat between us might convince him we needed to come to Bart's. He was taking far too long, however, and scrutinizing us much too closely.

I moaned louder and doubled over.

"Hurry up, man!" Lincoln snapped. "She needs help now or she'll lose the baby."

"Through there, cross the courtyard," the porter said, pointing. "Follow the signs."

Lincoln circled his arm around my waist, and I leaned against him. "Come, my dear. We'll be there soon."

"Is he still watching?" I asked once we'd gone several feet.

"Yes," he said without turning around.

"Your seer's senses know that much?"

"Yes."

We passed the north wing then doubled back on the other side, out of sight from the main gate and the porter. We hurried up the stairs, although I suspected Lincoln slowed his pace for me.

We heard the voices of Seth, Dr. Bell and Dr. Fawkner before we reached the top step. "You don't understand." Seth sounded exasperated. "You have to come with me."

"Don't be absurd," Dr. Bell shouted.

"Calm down, sir," Dr. Fawkner said. "Tell us why you think he's in danger."

"It's none of your bloody business," Seth growled.

"Unhand me!" Dr. Bell cried.

Lincoln and I raced along the corridor as other doctors and nurses emerged from offices and laboratories to see what the commotion was about. "Seth," Lincoln barked. "Let him go."

Seth looked like he wanted to faint with relief at seeing us. He let Bell go and moved away, hands in the air, only to step on Dr. Fawkner's foot. Poor Dr. Fawkner yelped.

"Sir!" Dr. Bell rushed up to us. He looked as if he were about to grasp Lincoln's jacket but thought better of it. "Where is he?" he blurted out. "Where's Mannering?"

"I don't know. Dr. Bell, may we speak with you in your office?"

"This way."

"Go back to work," Lincoln told the onlookers, including Dr. Fawkner.

We followed Dr. Bell into his office and shut the door. Seth remained near it, his arms crossed, scowling at Bell.

"Why didn't you tell me you worked for Mr. Fitzroy," Bell said to Seth.

"I didn't think that mattered," Seth said with a shrug.

"Of course it matters! My God, man, he knows how Mannering came back." Bell turned his wild gaze onto Lincoln. "Don't you? You know why a dead man broke into my laboratory last night and stole my papers."

"We work for a secret government organization that monitors threats to our national security," Lincoln said. "You and your research came to our attention recently through another investigation. We're concerned that you may be creating a serum or medicine for an unscrupulous person or persons who are operating against the interests of crown and country."

"Firstly, I know of no such government organization."

"Hence the secret part," Seth said with a shake of his head.

"Secondly, my patron has *only* England's best interests in mind. I wouldn't have accepted the commission otherwise."

"How can you be sure?"

"From the letter he wrote me. He swore that my medicine would be used only by the government to keep the nation safe."

"It's true," Seth said. "I read them."

"You said 'he' just now," Lincoln said. "Are you certain it's a man? Have you met him?"

"No. I'm not certain of anything regarding my benefactor's identity."

"Is there anything else you can tell us about him or her? Anything that may identify them? Think very hard, Dr. Bell."

Bell shrugged. "Nothing. You've seen the papers. There is no name, no monogram, no letterhead, and the signature cannot be made out. Money was left in a bag in here for me. I don't know who put it there. No one does."

"And you didn't ask for proof of his identity, considering the medicine would be dangerous if it was used by an unscrupulous person?" I asked. "That's very unwise."

"It must have been a lot of money," Seth muttered.

"It wasn't the money!" Bell snapped. "It was the challenge. Only a genius could succeed in creating such a medicine."

"Shame you couldn't do it," Seth sneered.

Bell ignored him. "I have questions for you, Mr. Fitzroy. How did Mannering come back to life? Was it a serum based on the analysis of his own blood, or something else entirely? Is my research into hematology important at all? Please, I've been floundering without getting close and now—"

"Enough," Lincoln ordered. "We have to leave. Now."

"Don't be ridiculous. I can't leave like this. I have work to do."

"It's not negotiable."

"Dr. Bell, please," I said. "You have to leave London and go into hiding until we catch this man. He's incredibly dangerous. He lied to you. He doesn't want the serum for good."

"How do you know?"

"He's murdering people to keep them quiet. Do you know any murderers out to do good for the nation?"

Bell fell back into his chair. He looked like an old man, worn down by years of hard physical labor, not scientific work in a laboratory. He lifted a shaky hand to stroke his beard. "Then what does he want it for if not for national security?"

Lincoln rounded the desk and pulled Bell to his feet. "We have to go. Now. Do you have family?"

Bell shook his head.

"I'll give you money to buy new clothes at your destination. Are there any personal effects from here that you wish to take?"

Bell simply stared at him as if he couldn't quite see or hear him.

Lincoln gripped his shoulders and shook him. "Move."

"But *you* managed to raise Mannering."

Lincoln let him go. Then he punched him. Lincoln caught the unconscious man before he hit the floor.

"Now how do we get him out without anyone seeing?" Seth asked on a sigh.

The door opened, knocking Seth in the back and pushing him forward. Dr. Fawkner stood there, gun in hand. It shook. "Stand all together over there," he ordered, pointing the gun at the far wall. He noticed Dr. Bell on the floor. "What did you do to him?" he cried in a squeaky voice.

"He wouldn't do as he was told," Lincoln said. "And if you don't do as you're told, the same thing will happen. Put the gun down."

Dr. Fawkner shook his head. "N-no," he stuttered. "I'm just following orders."

Orders! My God, *he* was the spy.

"Miss, go stand with him. You too," he said to Seth.

"Whose orders?" Lincoln asked as we joined him.

"I don't know. All I know is I have to make sure no one gets near Dr. Bell and his research. I didn't suspect you two at first, but then after I heard about last night..." He pursed his lips and expelled a breath. "Hopefully I can make up for my mistake now."

"You don't look like you want to use that thing," I said, wishing I felt as calm as I sounded.

Dr. Fawkner wiped the side of his face on his shoulder. It left a wet, sweaty streak on his jacket. "I will if I have to."

"Why?"

"Money. You know, that stuff that helps you put a roof over your dying mother's head and that young research assistants don't get much of."

"You're in danger too," Lincoln said. "Just as much as Dr. Bell. The man who gave you that money doesn't want any loose ends. He has killed everyone he ever employed on this project—and others—and you'll both be next."

"Why, if I haven't met him?"

"There'll be something that I could use to identify him. It won't be anything you suspect right now, but it could be enough for us if we put it together with other pieces of the puzzle."

"Only if I talk."

Lincoln merely stared at him. Fawkner sucked in his lower lip to stop it wobbling.

At that moment, Bell stirred. He got to his hands and knees, groaning.

"Dr. Bell?" I kneeled beside him. "Are you all right?"

"Stand up!" Fawkner shouted. He held the gun in both hands, yet it shook uncontrollably. His gaze darted between the four of us, and he licked his sweaty upper lip.

Lincoln crouched beside me and assisted me to stand. God knew why. I was perfectly capable of rising on my own. Even so, I was grateful for his steadying presence.

Even more grateful when I realized why he'd helped me. I registered the *click* of his knife blade locking into place the moment before it hurtled across the room. It must have been strapped to his leg or in his boot, somewhere the police hadn't checked.

The blade dug into Fawkner's shoulder. He cried out and fell back at the same time that Lincoln jerked me behind him. Almost as an afterthought, Fawkner pulled the trigger, but by then, the gun pointed harmlessly at the ceiling. A hail of plaster dust rained over Seth as he ripped the gun from Fawkner's grip.

Fawkner rolled around on the ground, clutching his shoulder and crying.

"That was bloody dangerous," Dr. Bell said, getting to his feet. "He could have shot one of us before the knife got him. Or what if you'd missed?"

Seth grunted. "He never misses."

"He was agitated and unused to firearms," Lincoln said. "I judged him to be an inaccurate marksman."

"He's also never wrong," Seth added as he checked Fawkner for hidden weapons. "Almost," he added with a glance at me.

Someone pounded on the door. "Dr. Bell! Dr. Fawkner, are you all right?"

Bell rubbed his jaw and gave Lincoln a dazed look. "You hit me."

"And I'll hit you again if you don't come with me. Or I could leave you here to die." He nodded at Fawkner. "He won't be the only one trying to stop you escaping."

Bell nodded and answered the door. "We're all right, but...we have to go away for a while," he said to the wide-eyed man standing there. "Penwick, you're in charge until further notice."

"But Doctor—"

"Just do as I say!"

Penwick nodded meekly and scuttled away. Bell rejoined me, looking rather forlorn.

"It'll all be over soon," I said.

Bell packed some things from his drawer into a medical bag then nodded at Lincoln. "Let's go. What'll you do with him?" He looked to Fawkner, whimpering on the floor.

"Take him with us," Lincoln said. "If we leave him, he'll be dead by nightfall."

"Why do you care? He tried to kill you."

Lincoln's hooded gaze flicked to me. "I don't care. But I care about the opinion of someone who does."

I took hold of Dr. Bell's offered arm, more to steady myself than from propriety. I felt quite unbalanced by Lincoln's pronouncement. His intense gaze didn't help either.

Lincoln removed the knife from Fawkner's shoulder, much to the injured man's horror, and tucked it up his sleeve. Fawkner almost fainted, but Seth pulled him to his feet and shook him. He put his coat around Fawkner, hiding the blood, and they followed us into the corridor.

Dr. Bell made excuses, telling his colleagues he needed to go away for a few days on a private matter. I don't think anyone believed him, but they could see he wasn't being coerced and they must have respected and feared him enough that they didn't want to pry.

We took them to the coach. Lincoln climbed in with Bell, Fawkner, and me. He ordered Seth to remain on the footman's perch at the rear and watch for anyone following. "King's Cross," he told Gus.

"Tell me how you did it," Bell once again asked Lincoln. "How did you make Mannering come alive?"

Fawkner spluttered a mocking laugh. "Have you finally lost your mind?"

"I *must* know!" Bell reached forward and grasped Lincoln's forearms.

Lincoln's stone-cold glare forced the doctor to let go and sit back again. "No medicine can bring the dead back to life, Dr. Bell. It's impossible."

"But I saw—"

"You saw someone who looks like Mannering. It wasn't him."

Bell's lips moved in silent discussion with himself as he considered this possibility. Perhaps he really was mad.

"It hurts like the devil," Fawkner whined, inspecting his bloodied sleeve.

"Do be quiet," I spat. "You made your bed, and now you must lie in it."

"I wouldn't really have shot anyone." He sniffed and slumped into the seat beside Bell. "Where are you taking me?"

"Home," Lincoln said.

"Where is that?" When Lincoln didn't answer, he asked again. "Where do you live?"

"In a mansion with an imposing central tower used for my prisoners. You'll like it there."

"No need for sarcasm," Fawkner said with a petulant sneer.

Bell didn't speak again until we reached the railway station. He sat in the corner, reluctant to move. The shadows around his eyes appeared deeper, darker, but that could have been because his face was paler. To look at him, one would think he'd lost a loved one. Perhaps, to him, his work was his closest and constant companion, and now that work lay ruined.

"Where will I go?" he muttered. "What will I do?"

"You'll go wherever the first train out of London takes you," Lincoln said, opening the door.

He got out and helped a doddery Bell descend the step. The doctor seemed to have aged ten years. Lincoln gave him a pouch full of money and spoke with him quietly before jerking his head at Seth. Seth jumped down from the footman's post and escorted Bell through the throng of passengers milling about the station.

Lincoln remained outside, watching, until Seth rejoined us ten minutes later. It felt like an interminably long time. Fawkner wouldn't stop asking me questions about our destination and about his fate. He wouldn't shut up, no matter how many times I asked him to, until Lincoln finally rejoined us.

We drove home in blessed silence. Lincoln and Seth escorted both Dr. Fawkner and me to the house via the service entrance. "Take him to the tower room," Lincoln ordered.

"Not the dungeon?" Seth pouted. "Pity."

Lichfield didn't have a dungeon, just a cellar; although it did feel like a dungeon down there once the door was locked. "I'll see to his wound in a moment," Lincoln said.

"You will not," Fawkner declared. "You're not a doctor. I'll do it myself."

"As you wish. Seth, once he's settled, fetch the medical kit and stay with him until he finishes then remove everything that could be used as a weapon."

Doyle and Cook watched Seth direct Fawkner past the kitchen. Fawkner walked meekly, his head bowed.

"How will we explain this to Lady Vickers?" I asked.

"She requires no explanation," Lincoln said, indicating I should walk ahead of him into the kitchen.

"That doesn't mean she won't demand one. I suppose we'll have to lie."

He asked Cook to make us something for a late breakfast then turned to Doyle. "See that Charlie's rooms are warm. Do you require a bath?" he asked me.

"God, yes. The sooner I get the stink of that cell off me, the better." I moved to the stove and helped Cook fry some bacon and eggs. Lincoln prepared two trays on the table.

"So what happened?" Cook asked.

I described our evening to him, and something occurred to me as I spoke. "No one has followed us this morning or tried to attack," I said to Lincoln. "Does that mean Fawkner was the only spy at the hospital, and since we caught him, the killer cannot be alerted?"

"To rely solely on someone like Fawkner would be an amateurish mistake," he said, leaning back against the wall near the pantry, his arms crossed over his chest. "Our killer isn't an amateur. It probably means they aren't willing to attack yet, so as not to show their hand too early. That's what I would do."

"Or perhaps it's not a committee member, after all. Perhaps whoever it is hasn't yet heard about our encounter with Bell last night."

"It's a possibility."

"Are you going to question Fawkner?"

"After breakfast. I can wait until after you bathe if you want to join me."

Why was he asking me to interrogate Fawkner with him? To involve me in the investigation? Or because he was afraid of the methods he'd use if I wasn't there to temper his violent streak?

"No, thank you. I'm tired. I think I'll rest."

"There you both are!" Lady Vickers stood in the kitchen doorway, the invisible barrier keeping her out of Cook's domain. "Who is our new guest? Seth wouldn't tell me. He suggested I speak to you about it."

"His name is Dr. Fawkner," Lincoln said.

"A doctor?" She pursed her lips in thought. "While I think you can do better, my dear girl, a doctor might suit if there are no other candidates. How fortunate that we can study his manner at close quarters. Do you know his connections, Mr. Fitzroy?"

It was so absurd that I couldn't help the bubble of laughter escaping. "Madam, I dislike Dr. Fawkner intensely."

She sighed. "Well, I suppose it's my own fault for telling you to set your sights high."

I rolled my eyes.

"I do expect you to be civil to him, Charlie," she snipped. "You must take tea with him and such. You may not like him, but you might like his friends. It's important to present yourself in the most agreeable manner to everyone. You never know how a connection will be made."

"Charlie won't be taking tea with him," Lincoln said. "No one will. He's not to be disturbed."

"Why not?"

"He's ill."

Her hand fluttered to her chest. "Nothing catching, I hope."

"It's highly contagious."

She gasped. "Good lord. Why isn't he in hospital?"

"It's a long story, and one I don't wish to go into right now."

That seemed to satisfy Lady Vickers. I expect the fact that Lincoln was the one to tell her had much to do with her believing the story. If I or someone else did, I doubt she'd be so trusting. Lincoln did have a rather straight way of delivering his lies so that I, too, found him utterly believable at times.

Lady Vickers left, muttering under her breath about diseases and cleanliness. Bella entered a moment later, and I suspected she'd been waiting for her mistress to depart. Lincoln told her about our new guest and repeated his warning about staying away. She, too, believed every word; so much so that when Seth returned, she screwed up her face and told him to scrub himself clean before he came near her.

"What have I done now?" he asked, throwing up his hands.

I left Lincoln to inform him and took my breakfast tray upstairs to eat in my room. After a warm bath and a quiet sit by the fire to dry my hair, I could no longer keep my eyes open. I fell asleep, only to wake up a few hours later from a nightmare. I'd dreamed that the Queen of Hearts' soldiers chased me into a prison cell where the disgusting Jenny, dressed in the queen's livery, belched in my face then drove a sword through my heart.

I went downstairs and found Seth and Gus in the sitting room with Cook and Doyle. Doyle jumped to his feet upon seeing me and flushed red to his hairline.

"It's all right," I told him. "Please, sit down. You're welcome to use the sitting room. Mr. Fitzroy won't mind."

"Thank you, but I have to speak to him anyway." He skirted around me as if I were a wild animal and slipped out.

"How's the prisoner?" I asked, touching the sides of the teapot on the table to test its warmth.

"Still alive, unfortunately." Seth lay stretched out on the sofa, his long legs dangling over the armrest, one arm under his head. "He's an annoying little turd."

"Did Lincoln question him?"

"Aye," Gus said. He sat on an armchair and wiggled his bare toes at the fire. "Fawkner told him nothin' about the person who employed him. Prob'ly because he knew nothin'."

"He received money and instructions in a blank envelope delivered to his house," Seth added. "He didn't see who left it."

Cook stretched out his legs and scratched his round belly. "He sounds like a toss pot. Who'd hire a fool like that?"

"He was closest to Dr. Bell," I said, "and desperate. Men like that are eminently employable. Apparently his mother is ill, too. That reminds me, we ought to find out where his family lives and concoct a story to explain his absence."

"Fitzroy asked me to do it later," Gus said.

Seth sat up to make room for me on the sofa. "Your mother would have a fit if she saw you sprawled out like this," I said. "Where is she, by the way? And why isn't Bella in here with you?"

"Bella's helping my mother dress for the dinner party."

I glanced pointedly at the clock on the mantel. It was only five o'clock and the dinner didn't begin until eight.

"Apparently it takes hours," Seth said. "Bella's hairdressing skills aren't up to snuff."

Gus snorted. "She ain't much good at anythin' round here."

Seth wiggled his eyebrows. "That's what you think."

"You're doin' it right under your mother's nose? Bloody hell."

"You be asking for trouble," Cook added. "Don't come crying to us if you get caught."

"I can handle my mother," Seth said around a yawn.

I chuckled into my teacup.

Lincoln entered and nodded at me. "You're awake."

Had Doyle been ordered to tell him when I woke? It would seem so. "Tea?" I asked.

"Thank you. Gus, make your visit to the Fawkners now. Seth, see if Dr. Fawkner needs anything."

"Why?" Seth whined. "I looked in on him not long ago."

Lincoln gave him a withering glare, and Seth sighed. He followed Gus out. Cook left too, without being asked. Lincoln had just made sure that we were alone. I suddenly felt trapped. Even more so when he shut the door.

I poured him a cup of tea but regretted it when I went to hand it to him. My trembling made the cup rattle in the saucer.

"Thank you," he said and sipped.

I sipped too and avoided his gaze. If he mentioned that kiss, I'd...I'd walk out. I wasn't ready to discuss such things with him. Intimacy needed to be avoided at all costs. By that measure, being alone with him should be avoided too.

"You'll need a new coat and gloves," he said.

"I have another."

"Even so."

We both sipped again.

"I expected the committee to come this afternoon," I said.

"As did I."

"Did you have a chance to look through the paperwork Mannering stole from Bell?"

He nodded. "It wasn't particularly helpful. There's nothing in it that we don't already know." He set his cup down and came to sit on the sofa beside me. "I want to talk to you. About us," he added, as if I were thinking of something else.

"I'd rather not." I went to stand, but he caught my hand. I snatched it away.

"I suspect you have some things you need to get off your chest."

"You want *me* to do the talking?"

"I want you to say everything you want to say to me now. Everything that's upsetting you. Don't hold back."

I straightened my spine and strode to the fireplace to gather my wits. "Very well, but be warned, you're not going to like it."

"I don't expect to."

I drew in a deep breath and let it out slowly. There was so much to say to him. The only problem was, where to begin?

CHAPTER 14

I twisted my fingers together behind my back and looked Lincoln in the eye. As always, it was an unnerving experience, and I wished I could look away again, but it was too late. I felt myself being sucked in by those pitch black orbs, unable to escape.

I cleared my throat. "The thing is, Lincoln, I think you know everything that I'm going to tell you already."

"I want to hear it from you."

"You are a glutton for punishment."

His gaze lowered, severing the connection and releasing me.

I gasped in a deep breath and let it out slowly. I could do this. I could tell him levelly what I thought without letting my emotions rule me. "You must know by now, from my reaction and that of the others, that what you did devastated me."

His only response was to look up again and swallow heavily. He didn't speak, and it would seem he was prepared to sit quietly without interrupting.

"You broke my heart when you sent me away, and you almost broke my spirit." My voice cracked, much to my horror. I'd wanted to present a strong front. I wanted to show him that he couldn't break me altogether. So far, I wasn't making a very good case.

He rose but I put my hand out to stop him coming closer. He sat again and passed a hand over his chin and jaw.

"Tell me honestly, Lincoln. Why did you send me away? I know it wasn't just to keep me safe."

He cleared his throat. "That was one reason. But mostly it was because you distracted me from my work. When I'm distracted, I don't work efficiently, and if I'm not efficient, dangerous things happen. People die. Killers slip through cracks. I forget to do important things."

Well. There it was. Now I knew, although I'd suspected. It was a relief, in a way, to hear him say it. It explained why he still cared about my wellbeing, although it didn't lessen the pain.

"I should have told you," he said heavily. "But I thought it best that you believed I'd had a change of heart. I truly wanted you to make a fresh start, away from here, with other people. Normal people. I wanted you to forget me, and you couldn't do that if you had hope that I...that I still cared."

I looked down at my slippered feet and twisted my fingers tightly behind me. My heart hammered against its cage, yet my mind felt clear. I looked up again and met his steady gaze. "You need to stop treating me like a child."

"I wasn't aware that I did."

"Perhaps not a child, but someone unworldly, innocent. I may have a friendlier, more open nature than you, but that doesn't make me an ignorant fool."

His lips clamped together and a muscle bunched in his jaw. I suspected he was trying very hard not to respond.

"I know the dangers of living here and being involved with the ministry," I went on. "And with you."

His gaze sharpened. His chest expanded with his breath.

"Did my absence help you focus?" Although I suspected I already knew the answer, I wanted to hear it from his lips.

"No. Sending you away was a mistake, in more ways than I can express." He leaned forward and rested his elbows on his knees. Some of his hair fell over his face, obscuring his eyes. He looked up at me through the curtain of lashes and hair. "I regret my actions, Charlie. I hope you know that."

My throat tightened. He looked so out of place, sitting on the sofa while I stood by the fire. It wasn't lost on me that the positions were usually swapped. "I do."

He suddenly stood and closed the short distance between us with two long strides. He went to grab my arms, but when his gaze met mine, he stopped at the last moment and put his hands behind his back. "You don't forgive me."

"No."

His nostrils flared. "I can only apologize again."

"I don't want to hear it anymore."

A frown sliced his brow. "Then...how can I make it right again?"

Tears burned the backs of my eyes. I hated that he could still make my heart ache like this; could still draw a reaction from me that I'd sworn never to have again. "You can't. I don't expect you to."

His gaze searched mine until I could no longer bear looking at him. I lifted my face to the ceiling, but he caught my chin. I braced myself and once again looked into his eyes. They swirled with raw, dark emotion that stripped all my remaining strength. I wished I'd seen coldness again, like the day he'd sent me away. It would be easier than seeing this vulnerability.

"Charlie..." he whispered. "There must be something I can do to earn your forgiveness."

I pulled away from his touch because my chin wobbled and it was one thing that he could see it, and quite another for him to feel it. I sucked in a breath and let it out slowly. It helped. "You sent me away because it suited *your* needs. You didn't think for a moment how it would affect me. You are a selfish man, Lincoln. You say and do whatever you want, and everyone else must fall into line or be trodden on as you charge toward *your* goal. I cannot forgive you for what you did." The damned tears, so near the surface, finally spilled down my cheeks. It was difficult to talk with my throat constricted, but I needed to finish my piece. "I can't forgive you, because if I do, I'll allow you back into my heart again. I can't risk it being broken a second time, and I certainly can't let you crush my spirit. It's the one thing that's truly mine—that's truly *me*—and I will guard it fiercely, from now on."

The silence that followed my words was absolute. Lincoln didn't move. He'd gone so still that he seemed not to be breathing. The strange thing was, I wanted to reach out and stroke his face, to soften the blow of my words. Part of me worried that I shouldn't have spoken with such brutal honesty. How did someone so inexperienced with emotions cope with the feelings that must be assaulting him now? Or was I mistaken? Did he feel nothing?

It was impossible to tell. Despite the small muscle pulsing high up in his jaw, his face gave away nothing.

Lady Vickers breezed into the sitting room, her hair around her shoulders. "Charlie, I need your help with choosing—" She stopped dead. "My apologies. I'll come back later." She turned and hurried out.

Lincoln took a breath. "Thank you for your time," he said, as if we'd just conducted a business meeting. "I won't keep you." He marched out. His hands, still clasped behind his back, twisted together in white-knuckled knots, much like mine.

I followed a few moments later and headed to my own room. I ran the last part along the corridor, hoping not to see anyone. Once inside, I threw myself into the armchair by the fire and burst into tears.

Much later, I realized my tears weren't born entirely from misery. While I did feel a little sick for dashing any hopes Lincoln may have had, I also felt lighter for unburdening myself. I was proud, too. I hadn't given in. I'd made my stance very clear and, best of all, I'd come through it unscathed. I didn't regret that I'd laid myself bare to him. He wanted to know what I thought and I why I couldn't forgive him. He *needed* to know.

Now, it only remained to be seen if the uneasy relationship we'd forged since my return would get better or worse.

***

The committee finally arrived while I ate supper in my rooms. My immediate reaction was to remain out of sight, but I quickly dismissed the idea as cowardly. The committee knew that I was back, so there was no point hiding. Besides, no one would dare attack me in front of Lincoln.

Heated voices signaled their presence in the drawing room. They all spoke over one another, but the theme was the same—they accused Lincoln of working without their authority. If Lincoln responded, he couldn't be heard above the noise. It was more likely he stood there, allowing them their say while somehow managing to seem above the squabbling.

I squared my shoulders, lifted my chin, and marched in. It proved an effective method of silencing them.

"Good evening," I said, going to stand by Lincoln at the fireplace. Whatever our personal differences, I wanted to present a united force, both to the committee and to him. They all needed to know that I was on his side and trusted his decisions in all matters regarding the ministry. "Is Doyle bringing tea?"

"Brandy," Lincoln told me. "Something stronger is called for." He did not look at me but at his guests, seated around the drawing room.

"So it's true," Lord Gillingham said. "You brought her back."

Lincoln didn't answer.

"Then what did you send her away for?" General Eastbrooke bellowed. His mutton-chop whiskers weren't as neatly trimmed as usual, and the lines on his face seemed more numerous. For once, he was showing his age.

The other committee members appeared more harried than usual too. Lady Harcourt's lovely face was paler and her eyes darted all over me, as if she were inspecting me for any signs of change. I wondered what she saw. Lord Gillingham rubbed the head of his walking stick, over and over. His face was a rather unhealthy shade of red as he spluttered his protest over my presence in the drawing room.

"Shut up, Gilly," Marchbank growled with more vehemence than I'd ever heard from him. Usually the composed one, he looked tired and worried.

It was this that gave me pause and had me glancing anxiously at Lincoln.

"We wanted her brought back, and now she is," Marchbank went on. "Stop harping."

"I didn't want her back," Gillingham protested. "I simply wanted to know where he'd sent her."

"As did I," Eastbrooke snapped. "As did most of us."

Four voices once again spoke over one another.

205

"She's back." Lincoln's voice cut through the noise. "She's back for good. That is the end of the matter."

Gillingham shot to his feet. "You do not tell us when the matter is ended!"

"Sit down," Lincoln growled.

He did not. He stepped toward us, but Lady Harcourt caught his arm.

"Please, Gilly," she said in a quiet, simpering voice that didn't sit well on her. "Let's keep this as civil as possible." She didn't look at me, but her brown eyes implored Lincoln.

Doyle wheeled in a drinks table. He poured brandies and handed them out. No one spoke until he left, shutting the door behind him.

"You may be wondering why we didn't come earlier," Lady Harcourt said.

"It crossed my mind," Lincoln said blandly.

"We needed to have a meeting to discuss the situation among ourselves first. It was...heated—and rather exhausting."

"That explains why your tempers are short and your eyes tired," I said, placing my glass on the mantel. I wanted a clear head.

Lady Harcourt's hand touched the corner of her eye, as if she were checking for new wrinkles.

"You allowed yourself to get caught by the police," Eastbrooke said. "What were you thinking, man?"

"And what the bloody hell were you doing at Bart's, anyway?" Gilly added. "What has the hospital got to do with anything?"

Lincoln shifted his stance. "I can't tell you yet."

"I beg your pardon!"

Eastbrooke stood. He was an imposing figure, but I wasn't afraid. Not with Lincoln beside me. "Careful, Lincoln. Be very careful of overstepping."

"You'll be told when I deem it necessary for you to know," Lincoln said. "No sooner. I am the leader of the ministry and this is my investigation."

Gillingham pointed the middle finger of the hand that held his glass at each of the committee members in turn. "*We* are the head of the organization."

"No, you are not."

"And we have the power to dismiss you."

I sucked in a breath.

Eastbrooke stood and held up his hands for calm. "Settle down, everyone. Let's not make any hasty decisions."

Decisions? Unease settled in my stomach, bitter and cold. I glanced at Lincoln but his stony face gave nothing away.

"Our decisions are never hasty," Marchbank said.

The general pointed a finger at his colleague. "You are not in charge here, March."

"Nor are you."

Eastbrooke's chest expanded and his chin thrust out. He sported the confident air of a man with an army under his command, whose word was never questioned and whose orders were always obeyed. "I am the most senior member of the committee. I have years of experience in strategy and planning, and dealing with men. Not to mention I am the closest thing to a father he has."

"No." The sharpness of Lincoln's voice had everyone turning to him. Lady Harcourt pressed her hand to her lips, and General Eastbrooke blinked. He hadn't expected Lincoln's disagreement. "You are not a father figure to me," Lincoln went on. "You are nothing like one, and never have been, so do not pretend otherwise."

"I raised you."

"You paid for a roof over my head and for tutors to teach me. That's not the same as raising."

"He's got you there," Gillingham said with a chuckle into his glass.

Eastbrooke tugged on his jacket hem. "Nevertheless, I am in charge here."

"You are not in charge," Marchbank shot back. "None of us are. That's why we have meetings and votes." Eastbrooke may have the bearing of a senior member of the armed forces, but Marchbank possessed what every nobleman did—a belief in his God-given right to be above everyone else. He also had the face of a battle-scarred warrior. It made him far more frightening and worthy of respect, in my opinion.

"Please, enough of this arguing," Lady Harcourt whispered. "My nerves are shattered enough."

"That's your own fault, Julia," Gillingham said, pointing his walking stick at her. "You can't blame any of us for your secret getting out. I, for one, didn't even know you were a dancer until I read about it in the papers. Tell me, do you know the cancan? Marvelously energetic dance. I wonder, would you give me a private show later?"

With a snarl and bearing of teeth, she flung herself at him. "How dare you!"

He put his hands up to shield his face, but not before her fingernails raked across his cheek and he spilled his brandy in his lap. It took both Eastbrooke and Marchbank to drag her off him and push her back down on the chair. Lincoln didn't step in to help.

Gillingham touched his bloodied cheek. "You bitch!"

"You disgusting, depraved little man." Her low growling voice held none of the velvety tones that usually came out of her mouth. Her body heaved with her deep breaths, and the swell of her breasts rose above her bodice.

"I am not the disgusting, depraved one here." Gillingham's gaze fell to her breasts. He grunted a laugh.

If Eastbrooke and Marchbank hadn't still been holding her, she might have flown at Gillingham again. As it was, she had to settle for a sneer.

"Enough!" the general shouted. "You're acting like children."

Gillingham dabbed at his cheek with his handkerchief then at his damp crotch. "This is why women shouldn't be allowed on the committee. One of the Buchanans should have taken over their father's place."

"What's done is done." Marchbank eased back warily, as if Lady Harcourt were a feral cat he'd caught but wanted to release, and he wasn't sure if she'd attack again. "Membership in the committee is not up for negotiation."

I watched the scene in wide-eyed wonder. Growing up, toffs had always been people to look up to and admire, with their lovely clothes, sparkling jewels, and regal bearing. They seemed to be above the sorts of things that I worried about, like where the next meal came from, or how I would change clothes without the boys seeing my breasts. Since meeting the committee, I'd learned that they were no different from anyone else. They could be just as petty and cruel as the lowest villain who walked the streets and preyed on the desperate. Watching the committee implode was a humbling experience, and yet satisfying too. With the exception of Marchbank, I didn't like any of them.

Lady Harcourt sniffed. Tears streaked down her cheeks, leaving tracks in the powder she wore on her face. Marchbank handed her his handkerchief, but she didn't take her eyes off Lincoln.

I glanced at him too. He stood with his hands at his back, his feet a little apart, his attention on the gentlemen. All three of them now stood.

"There is a point to this meeting," he said with bored indifference. "Will someone please get to it?"

Gillingham continued to dab at his cheek as if he hadn't heard the demand. Eastbrooke and Marchbank exchanged glances.

Eastbrooke shook his head ever so slightly. "It's a mistake," he said quietly.

"You were outvoted, General." To Lincoln, Lord Marchbank said, "At our meeting today, we discussed the immediate future of the ministry, and in particular, your role in it, Fitzroy. We decided that you will be stood down as leader, effective immediately."

"What?" I exploded. "You can't do that! The prophecy says he is the leader."

"For once, we're in agreement," the general said. "However, the other three voted for your dismissal, Lincoln."

"I can't believe you would do this! I respected you," I said to Marchbank. "But you're as foolish and arrogant as the others."

"The ministry has been exposed." Lord Marchbank sounded tired, older. "We no longer know where many supernaturals are, and Fitzroy refuses to keep us informed on important matters. He gave us no choice."

"There's no place for a rogue in the ministry," Gillingham said, refilling his glass from the decanter. "Particularly in the role of leader. He has to go."

"You can't do this!" How could I make them see? They couldn't do this to Lincoln. The ministry meant everything to him. Surely they hadn't thought it through. "You don't have the authority. No one does."

"Stop it," Lady Harcourt hissed. "Your puppy-like devotion is sickening. I'm surprised at you, Lincoln. You never did like overt displays of emotion, yet you stand there and listen to *her*."

"I listen to her because she has something to say that I want to hear. Or need to." He spoke with utter calmness, as if he hadn't just been dismissed from the job he was destined to do.

"You've become blind to reason, ever since she came here."

"Not blind," he said, while I was still gasping at her audacity in speaking to him like that. "Stupid, on occasion, but not blind. I should never have sent Charlie away. She belongs here." To Marchbank, he said, "I will willingly resign if my two demands are met. Lichfield remains mine, and Charlie is left alone."

I gasped again. "Don't you wish to think about it first?"

"I have thought about it. That is my decision."

"The house is yours," Marchbank said with a dismissive wave. "It always has been."

"As to the girl, she'll be treated as every other supernatural will be treated." I heard the smirk in Gillingham's voice, but I was too busy staring at Lincoln to see his expression.

"Lincoln...what are you saying?" I whispered.

"I agree to step down from the ministry," he said.

Gillingham snorted. "As if you ever had a choice."

CHAPTER 15

I blinked at Lincoln and shook my head, but he wasn't looking at me. Indeed, he seemed to be staring hard into the distance, purposely *not* looking at anyone.

"It goes against the prophecy," Eastbrooke said with a shake of his head. "Who else is qualified? He was raised to do it. No one else could be as effective."

"I agree." I touched Lincoln's elbow. "You don't have to accept their decision."

He turned slowly to me. His face seemed different, and it took me a moment to realize that it had softened. "Yes, I do."

He couldn't mean that. He couldn't simply step aside and let them take his life's purpose away from him. "Lincoln, you need time to consider what it means."

"I know what it means. It's what I want."

"But—"

"He's made his decision," Lady Harcourt bit off. "It's final." She put out her hand for one of the gentlemen to assist her to her feet. After a moment, Marchbank took it.

"I don't like it," Eastbrooke said with another sorrowful shake of his head.

"Your opposition was noted earlier." Gillingham stamped his walking stick on the floor. "As March stated, you were outvoted. It's time to consider the future."

"This is madness." I included Lincoln in that assessment and let him know it with a glare. "Who'll be leader now?"

"That's none of your concern," Gillingham said.

I appealed to Marchbank. "I thought you were on his side!"

"I'm not on any side. I do what I think is right for the ministry. In this instance, I believe Fitzroy has acted rashly in sending the supernaturals away and not informing us of their whereabouts—and yours." He extended his hand. Lincoln shook it. "Hopefully it's only temporary. If you bring the supernaturals back, all will be forgiven."

"Hardly," Gillingham muttered.

"I won't be accepting the position," Lincoln said.

I shook my head. I no longer understood him.

Gillingham was the first to leave, followed by Lady Harcourt, her head high. Even so, her stride lacked its usual grace and her back wasn't quite as stiff.

General Eastbrooke heaved a sigh and shook his head. "I would never have believed it, but you've gone soft, Lincoln." His glance at me left no doubt as to where he laid blame.

"Goodbye, General," Lincoln intoned.

Eastbrooke sighed again then left too. I followed, a little ahead of Lord Marchbank and Lincoln.

"It's not too late," Marchbank said quietly. "Bring back the supernaturals, or tell us where they are, and you can resume your position as leader."

"I won't be bringing them back while their lives are in danger. When you catch the murderer, which I sincerely hope you do, and they return to London, I won't be rejoining the ministry. It's time I moved on to other things."

"Very well. I accept your decision, even if I don't agree with it." We headed down the stairs to where Doyle stood handing out coats and hats. "I'll oversee the removal of your copies of the ministry files in the morning, as well as any notes on the search for the murderer."

"I'll write a report tonight. There isn't much to tell, I'm afraid. Be assured," he said, louder, so that the others could hear, "if anyone tries to harm Charlie, I will kill them."

Everyone looked to me. I wished I could hide behind the urn again, but I endured their scowls and disdainful sneers with what I hoped was a measure of dignity. None reacted with fear. Did that mean none of them was the killer? Or, if they were, did they no longer intend to kill me? Or did they think Lincoln wouldn't follow through on his threat?

"Your acceptance of our decision does you credit, Fitzroy," Marchbank said as he drew on his gloves. "To be honest, I expected you to fight it. Your reaction has been entirely selfless."

Selfless.

My god. *Now* I understood. I'd called Lincoln selfish only a few hours ago, so in an effort to prove that he could think of others, he'd set aside his own wishes and done what he thought was right. He'd agreed to step down as leader because he thought it was what I wanted, or perhaps what I needed. He had turned his entire life upside down, gone against everything he'd been raised to do, and given up his life's purpose *for me*. It was the most selfless thing he could have done.

But it was utterly wrong.

"Where is Seth?" Lady Harcourt asked, looking past Doyle to the shadows at the back of the entrance hall.

"At a dinner party with his mother," Lincoln said.

"Oh? Whose?"

"The Murrays. I believe Buchanan is there, too."

"Ah, yes," Gillingham said with a slick smile. "I was invited but declined. I believe all the young, popular set will be there, though. Didn't you get an invite, Julia?" His voice dripped with sugary cruelty.

She buried her chin in the gray fur of her coat collar. "Walk me out, General."

I waited until they were all gone, and Doyle retreated, before turning on Lincoln. "You didn't have to do that. You *shouldn't* have done that."

"I wanted to."

I smacked him in the shoulder. It was as effective as hitting rock. "Don't do this because you think it's what I want. It's not."

He crossed his arms over his chest and leveled his gaze with mine. "It's what I want." If he was lying, it was a bloody good act.

"You can't step away now. There's a murderer on the loose, and you're the best person to uncover the truth."

"They'll work it out."

"Eventually, perhaps, but in the meantime, the murderer is going to try again."

He gripped my shoulders. "I won't let anyone harm you. They wouldn't dare try."

"Oh, Lincoln, you can't be sure of that. And it's not just me. What about the evacuated supernaturals? They can't return to their homes until the killer is caught. You made them a promise that you'd help them."

His gaze shifted away.

I took his hands in both of mine. "Don't abandon them. Don't let the killer win."

"It's not a matter of winning or losing." He sounded so convincing, and yet he didn't look at me. I knew him. Lincoln would look me in the eye if he were telling the truth and needed me to believe it.

"It is, Lincoln. It *is* about those things. What it isn't about, is me—or us. This is something else entirely. Don't abandon the ministry and those people because you think doing so will win my favor. It won't. You aren't the sort of man who steps back from his responsibilities. It's not in your nature, and I wouldn't want your nature to change." I could have gone on to tell him that I'd fallen in love with him exactly the way he was, but that would lead to an exploration of whether I loved him still. I wasn't ready to test that slippery path.

His fingers tightened and his gaze flicked to mine then away. "I gave my decision. My decisions are always final." Even a stranger could have heard the uncertainty in his voice that time.

My eyes fluttered closed in relief. I was so glad that I hadn't been wrong, and he still wanted to be ministry leader. I didn't want to be the cause of him giving it all up. "Let them think you've resigned. That way, you can continue to search for the killer without the committee's interference."

"They'll learn what I'm doing, sooner or later."

"Let's hope it's later, *after* you've uncovered the murderer."

He looked down at our hands. I'd forgotten they were still linked and quickly pulled away. His formed fists at his sides. "Resigning may be the right thing to do," he said. "I've never considered what life would be like outside the ministry. I might like it."

More likely he'd go mad from boredom. There couldn't possibly be another job in the world that would keep him active, both in mind and body.

"I'll follow through on this case then decide," he said.

"Very well. If it's what you want." I folded my arms against a shiver. It was cold in the entrance hall. I longed for the fireplace again.

"You should ask Doyle to get the fire going in the library," he said. "I assume you'll stay up to hear Seth's account of the evening?"

I nodded. "What will you do?"

"I have a very vague report to write."

***

Lincoln, Seth and Gus joined me in the library upon their return. Gus crouched by the fire, his hands outstretched to the warmth, and sighed contentedly. The poor man had spent a lot of time out of doors lately, driving us around. The cold must be getting to him.

"Julia is upset that she wasn't invited, according to Buchanan," Seth told us. He cradled a brandy glass in his hand, although I wasn't sure if he needed it. His eyes were glazed enough, and he sported an air of devil-may-care mischief.

Lincoln didn't mention that we'd seen Lady Harcourt and the other committee members, so I kept quiet too.

"It's begun, you know," Seth went on. "This will be the first of many events that she'll not be invited to. The rumor mill is churning out all sorts of things about her, much of it bandied around tonight, despite Buchanan's presence. He probably started most of it. He certainly seemed to enjoy hearing the more salacious tidbits about his step-mother."

"I almost feel sorry for her," I said.

217

"Don't," Seth said. "She doesn't deserve sympathy, least of all from you. Besides, part of what was said tonight is true. I ought to know; I've participated in some of it." He held up his glass in salute. "But no longer. Particularly when there are so many other ripe little peaches ready for the—"

"Seth!" Lincoln's bark cut Seth off.

Seth chuckled into his glass.

"I thought your mother wanted you to marry one of those little peaches," I said wryly.

"She does. Doesn't mean I'm going to." He shrugged. "If I have to endure parties and silly conversation, I might as well enjoy myself. Spoils of war, and all that."

"You're a prick," Gus told him.

"Confine your dalliances to the widows," I said. "Don't go ruining any poor debutants."

"Poor debutants! You should have seen Miss Yardly. Practically had to break her fingers to pry them off me. She accosted me in the hallway when I went to use the privy and touched me in places that offended my delicate sensibilities. There's nothing innocent about her."

Gus snorted a laugh.

"Did you manage to speak to Buchanan about his movements on the day in question?" Lincoln asked. "Or were you too busy gossiping and fighting off ardent admirers?"

Seth smirked. "I did, as it happens, when we retreated to the billiards room. Through charm and the liberal application of alcohol, I managed to get out of him that he'd risen late from his mistress's bed and went home to freshen up, only to find his brother visiting. If Harcourt hadn't arrived in London that day, I doubt Buchanan would have recalled where he'd been or what he'd been doing. Apparently they fought over the younger brother's dissolute habits, then went their separate ways. Harcourt stormed out of the house, but Buchanan doesn't know where he went. Buchanan, meanwhile, made himself agreeable to The Honorable Jane Stebney-Green. He's in need of a wealthy wife, and she happens to be an heiress and available, albeit a quiet girl—not at all his type."

"How did he make himself agreeable to her?" I asked.

"By following her about as she shopped, made calls, and so on. Apparently he happened to bump into her and her mother on no less than three occasions that day."

"Don't sound so agreeable to me," Gus muttered. "More like a cough that can't be shook off."

"Someone ought to warn her about him," I said.

"No need," Seth said. "His methods didn't work. She has since told him, in no uncertain terms, what she thinks of him and is now being courted by a far more upstanding gentleman."

"Good for her."

"Amen. Fortunately for me, too, or Mother would see that I make myself agreeable to her."

"His story will be easy enough to verify with her maid," Lincoln said.

Seth pressed his hand to his heart. "It will be an honor to be assigned the task of interrogating the maid."

Lincoln nodded.

Gus stretched out on the rug in front of the fire and rolled his eyes. "You're a toss pot."

"But a toss pot who finds out things, like Harcourt's involvement with St. Bartholomew's Hospital." Seth downed the contents of his glass and set it on the table. "I mentioned Bart's in a passing comment about Gus's aunt's health, and asked Buchanan if he knew any good doctors there. He claimed to know nothing about the institution, but he said his brother does. Apparently Harcourt donates to research there."

"Which department?"

"Buchanan didn't know. The latest medical breakthroughs, is how he put it. He followed it up with a snide comment about his brother's excessive spending on strangers when he had family practically starving on his doorstep."

I laughed. "Buchanan's likening himself to a starving waif, now? The man is incorrigible."

"I'll look into it," Lincoln said.

"Right." Seth pushed himself out of the chair, wobbled a little, then wiped his mouth with the back of his hand. "I'm going to bed."

"Not yet," Lincoln said, and Seth plopped back down into the armchair. "There's been a development that you both need to be aware of."

"We know the committee were here," Gus said. "Cook already told us."

"That's not all of it." I glanced at Lincoln. He nodded at me to go on.

"You two have patched things up?" Seth asked us with a hopeful smile.

I cleared my throat. "Lincoln has resigned from the ministry."

"Um...what?"

Gus sat up. "Bloody hell! What'd you go and do that for?"

"They were dismissing him anyway," I said. "He simply agreed to it."

"Huh?" Seth rubbed his fingers over his eyes and blinked back at us. "You two really shouldn't be left alone with the committee."

We told them how the committee had met that day and voted to oust Lincoln as leader, and why, mentioning that Eastbrooke had been the only one against the decision. We went on to tell them what Lincoln and I had subsequently decided to do.

"Then, when all this is over, they'll happily reinstate you as leader," Seth said with a knowing tap of his finger on the side of his nose.

"Aye." Gus nodded. "They'll be bowin' and scrapin' and beggin' you to come back. Make sure I'm there. I want to see it."

"I'll reassess how I feel about the ministry after the murderer is caught," Lincoln said. "I might not return."

Two sets of eyes bulged. Then they both turned to me, as if I held the answer to why Lincoln had suddenly lost his mind.

I stood, wanting to cut off questions before they uttered them. "Goodnight, everyone."

"We go out for one evenin' and look what happens," Gus mumbled, helping Seth out of the chair. "We come home to a mess."

Seth nodded, but the action caused him to sway. Gus caught him before he fell back into the chair. "They shouldn't be left on their own with only the servants to keep an eye on them. We can't trust them."

I smiled as I headed out, feeling content for the first time in weeks.

***

"Finally!" Lady Vickers declared when I told her there was no need to keep my return a secret anymore.

"Finally?" I asked. We sat in the sitting room by the fire. Lincoln had taken Dr. Fawkner with him to Bart's to find out what he could about Lord Harcourt's investments. He'd promised the doctor he'd take him to see his mother and sisters afterward, as long as he did as he was told. A bleary-eyed Seth was visiting The Honorable Jane Stebney-Green's maid. Meanwhile, Gus kept watch over me, a job he took very seriously. He'd already ordered me back from the window when I went to sit there to soak up the morning sunshine. He remained alert while Lady Vickers and I sewed.

"Yes, finally," Lady Vickers repeated. "There is already interest surrounding you, thanks to my edited account of your intriguing past. Once I put out the word that you're available to attend parties, I expect the invitations to pour in. I'll begin today."

"So soon?"

She patted my knee. "Of course, my dear. There's no time to waste. You're not getting any younger."

I sighed and appealed to Gus for help.

"It might be fun," he said with a shrug. "You need a little fun. Ain't good for you to be cooped up in here."

"How did Seth fare?" I asked, eager to change the subject. "Did he meet any agreeable young ladies last night?"

"Several," his mother said with a preening smile. "He was very popular."

"Any in particular catch his eye?"

"Miss Yardly seemed to, and I know *he* caught *her* eye. She told me after dinner that he was utterly charming, and he amused her greatly."

Gus and I exchanged glances and suppressed smiles. Miss Yardly had been the debutant with the roving hands.

"He must like her," Gus said with a serious air. "He mentioned her last night, didn't he, Charlie?"

I glared at him until Lady Vickers looked my way, an expectant smile on her face. "Did he? I wasn't sure he took to her. She's not the prettiest girl, or the wittiest, but her father's business is doing well, by all accounts, so she's popular. Very much so." She lowered her sewing to her lap and frowned at the fire. "Although, her popularity is quite out of proportion to his wealth. All the gentlemen seemed to be trying to catch her eye last night. Indeed, they couldn't stop looking at her."

She sighed. "That's what happens when a girl with such a feminine shape wears a low-cut gown. At least you won't have that problem, Charlie."

My cheeks heated, but I couldn't protest. She was right.

Lady Vickers picked up her sewing again and attacked it with vigor. "Mrs. Yardly ought to point to Lady Harcourt as an example to teach her daughter some modesty. That woman doesn't know the meaning of covering up."

Gus's cheeks flamed, and he kept his gaze firmly on the window, pretending not to be listening. Lady Vickers seemed to have forgotten he was there.

"To be fair," I said, "Lady Harcourt has fallen prey to the gossips over her past as a dancer, not her clothing."

"Ah, there you are," Seth said, strolling in with a swagger. His eyes were brighter than when he'd left and the color had returned to his face.

"You look better," I said.

He grinned and pecked his mother on her cheek. "I feel better. The Honorable Jane Debney-Green's maid knows a wonderful tonic for curing the aftereffects of excessive drinking."

Lady Vickers clicked her tongue. "That's quite enough of that talk."

"I heard you discussing Julia just now. I forgot to ask last night, Charlie, but how did she seem when she was here?"

"Shaken, but whether that was from their earlier meeting, which I gather was quite heated, or from the gossip about her past, I don't know."

"She's only got herself to blame," Lady Vickers said.

Seth threw himself into one of the chairs. "You can't talk, Mother! You should have heard some of the things said about you after you left London."

She sniffed. "I bore it all with my head high and my dignity intact."

"You weren't even here!"

"The stigma followed me to America. The point is, I didn't let it upset me too much. I knew what would be said about me, when George and I decided to make our relationship known, but I did it anyway. Besides, my situation is different. I did what I did for love. Her motives are entirely avaricious, and everyone knows it. People are more forgiving when romance is involved, and I am being quite sure to tell them that George was the most romantic of men and that our life in New York was a fairytale."

"You cannot be serious," Seth said. "They believe you?"

She looked down her nose at him. "Where do you think you got your charm from? It's not your father, believe me. He had as much charm as a starving rat."

Seth looked like he was about to defend his father's honor then thought better of it.

"I'm sure Lady Harcourt would like a visit from a friend," I said to him.

He shook his head. "We're not friends, and she would try to manipulate me to her side. You shouldn't worry about her, Charlie. Julia is a survivor. She'll find a way back from this."

"Perhaps," his mother said.

Lincoln entered, carrying a tray with tea things. He poured while I served.

"I'll take mine to my room," Lady Vickers said, returning her sewing to her basket. "I have letters to dispatch. If all goes well, you'll be coming out to dinner with us tonight, Charlie."

"Tonight!" I looked to Lincoln. He set the teapot down with a clunk, but said nothing. "So soon?"

"Of course," she said. "Why wait?"

"Does this dinner include me?" Seth asked.

"Yes. I told you so last night on the way home, and you agreed to attend."

"I was drunk! You can't hold me to something I agreed to under the influence."

"You're going," she said with a stern glare. "As Charlie will be."

"If she goes, I go," Lincoln said.

Lady Vickers nodded stiffly. "I expected as much. Fortunately, Mrs. Overton is quite keen for you to attend too."

I heaved a sigh. The Overton girl only had eyes for Lincoln. Not that I cared, but I knew he would dislike being the object of her affections. Besides, she was wasting her time with him. He did not want to marry. I sighed again. It was going to be a long dinner.

Lady Vickers accepted a teacup and left us. Once she was out of earshot, Lincoln reported on his morning's work. "Fawkner introduced me to other doctors in the hospital. A microbiologist confirmed that Harcourt invests in his work on tropical diseases."

"That doesn't necessarily rule him out as a suspect," I said. "He might have secretly invested in Bell's work too."

"He may have."

"So now what do we do?"

"Marchbank will visit soon to collect the files and my report. I want to question him about his father."

"Won't he be suspicious?"

"I'll be subtle."

Seth, Gus and I exchanged glances. Lincoln sipped his tea.

Marchbank arrived later that morning with two of his footmen. Gus and Seth led the servants up the stairs to assist them with moving the files. None of us were particularly concerned with the files leaving the house.

Lincoln had memorized their contents and could easily reproduce them. Marchbank mustn't know that Lincoln's mind acted as a trap for information or he wouldn't have bothered.

Lincoln led Marchbank into the sitting room. "I'm glad you're both here," Marchbank said. "I wanted to tell you how much I didn't enjoy yesterday. It's not what I wanted."

"You voted for his dismissal," I pointed out.

"I had no choice. You'll be reinstated once you bring those people back, Fitzroy."

"Gillingham won't agree," Lincoln said.

"Gilly is a fool, but he's only one and we're three. Julia can be talked around, particularly if you speak to her. Eastbrooke is already on your side, of course." He crossed his legs and tapped his finger on the chair arm. "You know, he does see you like a son, in his own way."

I watched Lincoln closely, but he gave no sign that Marchbank's words affected him. "He never treated me as a father treats a child."

"Do you mean affection? Not all men are that way inclined."

"I mean with respect. As a person with an opinion— as an equal. He gave me little guidance and hardly any of his time. I didn't want his affection, I wanted—" His voice grew increasingly louder, tighter, and he must have heard it. "I wanted his friendship," he added quietly.

I'd never seen him discuss his childhood, or the general, with such vehemence before. It was always with indifference, as if he didn't care. Until now.

I curled my hand into a fist on my lap to stop myself reaching for him.

"He was a better father-figure when you were very small," Marchbank said. "You wouldn't remember, but he liked spending time with you in the garden, exploring, playing hiding games."

"Why did he stop?" I asked.

Marchbank shrugged. "I don't know."

"You never asked?"

"You don't ask a man like the general why he no longer treats his ward like a son."

"I suppose not." I couldn't imagine how such a conversation would even begin.

"Since we're discussing the past," Lincoln said, "there's something I've always wondered about *your* father."

I had to applaud him on his rather seamless transition. Nicely done.

"Ah. I was wondering when you'd ask." At Lincoln's raised brows, Marchbank added, "I knew you'd find out about it sooner or later."

"I've known for some time," Lincoln said, lying through his teeth and not looking even a little bit guilty.

"Have you now?" Marchbank didn't look like he believed him. "I suppose you want to know if my father's death at the hands of a hypnotist means I now hate all supernaturals enough to kill them."

He'd caught us, and after such a good attempt at lying, too. "Well?" Lincoln prompted. "Do you?"

"It was a long time ago, Fitzroy. Why would I wait until now for vengeance?"

Lincoln didn't speak.

"There is no reason," Marchbank answered for him. "Besides, why would I get my revenge on people who had nothing to do with that incident?"

"Vengeance against their kind," I said with a shrug. "Because you couldn't kill the hypnotist himself."

"That's the flaw in your theory. I *did* kill the hypnotist."

CHAPTER 16

I gasped. It was the only sound in the heavy silence.

Marchbank cast me a flat smile. "It's true. I killed him soon after he directed my father to throw himself off the bridge. So there you have it. I meted out justice all those years ago, so I have no need to do so now. Not that you're still investigating the case, however. Are you?"

Lincoln met Marchbank's steely glare with one of his own. "You knew the killer?"

"My father wrote about a fellow in his diary. A fellow so convincing and compelling that he could talk my father into doing the strangest things. Things that went against his character. My father guessed that he was a hypnotist, although he'd never met one before and had not known they were real. He wrote that the hypnotist didn't want his details recorded in our files, but Father had done so anyway, believing it for the greater good. He would tell the hypnotist that day, as was fair. That was the last entry. I came across the diary in his things after his death, and knew what must have happened as soon as I read it. So I killed the hypnotist—accidentally, of course. I confronted him over my father's death, but he began his hypnotizing chant, so I hit him with a fire iron to stop him. He collapsed and didn't wake."

"Did you question him first?"

"No."

"Make inquiries of independent witnesses?"

"No."

Lincoln sat back and I could swear I heard him draw a sharp breath.

Shock rippled through me, too. Lord Marchbank had killed a man based on very thin evidence. Accident or not, he'd committed a violent act. I wasn't sure how to take the news. Marchbank may not be the upstanding gentleman I thought him to be.

"There was no doubt in my mind, Fitzroy," Marchbank said. "Not after reading the diary. You would do the same."

"I would have got answers out of him first."

"That part I don't dispute. I wish I'd spoken to him about his hypnotism, and how it worked, why he was like that. His name was Christopher Eckhart, if you'd like to research his family."

"You should have given it to me earlier. It should have been recorded in the files, his family connections investigated and noted."

Marchbank acknowledged this with a nod of his head, but offered no reason for leaving it until now to inform Lincoln. "The thing is, Fitzroy, you assumed that I had a motive for killing those supernaturals—and Charlie—but I'm not the only one who worries about what people like her can do. Ever since Frankenstein showed us the possibilities of magic, and summoning Estelle Pearson proved how badly things can go wrong, the entire ministry has been on tenterhooks. We *all* distrust those who hold such great power over us.

Charlie may be an honorable person, but not everyone is like her, and she's not incorruptible."

"I'm quite sure I am, thank you," I snapped.

"Everyone should be wary of supernaturals, even other supernaturals. Even you. Both of you."

"I am fully aware of what people who possess magic can do," I said. "As is Lincoln. No one is more aware. But that doesn't mean we can murder all of them. Just because a person holds a knife, it doesn't mean they're going to stab someone."

Marchbank held up his hands. "I agree. That wasn't the point I was trying to make."

"Someone, however, disagrees."

"They do," he added quietly with a frown at Lincoln. I half expected Marchbank to tell us his own suspicions, perhaps even mention his thoughts about the other committee members, but he did not.

"I will be bringing the supernaturals back to London," Lincoln assured him. "After the killer is caught."

"A task that has now fallen to me. Unless..."

Lincoln handed him a single page document from his pocket. "My report."

Marchbank hesitated then unfolded it. After a quick read, he flipped it over, but the back was blank. "Is this it?"

Lincoln nodded. I'd read the report and agreed with him that much had to be left out. Marchbank was a suspect, and we couldn't let on how much we knew, even if he promised not to tell the others.

"What have you been doing all this time?" Marchbank asked.

"I've been pre-occupied with other matters."

Marchbank's gaze slid to me. "I see."

Seth peered around the door. "The last box is being loaded now, sir."

Marchbank rose and we walked him to the front door, where Doyle stood waiting with the earl's coat over his arm.

So what will you do with yourself now?" Marchbank asked, a hint of mockery in his gruff voice. Clearly he still didn't believe Lincoln would step aside from the investigation completely.

"I may take a holiday at the seaside," Lincoln said.

"But it's December!"

"The country is beautiful at any time of the year."

"I didn't peg you as an aesthete," Marchbank said, as Doyle helped him into his coat.

"I wasn't, until recently. I believe I became a lover of the countryside on my recent visit to Harcourt's estate in Oxfordshire."

Those few days out of London had been lovely, and I held fond memories of them. Lincoln had once told me that he'd not truly noticed how beautiful the countryside was until then.

"Grand place," Marchbank agreed. "You ought to come and visit Lady Marchbank and me at March Hall. You too, Charlie. Not in winter, though. Bitterly cold place is Yorkshire at this time of year."

Didn't I know it.

"That's why Elsa and I prefer to stay here until Easter." He tipped his hat and Seth saw him to his carriage.

"Well?" Seth said when he re-entered. "What did you learn?"

"He killed the hypnotist who killed his father," I said.

He whistled. "And I thought him the sane one."

Lincoln walked off without a word and took the stairs two at a time.

"Something got into his bonnet," Seth said, watching him go.

We headed to the kitchen and waited for Bella to leave before I repeated what we'd learned about Marchbank to the others. Lincoln still hadn't come downstairs and my curiosity eventually got the better of me.

I knocked on his door and he bade me to enter. He sat in an armchair in his sitting room, a sheet of paper in his hand and others scattered on his lap and on the table nearby. He looked up and seemed surprised to see me. He quickly stood and set down the paper.

After a moment, he said, "Is everything all right?"

"I was wondering what you were doing. You left in rather a hurry without explanation. Is everything all right with *you*?"

He indicated I should sit then he too sat. He picked up the paper again. "These are the documents Mannering stole from Bell. I decided to take another look at them."

"Any reason in particular?"

"Frustration at getting nowhere. I don't think Marchbank is our killer."

"Eliminating him is progress."

"Not enough. Not nearly enough." He rested his elbow on the chair arm and skimmed his top lip with the side of his finger. "Tell me what you think of these. A fresh set of eyes might reveal something I missed."

"I doubt it. You don't miss much." I accepted them anyway. They were mostly brief letters, asking for progress reports on the "assignment" with the occasional mention of payment. I read each one, some twice. I held the paper to the light but saw no watermark or other special markings. "There's nothing to identify the killer in these."

"True," he said, although I got the feeling he was holding something back.

I looked again. "I suppose they tell us a little of the sort of person he is. Or she."

"Go on."

"I think it's a man. The hand is neat but sharp. There are no feminine loops or flourishes."

"Almost too sharp." He leaned forward and pointed to the capital letters. All had small but noticeable ink blotches. "It's as if the writer thought for a moment after putting pen to paper, but before writing. As if they were consciously altering the style and shape of their letters."

I saw it now too. "So that doesn't eliminate a female writer."

"Perhaps not. It does indicate that the author is attempting to hide their identity. Because he knows we'll recognize his hand?" He moved his chair alongside mine and leaned in to read. It took me a moment to gather my scattered wits together and concentrate.

"The sentence formation isn't feminine," I said. "It's quite abrupt and to the point."

"Yes."

"That probably rules out Lady Harcourt, after all."

"And leaves in all the men." He stretched out his legs and rubbed his forehead.

"You're tired," I said.

"Frustrated with the investigation and this arrangement...it can't go on."

"Do you mean us both living here?" I hadn't thought it too terrible of late, but that could have been because we were both preoccupied and busy.

"No, I meant you having to remain inside. You should be out shopping, riding, and doing things young women do at this time of year."

"It hasn't been so bad, but thank you for the consideration. I think Dr. Fawkner has it much worse."

"He deserves it."

"We can't keep him forever. And we must consider the supernaturals too. It's almost Christmas, and they'll want to be home."

He drew in his legs and leaned forward, resting his elbows on his knees, his head bowed. His hair hung loose around his face, the dark twists obscuring his eyes. I ached to touch his shoulder to offer some comfort.

That thought shocked me to the core. When had I gone from hating him to caring? I didn't want to care. I didn't want to forgive. I didn't want to be at the mercy of his whims again.

I stood and looked away, but my heart remained heavy. "You know there's an easy solution. One that will draw the killer out."

"No, Charlie," he said with quiet conviction. "That is not a solution."

"It is. It's the only one we have."

He got to his feet. "I said no."

I lifted my chin and couldn't help the smile that stretched my lips. "You are no longer the leader. You can't order me about." I had him now.

He opened his mouth and shut it again. He seemed to be warring with himself. I wondered if he wanted to remind me that he could lock me in my room, or that he owned the house and was therefore still master here, but decided those were unwise words considering our history.

"You don't play fair," was all he said.

I laughed. "Says the man who wrote the book on devious play."

The corner of his mouth lifted. He took a step toward me, so I quickly retreated to the door and opened it. He wouldn't attempt anything foolish where others could see.

I was wrong. He caught up to me in the corridor and hooked me by the waist. His ragged breathing warmed my forehead, and his hand braced against my hip. He lifted the other hand to my face and gently stroked his thumb across my cheek. He tracked its path with his dark, heated gaze.

The exquisite touch thrilled me; yet it pained me at the same time. I wanted more of it, yet I wanted to shove him away from me. I wanted to wallow in his embrace, but I wanted to shout at him too. What was wrong with me? Why was I so conflicted? The choice should have been easy. Mere days ago, when he'd come for me at Inglemere, it had been easy. I'd been determined never to forgive him.

And now here I was, allowing him to tear my self-control to shreds and make a mess of my convictions.

He leaned in, and I closed my eyes. He did not kiss me, however, but rested his forehead against mine. "Charlie," he whispered.

With enormous effort, I drew away from him, out of his reach. I forced myself to hold his gaze, but it wasn't easy with the confusion I saw there. I hated seeing him like that.

"You can't keep doing this, Lincoln," I said. "You can't keep changing your mind. You want me, then you don't want me, now you want me again. It's hell on my nerves."

"I never stopped wanting you. Never." He leaned back against the doorframe and dragged both hands through his hair. "But I convinced myself that I was better off without you, and that I was strong enough to push my feelings aside." He folded his arms high up on his chest and tucked his hands away. "I was wrong."

I swallowed but the lump in my throat didn't move.

"Is there any chance...will you ever forgive me?" he murmured.

"I...I don't know. I think so, but it's not truly a matter of forgiving you. Not anymore. You see, I came to realize something while we were apart. It's not just that you sent me away, it's that I allowed you to do it."

"I don't understand."

"I allowed myself to be manipulated, and I allowed you to make decisions about my fate. I'm not sure when it happened, but at some point during our courtship, I stopped being *me*. I don't want to lose myself, Lincoln. Nor do I want to be at your mercy again, or anyone else's."

"You won't be. The cottage will see that you always have somewhere to go. You had no choices before, now you do."

"Perhaps. I don't know. I haven't had time to think it through."

"Take as much time as you need. I'll be here."

I tried to smile but it felt flat. I walked away, but it wasn't easy. Every piece of my heart wanted to turn around and throw myself into his arms. But my head told me to keep walking; not to give in to whims, or I'd regret it.

I was no longer sure which part of me should rule.

Lady Vickers cleared her throat, startling me. "Oh," I said. "I didn't see you." I glanced back along the corridor, catching Lincoln watching. He stepped back into his rooms. "How long have you been there?"

"Long enough to see you two," she said. "Don't worry, I couldn't hear anything. But I have eyes. I know what's what."

I sighed. "Please, I'm not up to a lecture right now."

"That's unfortunate, because you need one."

I got the feeling there would be no escaping her. I suddenly had immense sympathy for Seth. "Will it take long?"

She scowled. "Enough of your lip, young lady."

I laughed, in spite of my mood. "You think that's lip? You ought to come with me to visit my old haunts. You'll see and hear things that would make your hair curl."

Her lips turned white and her nostrils flared. If she stamped her foot, she'd resemble a bull preparing to charge. "As the senior woman of the house, and someone who has experienced love, loss and everything in between, I thought to offer you some advice."

"I don't want any advice," I said, walking away.

"That's too bad, because I'm giving it to you regardless." She trailed down the stairs after me. If I went to the kitchen, would she follow?

I headed to the sitting room instead, where Seth and Gus sat, talking quietly. Lady Vickers wouldn't dare upbraid me in front of her son and one of the servants.

Once again, I was wrong. "How long are you going to punish him for sending you away?" At least she didn't waste time skirting the point.

"I'm not punishing him," I said breezily, sitting on the sofa. Both Gus and Seth gave us their full attention. It would seem they were as interested in my answers as Lady Vickers.

"Aren't you?" she asked mildly.

"He did a heinous thing, Mother," Seth said before I could respond. "He sent Charlie away from her home."

"Aye," Gus chimed in. "She'd been livin' on the streets for years, with no home, no one to care for her, and just when she gets settled here, he sends her off."

"I know her history," Lady Vickers said crisply.

I looked from one to the other, my heart in my throat, tears in my eyes. I ought to stop them, and remind them that I was right here, but I couldn't.

"You know it, but you don't truly *know* it, Mother," Seth went on. "Let me explain. Charlie was only a little girl when her father banished her. Girls are supposed to trust their fathers. It's the one person a girl should know is on her side, and Holloway wasn't. He pushed her off the end of the pier and she had to swim or drown. She swam, but only just. Then she comes here, and just as she begins to hope that she could once again have a home and is surrounded by people she can trust, Fitzroy does exactly the same thing as her father did. He took away her home, her family, and dropped her off the end of the pier." He shook his head. "He *ought* to be punished."

"I'm not punishing him!" I swiped my damp cheeks and stood.

Lady Vickers caught my hand, but I wrenched free and ran out of the room. I halted in the doorway. Lincoln stood there, his eyes huge black pits surrounded by deep shadows. He stared at me, unblinking, not breathing, his hands fisted at his sides. He'd heard everything.

"I didn't get to finish," Lady Vickers announced, joining me.

"I don't want to hear it!" I snapped.

"Very well." She cleared her throat. "This letter came for you. That's why I was looking for you, but then I saw...." She handed me the letter then returned to the sitting room.

Lincoln didn't move. He seemed to be waiting for me to do or say something first. I couldn't think what. I'd said everything I needed to say already.

I opened the letter because I could no longer bear to look at his haunted eyes. I drew in a steadying breath, but my hands still shook as I read. It was from Alice, and she had news. Dreadful news.

CHAPTER 17

Lincoln strode to my side but didn't get too close. "What is it? What's happened?"

"Alice's dream came to life again." I showed him the letter. It was brief, only a paragraph long, but it told me everything I needed to know. Alice's parents refused to keep paying for her place at the School for Wayward Girls, and had forbidden her to return home. They'd disowned her, and Mrs. Denk had given her until Christmas to leave. That very night, Alice's dream had come to life again. This time, two fat twins visited the school looking for her, both of them bumbling fools, according to Alice. She'd met them often in her dreams. Two portly idiots were better than an army, but Mrs. Denk became cross and ordered them to leave. Apparently the men wouldn't listen to her. I wondered if she marched them down to the dungeon to teach them a lesson.

"Alice will come here," Lincoln said, handing the letter back to me. "Write to her today and send her some money for the journey."

I nodded through my tears. Why was I still crying? I was happy to be seeing her again, yet I couldn't stop. "Thank you, Lincoln."'

"Don't thank me." He walked away and did not look back.

"What is it?" Seth asked, joining me.

I showed him the letter. "Alice is coming to stay."

He laughed as he read. "I hope we get to experience these dreams of hers. Her fat twins will get along superbly with Gus and Cook."

"Hopefully a safe environment will put an end to that."

"How safe is it here at the moment?" He put his arm around my shoulders. "Let's go see Cook. You look like you could do with a slice of one of his cakes."

***

The evening at the Overtons' dinner party began well enough. Miss Overton stuck to her mother's side, so I simply avoided them both during the pre-dinner drinks in the drawing room. Lincoln managed to slip out of their trap, too, thanks largely to Lady Vickers accosting Mrs. Overton. Catching one Overton inevitably led to the capture of the other.

"Two birds, one stone," Seth muttered in my ear. "But my mother needs to think again if she's setting her sights on that girl for me."

"She might be quite lovely, when she's separated from her mother's skirts," I said.

"How will we ever know? I prefer a girl with a mind of her own."

"Like Miss Yardly?" I nodded at the buxom woman giggling at something Andrew Buchanan had said. I'd been prepared to like her for her spirit until I saw her fawning over him. He was a cad and not very good at hiding the fact. Clearly she had poor taste.

"*Not* like Miss Yardly." Seth turned his back on the couple and gazed over my head at the rest of the party. There were twenty, mostly young and eligible—the girls with their chaperones, of course. It would seem Mrs. Overton had matchmaking in mind.

So did Lady Vickers. The two of them put their heads together and nodded at various members of the party as they talked. I suspected they were pairing us up in some sort of game.

"Vickers," declared a gentleman, clapping Seth on the back. "Good to see you again. It's been a while."

Seth shook the man's hand. "A long while. I thought you'd left London."

The man grinned. He had straight, white teeth that dazzled against his tanned skin. His hair was as fair as Seth's and he was just as tall. If it wasn't for the three scars on his cheek, he'd have been very handsome.

"I did." He pointed to his scars. "Been in Africa."

"What creature did that?"

He threw his shoulders back, pushing out his chest. "Lion."

"Bloody hell." Seth drew me over. "Charlie, this is my old school friend, Mr. Martin Seacombe. Seacombe, this is Miss Charlotte Holloway, my mother's companion."

Mr. Seacombe did the oddest thing. He held out his hand for me to shake. Most men bowed or kissed women's hands, but he did not. I shook it with a firm grip.

His face pinked and he quickly removed his hand. "Sorry. I've been away so long I've forgotten how to behave around gentler company."

"Don't be sorry," I said.

"Don't worry," Seth said with a grin. "Charlie's not at all gentle." He nudged me with his elbow. I wanted to kick him.

Lincoln joined our party, and Seth introduced him then asked Seacombe about his travels. He regaled us with the story of how the lion he'd been hunting outsmarted him and hunted him instead.

"He won the battle," Seacombe said with a grin that made his scars pucker. "But I won the war."

We three stared at him. "You killed the lion?" Seth asked.

Seacombe puffed out his chest. "I did."

"Oh."

"The skin and head make an impressive rug on my library floor, as long as you watch your step." He laughed. "What's wrong, Vickers? Lion got your tongue?" He snorted.

"I suppose I don't see the appeal of killing animals for no particular reason."

"That's because you've never experienced the thrill of the chase. It makes you feel alive. When it's a matter of kill or be killed, everything becomes so much clearer." He clapped Seth on the shoulder again. "Wouldn't expect you to understand. You've never been to Africa."

"I have," Lincoln said, sounding bored.

Seacombe gave him an appreciative look. "Shoot anything?"

"Yes."

"Lion? Elephant?"

"Englishman."

Seacombe lowered his glass. Some of the contents tipped onto the floor.

"He talked a lot," Lincoln went on. His face was as hard and blank as ever, but I knew he was mocking the fellow. "I found it annoying." He strolled away only to be hailed by Andrew Buchanan.

"Odd company you keep these days, Vickers," Seacombe muttered into his glass, his gaze following Lincoln.

"Not as odd as it used to be," Seth replied.

The dinner gong sounded, and I silently thanked the staff for their excellent timing, freeing me from any more of Seacombe's banal chat. Or so I thought.

I ended up sitting next to him. Lady Vickers bent to my level as I sat. "I asked Mrs. Overton to put you beside Seacombe," she whispered. "I saw you two talking, and I knew instantly that you ought to be seated together."

"I don't like him," I whispered back.

"Oh, I don't expect you to. He's an arrogant peacock. No, I sat you next to him to make Fitzroy jealous." She tapper my shoulder with her closed fan. "No need to thank me."

"So you're old Lady Vickers' companion, eh?" Seacombe said to me. "Quite an entertaining woman, that one. Careful you don't follow in her footsteps, though." He laughed. "Wouldn't want to find yourself the object of scandal and gossip."

"Mr. Seacombe, how much do you know about me?"

"I know your name."

I smiled and lifted my glass in a toast. "To scandal and gossip, then."

He shrugged and toasted too. "Tell me about yourself. What's your story? How did you get to become Lady Vickers' companion?"

"My mother died, my father disowned me, and I lived in the slums for five years until Mr. Fitzroy kidnapped me. Seth was already working for him, so when his mother returned to England, she came to live with us." I thanked the footman for placing my soup in front of me.

"Well then," Seacombe said with a sniff, "if you don't want to tell me, you only had to say. No need for sarcasm." He presented me with his back and fell into conversation with the woman on his other side.

The question came up again, however. Mrs. Overton, sitting all the way down at the other end of the table, called for silence to ask me. "Who are your parents, child?"

"They're dead." My blunt answer caused Lady Vickers to cough into her napkin, but it didn't put off Mrs. Overton.

"When did they die?"

I decided to tell her about my adopted parents, not my real ones. That real story was too complicated to go into. "My father only a few weeks ago, and my mother when I was thirteen."

She frowned. "Only a few weeks ago? But you've been at Lichfield Towers for months, have you not?"

"I have."

"Why not with your father?"

"Because he threw me out of the house when my mother died."

The collective intake of breath made the ensuing silence seem even louder.

"It's a complicated situation," Lady Vickers said, giving me a hard glare.

"But where did you live before Lichfield and after your father threw you out?"

"Here and there," I said.

"Where?"

"She was passed around between family and friends," Lady Vickers said quickly. "No one you know. All reputable people, of course, but not like us."

"In London?" Mrs. Overton asked.

"Yes," I said at the same time that Lady Vickers said, "No."

"Well, if they're in London, perhaps I have heard of them. Where do they live, these family and friends?"

Lady Vickers shot me another fierce glare that had me shutting my mouth before I rattled off the numerous slums I'd lived in before coming to Lichfield. It wasn't fair of me to thwart her efforts like this. It was important to her that I be accepted, and it would reflect badly on her if my true story got out. Her own reputation hung by a thread, and that thread could be chopped off if her peers knew she was championing a street rat who'd lived with boys for five years.

"Down south," Seth said. "Charlie has distant cousins in Cornwall."

Mrs. Overton eyed me warily. "She doesn't have a Cornish accent."

"That's because she also has cousins up north," Lady Vickers said, "and in the east. Not the west, though, thank God. Her accent has been smoothed out with all the to-ing and fro-ing, going between cousins. It was no life for her, so when my own dear cousin told me of her plight, I decided to have her sent to Lichfield, where I knew Seth would see that she settled."

Miss Yardly sniggered into her wine glass. One of the other girls colored. No doubt they were imagining all the ways Seth had helped me settle.

"She became my ward," Lincoln told them, his cold-as-ice voice stopping all giggles and blushes. "Seth asked me to take her in, so I did. If anyone thinks there's anything unseemly in that arrangement, feel free to discuss it with me outside."

Oh, Lincoln, resolving things with brute force again. To be fair, there was no way to avoid scandal. I was steeped in it. We all were. Lady Vickers was a fool to believe she could steer us clear of it. I hoped she wasn't too upset with how the evening was turning out. Seth had a female admirer on either side of him, and he seemed to be enjoying himself. She might salvage something from the disaster after all.

"What a curiosity you are," Seacombe said, leaning much closer than was necessary or polite. The smoldering gaze and slick smile told me precisely why he'd deigned to speak to me again. "I find you intriguing, Miss Holloway. Very much so. Perhaps I'll be permitted to call on you soon at your home."

"Yes, of course, but you'll need to confer with both Lady Vickers and Mr. Fitzroy first. I must do as they both wish."

He eyed Lincoln. Lincoln stared back, a wicked curl to his top lip.

Seacombe gulped. "I'll check with my assistant to see when I'm free. I've got a busy schedule ahead."

"I don't doubt it. You must be in demand to speak about your African adventures."

That set him off again, and he spent the rest of the dinner regaling me, and the woman on his other side, with stories.

Dinner seemed to last an interminably long time. I was glad when the gentlemen and ladies finally separated, and hoped we could leave as soon as the gentlemen rejoined us in the drawing room. Unfortunately we did not. Lady Vickers appeared keen to stay, and Lincoln made no motion to go. Even worse, Andrew Buchanan cornered me.

"Where *did* you go while you were away?" He sprawled in the spindly-legged chair beside me, a glass at his lips. He looked as if he didn't have a care in the world, yet mere months ago, he'd needed rescuing from Bedlam. He'd been appreciative then. I preferred that fellow to this cocky bore.

"North," I said.

"Where, precisely?"

"That is none of your affair, Mr. Buchanan."

He grunted into his glass. "Very well, keep your secret. May I say what a pleasure it is to see you again. I hope you've resettled back at Lichfield."

"I have, thank you." I looked around for a conversation to escape to, but Seth was talking to Seacombe, and Lincoln had been accosted by the Overtons. Buchanan seemed like the lesser of three evils.

"There was quite a to-do while you were away," he went on. "The circus murder, for one thing. Do you know, Fitzroy thought *I* killed the strongman? Me! I haven't got a violent bone in my body."

"He must have had his reasons." Lincoln had told me about the arrangement between Buchanan and the circus dancer who'd also been in a relationship with the murdered strongman. I would have suspected Buchanan too, given that knowledge.

"It wasn't only that fellow's murder that set my household on edge. Julia has been dealt quite a blow too."

"So I read. Lady Vickers pointed out the article in the newspaper. I imagine it's upsetting to be the object of gossip."

"Devastating. You'd think the world was coming to an end any day now."

"I suppose it is, in a way. Her world, that is."

He sipped thoughtfully. I expected him to mock his stepmother's situation, to take the opportunity to grind his heel in, now that she was laid low. This pensive quietness was unlike Buchanan, and it was certainly out of character for their relationship. They'd always been so bitter toward one another in my presence, as if they were locked in some kind of battle. Yet he seemed almost sympathetic.

"It's interesting," he said to his glass.

"What is?"

"The change in her."

I wasn't sure interesting was the word I'd use.

"It's good for her to be reminded of where she came from," he went on. "Her horse had become a little too high. I warned her that she'd be thrown off it one day, and now that day has finally arrived." He drank the contents of his glass in a single gulp. "Definitely interesting."

Could he have been the one to inform the newspaper of her past? It was difficult to tell from his response, yet I could see him betraying her as revenge for her rejecting his advances in favor of his rich, titled father.

Lincoln joined us and announced it was time to leave.

"So soon?" Mrs. Overton pouted. "What a shame. Isn't it, my dear?" she said to her daughter.

"Such a shame," Miss Overton repeated without an ounce of sincerity. It would seem she no longer considered him a prospect, although her mother still did. Perhaps the conversation with him had cured Miss Overton of any tender feelings she once held. Knowing Lincoln, he would have made conversing difficult. Idle conversation wasn't his strong suit.

"Do come again," Mrs. Overton said to Lincoln as we made to leave. "Your presence is always welcome here, sir. As is your ward's," she added as an afterthought.

Lincoln and I thanked her.

Mrs. Overton elbowed her daughter. Miss Overton cleared her throat. "I've enjoyed your conversation tonight, Mr. Fitzroy."

"And I yours," he intoned.

Gus brought our carriage around, and we piled inside, snuggling into our fur coats and the blankets set out for us.

"Poor Gus, out there in the cold," I said.

"Poor Gus!" Seth patted the blanket around his lap. "He's been having a right old lark in the mews, lucky prick. He hasn't had to listen to bloody Seacombe go on about his dead lions. I don't remember him being such a bore."

"I do," his mother said.

"Then why did you want Charlie to sit with him?" Seth asked. "I heard you pester the Overton woman to change the arrangements."

She sniffed. "Reasons, dear boy, reasons."

"Did you enjoy yourself?" Lincoln asked me.

I sighed. "Not really."

It was dark in the cabin, but I could swear he smiled.

"It's not about enjoyment," Lady Vickers declared. "It's about making connections, angling oneself into the right set. Seacombe is rich and spends most of his time traveling. His wife would be very comfortable here and able to be her own person without interference from a demanding husband. I happen to think that arrangement would suit Charlie well."

"Charlie wouldn't want it that way," Seth said.

"Charlie can decide for herself, thank you," I said snippily.

Seth groaned and tipped his head back. "I should have drunk more. *Then* it would have been a good night."

"I have a suggestion," I said. "One that came to me as we sat in the drawing room, waiting for the men to join us. You're not going to like it."

"In that case, the answer's no," Seth said.

"Agreed," Lincoln said. "We are not using you as bait."

Either he'd guessed or used his seer's powers.

"Bait?" Lady Vickers asked. "Does this have anything to do with Seacombe?"

"Seth will explain later," Lincoln told her.

Seth tilted his head forward. "I will?"

"Tell her everything."

Seth groaned. "This evening suddenly got worse."

"We need to do this," I said to Lincoln. "It's the only way and you know it."

"What are we doing?" Seth asked.

"Having a dinner party and inviting the committee members, Andrew Buchanan and Lord Harcourt. Tomorrow night."

Lady Vickers pulled a face. "What an interminably dull group. I think I'll be out tomorrow night, if that's all right with you."

"Good idea," Lincoln said darkly. "The evening might become too interesting."

I tugged the blanket higher. I hadn't expected him to agree. "It'll be all right, Lincoln. We'll be well prepared."

He turned to look out the window, even though nothing could be seen except his own reflection.

***

I helped Cook in the kitchen most of the next day. We rarely had guests to dinner and never so many at the one time. Cook, in his quest for perfection, became more dictatorial than General Eastbrooke. He issued Bella and Gus with a long list of ingredients to purchase, while Seth and I helped him with the tasks that could be started while we waited for the shoppers to return. Doyle spent the entire morning setting the table and considering wine options, although I suspected he was simply avoiding the kitchen. Even Lincoln joined us when Gus and Bella returned. Cook set him to chopping carrots, and he silently obliged, much to everyone's surprise. Only Lady Vickers stayed away.

"Have you issued invitations?" I asked Lincoln, as I collected his pail of peel and scraps.

"Gus and Bella did, this morning," he said. "And they're not invitations. They're demands."

"That'll go well," Seth muttered.

Bella offered to take the pail outside for me, and I handed it to her. Once she was gone, I asked Seth, "How did your mother take the news of our...work?"

"She thought I was joking, at first. I had the devil of a time convincing her I spoke the truth. I'm still not sure she believes me. That reminds me, Charlie, expect her to ask you to raise the spirit of my dead father."

"As proof?"

"And to blame him for leaving us in debt. She never had the chance before he died, and she wants to do it face to face. I tried to tell her she won't be able to see him, unless you raise his body. That quickly put an end to the notion, but she still wants to speak with his spirit."

Cook tossed a potato at Seth, and Seth only just managed to catch it. "Stop talking and either get to work or leave."

"You mean I have a choice?" Seth tossed the potato to Gus, who juggled it before securing it in his broad hands.

Despite the frenzy of activity in the kitchen, the afternoon dragged interminably until it was time to dress for dinner. Bella helped me with my hair and dress, and she was just about to leave when there was a soft knock on the door. She let Lincoln in, bobbed a curtsy, and left. She shut the door before I could think to ask her to leave it open.

Lincoln always managed to look handsome, no matter what he wore, but a formal tail coat, white bow tie and black waistcoat added a layer of aloofness that more casual attire didn't. With his dark hair neatly tied back, it was easy to imagine him dining with the royal members of his family, if they ever invited him.

"I see you have the imp," he said, nodding at the amber orb around my neck.

I touched it, relieved to feel it throb. I hoped I wouldn't need to call on it tonight, but it was a comfort knowing it was there.

He cleared his throat and approached my dressing table where I sat. He held out a blue box. "For you, to wear tonight."

I stared at the box and a well of emotion threatened to consume me. Why would he continue to do this? Why was he making everything so...complicated? "Isn't the house enough?"

He lowered his hand and his gaze dropped too. His shoulders lost their rigidity.

I felt sick. There was no need for such ungratefulness. "I'm sorry, Lincoln. I spoke without thinking." I held out my hand. "If you're still offering it, I'd be pleased to accept it."

He handed me the box and I opened it. A bracelet nestled against the blue velvet bed, a dozen circular amber gems positioned all the way around. They were the same shade as the orb in my necklace.

"It's beautiful." I held it up to the light and laughed quietly. "No imps?"

"I couldn't find a jeweler who sold them. I'll keep looking."

"Thank you, Lincoln. I like it." Very much, I could have added. It was lovely, and thoughtful too, matching it to the necklace I had to wear tonight. Damn him for being so considerate.

He bowed and turned to go.

"We haven't discussed how to draw out the killer," I said. "Do you have a plan?"

"No. Do you?"

"I could claim to have an upset stomach and leave the dining room. Hopefully the killer will follow, then you can follow him."

"It's a good plan."

"You're flattering me," I said with a shake of my head. "It's a terrible plan."

"It's the only one we have."

"But what if the killer doesn't follow? What if he produces a gun and I can't call the imp quickly enough?"

"I doubt he'll have a gun. If he tries to kill you, it'll be in such a way that can't be blamed on him. Watch your drinks and your food at all times. Poisoning is a very likely possibility."

I drew in a deep breath and let it out slowly. He was right, but it didn't help settle my stomach. I doubted I could eat anything anyway.

He crouched before me and clasped my hand in both of his. "Don't worry, Charlie. I won't let anything happen to you."

I nodded and withdrew my hand. "Will you help me put the bracelet on?"

He hesitated before picking up the bracelet. I held out my wrist and instantly realized the mistake I'd made. The touch of his fingers sent my already shaky nerves into a spin. His warmth, the smell of his spicy soap, the sheer closeness of him played havoc with every piece of me. I forgot my conviction. I forgot to listen to my head, and instead could only hear my heart telling me to forgive him, to stop punishing him. And to kiss him.

CHAPTER 18

"Charlie," he said, rocking back on his heels and studying me with a thoughtful frown. "What Seth and Gus told Lady Vickers yesterday...about homes and you not having one for so long until now...I never understood. Not really."

"How could you not understand, Lincoln? You're not completely devoid of emotion or empathy. I know you're not. So how could you not see what this place meant to me?"

"I've only ever lived here—and at the general's house before that." He glanced to the ceiling, the walls, and the fireplace behind me. "Both places are nothing more than bricks, wood and glass to me. When I'm absent, I've never felt a longing to be back. Not to the building itself." His gaze rested on mine. It was the softest I'd ever seen his eyes, the most guileless. For once, I didn't feel as if he were trying to compel or convince me, just speak to me with honesty. "When I do want to come home, it's because there's someone there I want to see."

My throat tightened. He didn't need to say as much, but I knew he meant me. It was all there in his eyes.

The knock on the door made him turn away, giving me an opportunity to dab at the corner of my damp eyes with my little finger.

Seth gave us both a grim nod from the doorway. "They're beginning to arrive."

Lincoln drew in a deep breath before turning back to me. "Ready?"

I pulled on my long gloves and stood. "Ready."

He held out his arm and I took it. He must have felt my hand shaking because he placed his hand reassuringly over it. "You look beautiful, by the way. You always do."

***

The general was the first to arrive. He marched into the drawing room and shook Lincoln's hand. "Glad to see you've come to your senses. Don't worry about the others. Between us, we can talk 'em round."

"I'm not resuming my role as leader," Lincoln told him.

Lord Gillingham's entrance distracted me from Eastbrooke's gruff response. "Why are we here?" Gillingham demanded, leaning heavily on his walking stick. "What's the meaning of this, Fitzroy?"

"I wanted to clear the air," Lincoln said. "To show you I don't regret your decision, and I am at peace with it. Dinner is purely social."

"You don't have to accept the decision," Eastbrooke said.

"Do be quiet, General," Gillingham muttered. "You lost this one. Accept defeat graciously, for once, instead of stewing over it."

The general stormed past Doyle, almost knocking him off his feet. The tray he held wobbled dangerously, but he managed to avoid any of the drinks on it from spilling. Eastbrooke towered over Gillingham. He might be older, but he was far more physically imposing than the smaller man.

Gillingham backed up a step and gripped his walking stick hard. I would never forget how he'd used it on me as a weapon. Would he dare try to use it on Eastbrooke?

"You're a coward, Gilly," Eastbrooke sneered. "Weak. A *man* never accepts defeat."

Lincoln stepped between them just as Lady Harcourt and her two stepsons appeared. "Not in front of the ladies," Lincoln said.

Eastbrooke stepped down but continued to glare at Gillingham from across the room.

Lincoln repeated his explanation for the dinner invitation for the benefit of the newcomers, and finally for Lord Marchbank, the last to arrive. "I hope your wives aren't offended," he said to Marchbank and Gillingham, "but I didn't want to alarm them with any talk of the supernatural, if it should arise."

Gillingham tried to hide his blush behind his glass, downing the contents in a single gulp.

Lord Harcourt checked his watch, frowned, then slipped it back into his waistcoat pocket. *Yes*, I wanted to tell him, *it's going to be a long night.*

"So you're now a gentleman of leisure," Andrew Buchanan said, raising his glass to Lincoln. "Congratulations. All the best fellows are. You ought to join me at the club. Or come with me to the races. It would be a lark. Bring Charlie." He winked at me.

Ugh. Perhaps he'd arrived drunk. His eyes certainly seemed glassy and he hadn't even finished his first sherry.

"Shut up, Buchanan," Seth snapped. "Nobody wants to go anywhere with you."

Buchanan's nose wrinkled. "You've become an egalitarian, Fitzroy. Allowing the *help* to dine with the honored guests, now, eh?"

Seth simply rolled his eyes.

"Stop it, Andrew." Lady Harcourt pressed her fingers to her temple. "This is trying enough without you making it worse."

"That's what happens when several of your paramours happen to be in the one room together. It becomes *trying*." He held his glass out to Doyle to refill. "Hurry up, man. I need the fortification if I'm to survive."

"Enough!" Eastbrooke bellowed. "Or I'll throw you out myself."

"I'd like to see you try, old man."

"Andrew!" Harcourt snapped at his brother. "Don't!"

Buchanan snapped his heels together and saluted, first at his brother then the general.

"Arse," Seth muttered.

The company broke up into small groups, although Lincoln remained no more than an arm's length from me as he conversed with Lords Harcourt and Marchbank. Seth remained on my other side, so close that I felt him bristle when Lady Harcourt sidled up to me.

She wore deep black with her usual plunging neckline that displayed her bosom and jewelry in all their perfection. She never ceased to dazzle me with her beauty and wealth, although nothing could hide the tiredness in her eyes and the worry lines around her mouth. The gossip was taking its toll.

"That necklace is unusual," she said, reaching out to touch the orb. I pulled back, out of instinct, and she laughed. "I'm not going to steal it, Charlie. I simply wanted to admire it. It's interesting. Where did you get it?"

"It belonged to my mother."

"Oh? And the bracelet too? Are they a set?"

"Lincoln gave that to me."

Out of the corner of my eye, I saw Seth's gaze shift from me to Lincoln. Lincoln didn't appear to be listening.

"And you didn't give it back when your engagement ended?" Lady Harcourt asked. "My dear, what sort of signal are you sending him? I know you don't have a mother to guide you through the proper etiquette, but I expect more from Lady Vickers. She ought to tell you that when a woman breaks an engagement, she returns all gifts."

"I didn't break the engagement, he did. And this bracelet was given to me only this evening. It was a gift from a friend, not a fiancé."

The odd little smile on her face froze. "I see," was all she said before moving away to speak to General Eastbrooke.

"I don't think it's her," Seth said to me from behind his glass. "She's too preoccupied with her own problems to orchestrate the murders."

"What about the others?" I muttered. "Buchanan seems too drunk. If he were going to attempt to murder me tonight, wouldn't he want to be sober?"

"Definitely. Have you noticed how the general keeps glancing at the door?"

"Perhaps he's hungry."

Seth chuckled. "Gillingham has a firm grip on his walking stick too. It could house a sword or some other kind of weapon."

"By the same token, Lord Harcourt might have a weapon in his jacket pocket. He pats it every now and again, as if checking for something. There! He did it again."

I continued to watch the guests while attempting to make light conversation. It wasn't easy with Buchanan growing louder and continuing to wink at me, Lady Harcourt, General Eastbrooke and Lord Gillingham ignoring me, and Lord Harcourt and Marchbank keeping to themselves.

It was a relief when the dinner gong sounded. Lincoln offered me his arm, even though he should have escorted the highest ranked female, Lady Harcourt. She reacted to the snub with a flare of her nostrils and a hardening of features. The others noticed too, but most kept their opinions to themselves. Only Lady Harcourt's stepsons glanced at one another. To my surprise, it was the elder brother, Lord Harcourt who smirked. Buchanan's lips flattened.

We filed out of the drawing room, but due to a misunderstanding, Lord Harcourt went one way and I the other and we bumped elbows. "Apologies," he muttered. "Didn't see you there."

"I'll join you all shortly," Buchanan said just before we sat down.

I watched him go, unease settling into my stomach. Lincoln gave a slight nod, which I guessed meant he was suspicious too. He glanced at Seth, who slipped quietly out. His departure was noticed by most of the guests.

Seth and Buchanan returned some minutes later, ahead of Doyle who pushed the dinner trolley into the dining room. He'd been given strict instructions not to let any food out of his sight between the kitchen and dining table, but even so, I waited for everyone else to try their soup before I dipped my spoon in.

"Delicious," Gillingham said from the other side of the table. "Always did say you had an excellent cook."

I had to tilt my head a little to the right to see him past the large central candelabra. He appeared to be sincere. The fool had forgotten that he'd once employed Cook himself.

Next came the oysters and shrimp, after which I made my excuses.

"Are you all right?" Lincoln asked with convincing concern.

"Just a little stomach ache," I said, heading out. "I'm sure it's nothing."

I made my way upstairs, pausing on the landing. I glanced down and stifled a gasp. Andrew Buchanan followed me. He lumbered up the stairs, stumbling once, a leering grin on his face.

I clutched my amber orb. "What do you want?"

"A little kiss from a pretty wench," he slurred.

The words hadn't even left his mouth when Lincoln appeared behind him. "Touch her and I'll hurt you."

Buchanan raised his hands in surrender. "I thought you two were no longer together. If you still want her for yourself, Fitzroy, you should have said earlier."

Lincoln moved up to the same step as Buchanan.

Buchanan swallowed. "I wasn't going to ravish her. Not unless she wanted me to, that is. Sometimes they do, but I suppose you're aware of that."

If he didn't shut up soon, he might find his mouth shut for him by Lincoln's fist.

"What's going on here?" the general called from the foot of the staircase. "Lincoln?"

"Buchanan was just returning to the dining room," Lincoln said.

Buchanan backed away and would have fallen down the stairs if Lincoln hadn't caught his arm. He did not let go and escorted him the entire way down. All three men returned to the dining room, and I continued up.

I remained in my room for a few minutes then returned to the dining room. Everyone looked up as I re-entered.

"Feeling better?" Marchbank asked.

"I am, thank you."

Gillingham picked up my wine glass and passed it to me. "I find a glass of red does wonders for the constitution."

Why was he so eager for me to drink? Not only had I been out of the room, but so had Lincoln. While Doyle hovered nearby, I couldn't expect him to watch every guest during our absence. I accepted the glass and waited until the attention was no longer on me then set it down without drinking.

Gillingham, however, noticed.

"Are you any closer to finding the circus murderer?" Buchanan asked Lincoln in what was a surprisingly sober manner.

His brother slammed the knife and fork down on his plate. I'd be surprised if the plate didn't chip. "For God's sake, Andrew, not at the dinner table."

"Why not? I think everyone here is well versed in blood, gore and the supernatural."

"There are ladies present."

"They're hardly delicate flowers, Donald."

"Even so," the general said. "Not appropriate."

"Very well." Buchanan concentrated on the three different roasted meats and poultry on his plate, but I got the feeling he wasn't finished with the topic. "Tell me," he said, when no other conversation began, "what will you do now that you're no longer part of the ministry, Fitzroy?"

"Travel," Lincoln said simply.

"No," the general cut in. Everyone looked at him. His gaze, which had been watching the door behind me, settled on Lincoln. "Stay here in London. You will be recalled."

"He isn't needed, General," Gillingham said. "We can investigate without him. We have the resources and means."

"I disagree."

Lady Harcourt dabbed at the corners of her mouth with her napkin. "Gentlemen, please, my nerves—"

"Are fine," the general cut in. "Stop exaggerating, Julia."

Lady Harcourt's eyes widened. I'd wager she hadn't been addressed so disrespectfully in a long time.

"I say," Buchanan said, "that wasn't called for."

"Again, I disagree." The general turned to Lincoln but did not get a chance to speak.

"There's no need to be so abrupt," Lord Harcourt said. "For once, I agree with my brother. Whatever your differences with Julia, she is a lady and deserves your respect."

Abrupt.

I blinked at Harcourt. He was right. The general did have an abrupt and to-the-point way of speaking. Just like the letters written to Dr. Bell. Not only that, but he looked to the door frequently. Why? Who was he expecting to walk in?

I tried to catch Lincoln's attention, but it was focused on the general too. Had he also made the connection?

I pressed my hand to my stomach and rose. "Excuse me," I murmured with what I hoped was a pained expression.

Several gazes burned into my back as I walked out, and once again, I reached the stair landing before a guest caught up to me. It wasn't the general, as I'd expected, but Lady Harcourt with Lincoln not far behind. She hurried up the stairs and paused beneath the chandelier. The dozens of little gas lights picked out the gems in her hair and the cruel gleam in her eyes.

"Tell me once and for all, are you and Lincoln together?" she said.

Lincoln slowed. His footsteps were so light, she hadn't heard him. I clutched my imp's necklace.

"That is not your affair," I told her.

"It is very much my affair, you little sewer rat." She raised her hand but I deflected her slap with ease. I may not have resumed my training since returning to Lichfield, but I hadn't forgotten some of the defensive moves Lincoln taught me.

I put out a hand to stay Lincoln. I wanted to deal with her without his interference. "Sewer rat? Have you nothing more original?"

"He's mine," she hissed, baring her teeth. I'd never seen her so wild. Despite the jewels and elegant clothes, she looked as desperate and vicious as a slum whore defending her territory. "You cannot possibly be interesting enough for a man like him."

"He's not yours, Lady Harcourt, no more than he is mine. He's never going to *belong* to any woman. If you knew him well, you'd know that." I glanced past her to Lincoln. His gaze flicked to mine then back to her, but I saw the brief flare in it. A flare of hope.

Buchanan stood a few steps down from Lincoln, an ominous scowl on his face. He stared at Lady Harcourt's back, pressed his lips together, then spun on his heel. "Doyle!" he shouted as he trudged down the stairs. "My coat! I'm leaving."

Lady Harcourt turned and gasped upon seeing Lincoln there. She staggered a little until she caught the stair rail. "You can't take the carriage," she said to Buchanan.

"I'll walk. Doyle!"

The butler appeared, as did all the other guests, jostling one another in the dining room doorway to get a better view. Lady Harcourt descended the stairs like a queen, her head high and an air of unattainable aloofness about her. Sometimes I wished I could be as outwardly calm. I followed her and rejoined the guests.

"Why are you leaving?" Lord Harcourt asked his brother.

"I've had a viper spit in my face one too many times." He snatched his coat and hat off Doyle and shot a vicious glare at Lady Harcourt. "I've had enough."

"It's freezing out there! You can't walk all the way home."

"Let him go." Lady Harcourt presented Buchanan with her shoulder. "Allow him his dramatic exit."

"God, how I hate you," Buchanan spat. "I wish you'd crawl back under the rock you came from."

"Enough," Marchbank ordered.

Buchanan jerked the door open just as a gunshot resonated from deep within the house.

"Fuck!" came Gus's distant cry from the same direction.

Oh God.

"What's going on?" Gillingham asked, edging toward the front door. "Fitzroy, is this some kind of sick joke?"

Lincoln pulled out a gun from the waistband of his trousers at his back where his jacket had hidden it. Lady Harcourt gasped and sidled up to the others. I moved toward Lincoln and Seth.

"Everyone stay here." Lincoln's order may have been directed at all of us, but he looked at Seth as he spoke then at me. "Don't follow, no matter what you hear."

"You cannot go back there!" the general bellowed. But Lincoln was already striding away.

Seth put his arm around me. He stared at the door that led to the service rooms at the back of the house. It swung closed behind Lincoln. "It'll be all right," he muttered. "Gus is fine. That ugly prick is always fine.

Nothing keeps him down. He'll be fine." He passed a shaky hand over his mouth.

I put my arm around his waist and squeezed, but it didn't ease my own concerns. My heart hammered in my throat, and I suddenly felt so cold, even though the front door was shut again. Buchanan hadn't left. No one moved. It was like time stopped as we waited to hear from Lincoln.

"Back into the dining room." The general's bark startled me. "Everyone! Now!" With large sweeps of his arms, he herded the others. "You too," he said to Seth and me.

"I hate not knowing," I said, ignoring him. "Perhaps we should check."

"He's capable of dealing with whatever is happening back there." The general didn't sound entirely convinced by his own words. "He'll want you to be safe, Charlie. Go with the others."

"He's right," Seth said. "I've got a bad feeling about this."

I allowed Seth to steer me into the dining room, but clutched my orb to ease my anxiety. All the others, including Doyle, waited inside, their gazes focused on the door. I joined them, Seth and Doyle flanking me.

Then the candles went out.

"I say!" Gillingham cried, louder than the other protests.

"Who blew them out?" the general demanded.

I hadn't seen. My attention had been on the door.

"Doyle!" Lady Harcourt's screech grated like nails down a chalkboard. "Doyle, re-light them!"

"Yes, ma'am." I felt him move away, the sudden absence of his solidness turning my blood cold. I couldn't see a thing in the dark, not even outlines. The scent of candle smoke filled the room.

"I release you," I muttered, but my imp didn't emerge from its cocoon.

Seth's arms circled me. "Stay close," he murmured in my ear.

I had every intention of doing so. But my arms were suddenly grabbed from behind, and I was wrenched away and flung face down on the floor, my hands clasped at my back by large, strong fingers.

"Charlie!" Seth shouted. "Charlie! Where are you?"

"Here!" I managed to call back before a fist slammed into my mouth. My head hit the floor, dazing me.

Noise. So much noise filled my head. Screaming. Shouted orders. The pounding of my blood.

Then a knife pressed into my side, its cold, sharp point pricking my skin through the layers of clothing.

I struggled, kicking out, but a heavy body weighed me down. My pathetic efforts achieved nothing. It was definitely a man, and not Gillingham either. He wasn't big enough.

The knife cut me.

I screamed but it was drowned out by an explosion. The floor trembled beneath me. Glasses and plates rattled. The shouts suddenly stopped and an eerie silence followed.

"No," gasped the man on top of me. "Not yet." The pressure eased enough for me to flip over and punch upward in one fluid movement. My fist connected with a satisfying but bruising crunch.

"Charlie!" Seth cried.

"Down here!" I shouted, lashing out again.

I must have stunned my attacker because he fell back but did not get off me altogether. I wriggled and shoved at him, managing to free myself. Doyle relit a candle, and in the wan light, I realized I'd only wriggled free because Seth had pulled the attacker off me.

266

"You!" both Seth and I snapped at General Eastbrooke.

He breathed heavily and sweat dampened his brow, but he did not look at us. He stared at the door. "Lincoln," he muttered, eyes wide. "It wasn't supposed to go off yet. Lincoln...my son."

I scrambled to my feet, picked up my skirts, and sprinted out the door. "Lincoln!"

CHAPTER 19

A wall of heat and smoke slammed into me when I reached the kitchen. It was impossible to see how much of the room was on fire through the dark, billowing smoke. "Lincoln!" I screamed.

No answer. Only shouts behind me and the crackle of flames in front. Tears burned my eyes, blurred my vision. I buried my mouth and nose in my arm and pressed on. I had to find him. He must be safe, somewhere, alive. He *had* to be.

Otherwise...

I choked, as much from the suffocating fear and tears as from the smoke itself. I squinted into the gray pall, tried to make out human shapes, but could only identify the table and stove, no people.

Someone coughed and spluttered. Lincoln! Or Gus or Cook, perhaps. I had to get in there, but the air squeezed out of my lungs and smoke rushed in. I coughed into my arm and inched forward.

The amber in my necklace pulsed. The imp! It wouldn't save the others, but it would save me.

Voices sounded behind me, a jumble of incomprehensible shouts. Then the general suddenly emerged from the dark. With a snarl, he lunged at me.

I plunged into the smoky haze filling the kitchen. Searing heat smacked into my face and stole the remaining breath from my lungs. Smoke clogged my throat. I couldn't breathe. Dizziness swamped me. I fell to my knees, but managed to wrap my hand around the rapidly beating orb.

"I release you," I choked out.

Light flashed, and the imp rose large and real before me. Its hairless body reared up and its slanted green eyes pinned on a point behind me, as if daring the general to attack.

"Devil!" Gillingham cried in a high-pitched voice. "She's a witch!"

"Get back!" the general ordered. "All of you, stay back!"

My chest hurt. My throat ached. Heat swirled around me, more intense near the pantry door, engulfed in flames. I put my hands out like a blind person and shuffled forward. *Trust the imp.*

The imp suddenly changed shape. The cat-like creature whirled around and around until it became a blur. Smoke swirled around it, caught in the force like dust in a whirlwind. The imp spun out of the kitchen, scattering the panicked onlookers, drawing the smoke along in its wake.

I breathed in two deep breaths of semi-clear air, before more smoke billowed from the flames. Through the sting of my tears, I could just make out three bodies and a dismembered leg on the floor amid broken pieces of furniture, crockery and splattered food. I recognized Cook, Gus and Lincoln. Only Cook coughed. The other two didn't move.

Oh God, oh God.

"Water!" Seth shouted. "Put out the fire before it spreads."

"Stay there," the general growled, pointing a small handgun at Seth. "No one move."

"Enough, General," Marchbank snapped. "Put the weapon away, and let us save them."

"Get Lincoln out," the general said. "No one else."

"Are you mad?"

"He's my son!"

"No," I rasped. "He's not."

The general pointed the gun at me. "You corrupted him. You changed him. He was loyal, and content to do his duty for the ministry, until you appeared."

I couldn't protest. A coughing fit assaulted me, and snot streamed from my nose and tears from my eyes. My imp was gone, and I couldn't attack the general from my weakened position, hunched on all fours.

"Damn you, witch. You're going to hell, where your kind belongs." He pulled the trigger and a shot rang out.

Yet I didn't die. I opened my eyes—I hadn't realized I'd shut them—to see the imp on its hind legs, a bullet in one paw, a pail in the other. It splashed water from the pail over the flames licking the pantry doorframe, as if it did that sort of thing every day and had not just saved my life.

Seth grabbed the gun as the general stared dazedly at the imp.

"What *is* that thing?" Gillingham murmured from behind Lady Harcourt.

"Move aside," Marchbank ordered, pushing past. He, Buchanan and Harcourt rushed in, pails in hand. They tossed water over the flames. Between them and the fast-moving imp, the fire was soon put out.

The kitchen was a charred, ruined mess. I scrambled through the shards of crockery and splintered furniture to Lincoln's still body. Too still.

I brushed his hair off his face and pressed my ear to his mouth. His shallow breaths wheezed. Despite my parched throat, I began to cry.

"Does he live?" Lady Harcourt knelt at my side, a candlestick in hand. Now that the fire was out, it provided the only light.

I nodded and she let out a low wail. The general murmured something at the ceiling and lowered his head. "My boy."

I was too exhausted to tell him Lincoln did not see himself as the general's son.

"Doyle," I rasped. "Fetch Dr. Fawkner."

The butler nodded then disappeared.

I stroked Lincoln's face. Except for the blue-black lump on his forehead, he was so pale. He looked younger, but that could have been because I'd never seen him so helpless. I pressed my lips to his, half kissing, half breathing in the hope that I had the power to keep him alive.

"Get away from him," Lady Harcourt hissed. "You're smothering him."

I cradled his head in my lap and continued to stroke his hair and watch for signs that he would live. But there was no flutter of eyelashes, no parting of lips, and he remained deathly pale.

"Fool!" the general spat. "He wasn't supposed to set it off yet."

I followed his gaze to the dismembered leg, still clad in trousers and a boot. It belonged to neither Cook, Gus nor Lincoln.

"You orchestrated that explosion?" Marchbank demanded. "Are you mad?"

"We could have all been killed!" Harcourt growled.

"Idiots!" the general snapped. "All of you! There can be no battle without casualties, but not once did I put *your* lives in danger. Only those who are expendable."

"Lincoln is not expendable!" Lady Harcourt screamed.

The general's face fell. His gaze softened as he looked at Lincoln. "Something went wrong. The explosion shouldn't have gone off yet. It was too soon. Too damned soon."

"You tried to kill Charlie in the dining room," Seth snarled, pulling hard on Eastbrooke's arms.

The older man winced. "She's a danger to society! Every single one of you knows it. Even you, Vickers."

Buchanan wound up his fist to punch the general, but he moved and hit Seth's jaw instead. Seth fell back and must have loosened his grip. The general muscled free and scooped up the gun I recognized as Lincoln's from the floor. He aimed it at me.

"Damned idiot, Buchanan," Seth snapped, rubbing his jaw. He went to raise the gun, but the general aimed his at me. Seth swore and lowered his weapon.

The imp straightened and stretched tall again.

Eastbrooke eyed it with a mixture of fear and wonder. "It only saves you, doesn't it?" With a derisive snort, he aimed the gun at Gus, now coughing and spluttering on the floor. Blood dampened his shirt at his waist.

Cook sat up, swayed, and rubbed his eyes. He quickly took in the situation and tried to come toward me, but the general ordered him to stay.

"All of you stay," he said. "Or I *will* kill him."

"What do you think will happen?" I asked. "You think Lincoln will treat you like a father after this? You truly are mad if you believe that."

"You've turned his head." He momentarily aimed the gun at me before pointing it at Gus again.

I closed my eyes and muttered a prayer, a familiar one I hadn't recited in so long.

"That's why he agreed to the committee's vote to end his tenure as leader," he went on. "Because of you. Because he thinks it's what you want. He won't listen to anyone else."

"Why do you want him to be the leader so desperately? Because of an ancient prophecy, the origins of which no one can trace?"

"Forget the prophecy. I want him to be leader because it's who he is. It's part of him, like being an army man is part of me, and a necromancer is part of you. It's his life, his *essence*." His tongue darted out and licked his top lip. "What is he without the ministry?"

My hand stilled on Lincoln's cheek where I'd been absently stroking him. As much as I hated to admit that the general was right, he had a point. Lincoln and the ministry were tied together as much as my necromancy was part of me. While I didn't want to be labeled as a necromancer—or a gutter rat, or an orphan—I couldn't deny that I was all of those things. I was the sum of all my experiences, yet I was so much more, too.

I couldn't let Lincoln give up the ministry leadership for me, no more than he would ask me to stop being a necromancer. He'd tried that and it hadn't worked. He'd learned from his mistakes. It was important that I didn't make the same mistakes now, with him.

"Put the gun down," Seth said calmly. "You don't really want anyone to get hurt."

The general grasped the gun in both hands to steady it. "If you believe that, then you don't know anything. I've killed vast numbers of men, Vickers. More than you'll ever know. I've led my own men into certain death." He choked then wiped his nose and mouth on his shoulder.

"The campaign in Bhutan?" Marchbank asked. "I recall when you returned. You were...a different man."

"Twenty-five years ago. So many dead...my boys. It was supposed to be an easy battle against a weaker foe, but...it was a bloodbath."

"So you wanted to raise them, using a serum," I finished.

"It's too late for them but not for others. Imagine if we had an army that kept rising and rising again. We wouldn't need fresh soldiers. So many lives could be spared. No more fine young men would be cut down."

His honorable reasons made it all so much more tragic. "Why now?" Lady Harcourt asked.

"I've been trying for years. No one has come close until Bell. Then *you* spoiled it, witch, by convincing Lincoln to remove him."

"Bell wasn't close to producing a serum," I said.

"He was. He wrote to me only the other night, claiming he raised the body of Mannering, a recently deceased colleague."

"I raised Mannering."

Eastbrooke's lips parted. A trickle of sweat dripped into his eye and he blinked. "You?" he whispered.

"I meant why all the murdering now?" Lady Harcourt said. "If you hate supernaturals, why not kill them earlier? You've had years."

He licked his lips. "Because it wasn't until *she* appeared, and Frankenstein sought her, that I realized what could be done. He could use her to raise the dead himself. She was the key to his experiments. Her and others like her. I had to eliminate *all* supernaturals who could be potentially used for such inhumane purposes."

"But *you* wanted to raise the dead too," I said. "How was Frankenstein doing anything different?"

"At least with me at the helm, the serum would be used for England, for defeating our enemies. Imagine if an unscrupulous monster perfected Frankenstein's experiments and sold them to another country, along with the necromancer. Imagine what our enemies would do with such powerful magic. At least with a serum controlled by me, there would be no risk of rogue supernaturals selling themselves to the highest bidder. My serum would be kept here, safe, and used only in times of war."

"I am not a danger, General," I said with a sense of calm authority that surprised me. I felt anything but calm. "No more than anyone else. You cannot play God like that."

His nostrils flared. "Nor can you."

"Don't think we're going to let you go," Marchbank said. "There has to be punishment."

Gus stirred. His eyes opened and he muttered something I couldn't hear. Eastbrooke looked down at him.

"Don't shoot!" Seth slowly, slowly approached them, the general's small gun still in his hand. He aimed it at Eastbrooke's chest. "There's no point. You kill him, and I'll kill you. It's as simple as that."

Eastbrooke blinked at Lincoln, lying in my arms. Tears dampened his eyes. "Get him a doctor. Tell him I'm sorry." He aimed the gun at his own throat and pulled the trigger.

I closed my eyes just in time to avoid seeing the mess, but I opened them again to watch the general's spirit drift out of his body and form his shape in the air. He hovered there, staring sadly down at Lincoln. My heart pinched.

"I'll tell him," I told the spirit.

He glanced at me and nodded before the mist dispersed and floated away. I let out a breath.

"Has he gone?" Lady Harcourt whispered, her lips trembling.

My imp shrank to its normal cat-size and nestled into my skirts with a soft mewl. "Go back," I told it. "Return and rest now."

The flash of light brightened the dark room but only for an instant.

"You have a lot of explaining to do, girl," Gillingham snapped at me. Now that the danger was over, he stood like a peacock, his chest puffed out, his stance wide. He'd left his walking stick behind.

"Do be quiet," Marchbank said, sounding tired.

Dr. Fawkner rushed in and took in the bloody scene with a mixture of horror and curiosity. "You mentioned there'd been an accident," he said to Doyle, "but I hadn't expected this...chaos." He picked his way carefully through the mess to where I sat with Lincoln. Doyle nipped at the doctor's heels, carrying the medical bag that Lincoln kept in his rooms.

Fawkner bent over Lincoln, while Seth rummaged through the bag and pulled out cloths. He lifted Gus's shirt and silently cleaned away the blood to inspect the wound. It didn't look deep, thank God.

"Will he be all right?" Lady Harcourt asked Fawkner.

"Hard to say." Fawkner opened Lincoln's jacket, waistcoat and shirt then inspected him. "The blow to the head must have been severe, but I can't see any other wounds."

"He be closest to the explosion," Cook said, pulling the general's dead body away. "Aside from Eastbrooke's driver." He nodded at the charred pantry, where perhaps the rest of the driver lay. I didn't want to look. "The blast's force pushed Fitzroy back into the wall, but that's all I saw before I got hit." He picked up a stool leg, as if that were the culprit. "Something must have hit Fitzroy in the head, too. Gus—he got shot before Fitzroy came in." He crouched beside Seth and clasped Gus's forearm. They exchanged grim smiles, perhaps relieved to see they'd both survived.

"It's not too bad," Seth said with cheerfulness that I didn't believe for a moment. He was as worried as the rest of us. "Stop looking for sympathy from the ladies."

Gus clapped Seth's shoulder. He glanced at me and then Lincoln. "He all right, Doc?"

"We need to make him comfortable," Dr. Fawkner said. "Hopefully he'll wake up soon."

"Hopefully?" Lady Harcourt cried. "Is that all you can do? Hope?"

Fawkner took a wary step away from her and almost tripped over a pot. "Head injuries are unpredictable. I...I'm sorry."

"Take Lincoln to his rooms," I told no one in particular. Buchanan and Harcourt came forward and lifted him. They carried him out, led by Doyle who held two candlesticks aloft.

To Fawkner, I said, "You may go home now. The danger is past, and you're free." I looked at the general's feet, avoiding seeing his face. "We'll notify Dr. Bell tomorrow."

Fawkner stretched his neck out of his collar and eyed Lady Harcourt carefully. She, however, only had eyes for her stepsons as they carried Lincoln away. I resisted watching too, even though every part of me wanted to race after them.

"I'll check on your friends first," Fawkner said.

I touched his arm. "Thank you."

Seth drew me into a brief hug. "Go and be with him, Charlie. I'll see to everything down here."

I walked off, only to have Lady Harcourt attempt to race ahead of me.

Seth caught her. "No," he growled. "You have to help clean up."

"I do not clean," she said with the defiance I expected from her but hadn't seen of late. "I am Lady Harcourt."

I caught up to her stepsons as they laid Lincoln on his bed. They removed his jacket and waistcoat, but left his shirt on. I thanked them and sat on the edge of the mattress. I wasn't aware they'd left the room until I heard the door click closed.

Lincoln lay motionless, the bruise on his forehead a deep black against his pale skin. It wasn't right. Someone with Lincoln's vibrancy and strength shouldn't be rendered weak. He would hate it, and he would hate me seeing him like this.

I touched his cheek. It felt cool so I pulled the bedcovers up and tucked them around him. His eyelashes fluttered, and I held my breath, but he didn't wake. I stroked his cheek, his forehead, traced the line of his brow to the edge, beneath the bruise. Injuries to the head were unpredictable, so Fawkner said. Lincoln could wake with memory loss, or his speech could be affected, or his body. Or he might never wake.

My stomach lurched. Tears spilled, even though I thought I'd shed enough. If he died...the hole his absence would leave in my life and heart would never close.

Soft footsteps approached. "Charlie," Doyle whispered from the door. "I brought you tea. I thought you may need it." He set the tray down on the bedside table and poured me a cup.

"Thank you." I took my cup out to the adjoining room with the butler. "How are the others?"

"The guests have left. It was decided that the police will not be informed. The gentlemen removed the general's body and, er...what remained of his coachman. The coachman will be disposed of and his family informed, but they will not be forthcoming on the particulars of the disposal. The general's body will be left in his carriage near his house. Any questions from the police will be quashed by their superiors and the proper arrangements made for the funeral *et cetera*."

"He had no family," I said, numbly. "Only Lincoln, of sorts."

"Seth and I are seeing to the clean-up in the kitchen with Cook overseeing proceedings. I had to make tea in the drawing room fireplace."

"Be sure Cook and Seth get some rest, too. And Gus?"

"In bed."

"Good. Thank you, Doyle."

He gave me a flat smile. "Let's just be glad Bella was given the evening off and her mistress is out."

I checked the clock on Lincoln's desk. "She'll be home soon." I sighed, not looking forward to the explanations. "I'll come downstairs and help."

"It's not suitable work for a young woman. Stay here and watch over Mr. Fitzroy."

"I've cleaned up blood before." And bits of brain and skull—belonging to Lord Harcourt's brother-in-law.

"Seth will have my head if I allow you downstairs. Rest in here or your own room."

"Very well. Thank you, Doyle. You're a marvel."

He left, but I neither rested nor returned to Lincoln's bedroom. I was too tightly wound to sleep. I set my teacup down on the desk and began searching for a list of the supernaturals and where they'd gone. The task helped distract me from the man lying on the bed and what had transpired. I didn't want to think about the general, of what he'd done or tried to do. Nor did I want to explore the emotions rolling through me.

Yet I couldn't help it when I saw my engagement ring in its box. The box was open, as it had been every time I came into Lincoln's rooms.

I rummaged through drawers, willing myself not to think about our broken engagement, of what might have been if he'd never sent me away. But I couldn't help it. The ring drew me back, again and again, until I finally picked up the box. It was a beautiful ring, with its multi-faceted diamond, but it was no longer mine.

Unless I wanted it. I suspected Lincoln wanted me to be his fiancée again, but I couldn't go back to the way things were—the way *I* had been. I wasn't that girl anymore. I wasn't foolishly in love with the perfect man. Lincoln wasn't perfect.

Nor was I.

The pad of heavy footsteps coming from the bedroom had me drop the ring box and leap out of the chair. Lincoln appeared in the doorway, looking disheveled and groggy but *alive*. "Charlie," he croaked.

"You're awake," I said, going to him. I kept my arms folded over my chest and dug my fingernails into my palms to stop myself from going to him.

He slumped against the doorframe, his shoulders stooped and tangles of hair falling over his eyes. "Barely." He touched the bruise on his forehead and grunted.

I blinked back tears and bit the inside of my cheek to hide my grin. It was so good to see him alive and talking, even if he looked like he'd just survived the apocalypse. "You should rest some more."

He suddenly looked up at me and stumbled forward. I caught him as he put a hand out to the doorframe. He managed to stay upright, but I clung to him as tightly as he clung to me. His shirt was still open from when Dr. Fawkner had unbuttoned it, and I pressed my cheek to his chest. The steady, rhythmic beat of his heart was the most wonderful sound I'd heard all evening. I closed my eyes and drew in his smoky scent.

His breathing fanned the hair on the top of my head, and he lightly stroked my neck. "You're unharmed." His voice rumbled in my ear, more gravely from the smoke but no less rich.

"Yes."

"Gus? The others?"

"Gus is wounded but not badly. Cook and Seth are fine. General Eastbrooke is dead."

He seemed unsurprised, and I realized he must have known the general was our villain once he saw his coachman in the kitchen with the gun that had shot Gus and the explosive device that had caused so much damage.

"How long have I slept?" he asked.

"Not long." Reluctantly, I pulled away. He reached for me, but I caught his hand and held it instead of letting him draw me close. He looked exhausted. The shadows around his eyes were almost as dark as the bruise on his forehead. "You must rest, Lincoln."

"I can't."

"You can."

"I need to—"

"No." I put up my finger. "The only thing you need to do is rest. Dr. Fawkner said so. The danger has passed, and everything is being taken care of."

"You're beautiful when you're ordering me about."

I sucked in a breath. *Be strong, Charlie. Don't give in.* "Did you keep notes on where the supernaturals have gone, or is it all in your head?"

"Both. There's a coded document in the middle drawer of my desk. It lists the names and locations of them all."

"And the code?"

He tapped his forehead.

"That's not very helpful. What if you'd—?" I bit my lip because it threatened to wobble.

"The code is kept in a safety deposit box in my bank. It's one of many. If anything ever happens to me, remember to check it. The bank details are in my wall safe." He nodded at the painting of an idyllic country scene on the wall. "I change the code regularly, but the current code is your birth date."

I blinked.

"I'll keep you informed every time I change it," he went on. "None of that's necessary now. My memory is fine. I'll write down the cipher and you can decode my list." He walked more steadily to the desk than I expected but sat heavily.

He reached for the inkstand but paused when he saw the engagement box had been moved. He picked it up and cradled it in his palm before setting it down again in its original position near the back of his desk.

A few minutes later, he handed me the paper. The code was ridiculously long. "Your memory is better than fine," I said.

"Unless this doesn't work and you end up with a laundry list instead."

I smiled with relief. If he was making jokes, he must be all right. "Go to bed, Lincoln. You look tired, and I suspect your head aches."

He bristled. I may have insulted his manliness, but I didn't care. "I don't want to sleep. I want to talk to you."

"There'll be no more talking tonight. Tomorrow. I promise."

He lowered his head and I touched his chin. He looked up at me, hopefully.

"Goodnight, Lincoln."

He eyed the sofa. "I'll stay out here with you, to help with the code if necessary."

If he didn't look so weak, I'd thump him. "Do you need help getting to the sofa?"

"I can manage." He rose and stepped away, then paused. "I think I do need help. If you could put your arm around me..."

It was a bare-faced lie and I knew it. What's more, if the slight curve of his lips was an indication, he knew that I knew it. Even so, I tucked myself into his side and put my arm around his waist. He circled his arm around my shoulders, but didn't put any of his weight on me, and allowed me to steer him to the sofa.

I positioned two cushions at one end and he lay down, his legs dangling over the edge at the other end. I helped him off with his shoes only to stop at the sight of the bandages wrapped around his feet. I'd forgotten about the cuts he'd inflicted by walking over broken glass in this very room.

I rested my hand on the top of one his feet and swept my gaze up to his face. He quickly closed his eyes, but I knew he'd been watching me. *Oh, Lincoln, you're a broken, battered mess.*

I resisted the urge to kiss him, although it wasn't easy. I lit a fire in the grate and returned to the desk. It took some time to use the code to write out all the names and new addresses of the supernaturals. When I finished, I glanced at Lincoln. He slept in exactly the position I'd left him, his arms crossed over his chest. The color had returned to his face, and his breathing sounded steady, thank God.

Another two hours later, I'd written letters to every supernatural in my best hand, and I left a space for Lincoln to sign when he woke. Then, after casting a long look at him asleep on the sofa, more at peace than I'd ever seen him, I left.

CHAPTER 20

"He's awake," Doyle announced, as he brought in luncheon to Lady Vickers, Gus and me in the sitting room the next day. She had been told what had transpired in her absence, and she had taken it remarkably well. That could have been because she hadn't seen the kitchen, the dismembered body parts, or the general's dead body. "He asked me to post these." Doyle set the tray down and picked up the stack of papers. It was the letters, all signed.

"He's not coming down?" I asked.

Doyle shook his head.

For Lincoln to remain in his room, he must feel very unwell. "Is it his head?"

"He wouldn't say, but I suspect so. I opened the curtains, but the light hurt his eyes. And he can't keep anything down this morning."

"Oh." I stared at the letters in Doyle's hand but hardly saw them. "I should see if he needs anything."

Lady Vickers pulled a face as she accepted her plate of sandwiches from Doyle. "If you want my advice, stay here, Charlie. Capable men like Mr. Fitzroy don't like their paramours to see them when they're low."

"We're not paramours."

"You know what I mean. Send for the doctor, Doyle."

"He's on his way, madam." Doyle bowed. "Thank you for your advice."

He left and I tried to eat my lunch, but I wasn't hungry. I'd been shooed out of the service rooms earlier, as Seth oversaw the continued clean up, and had sat with Gus in his room for a while until he decided he was well enough to come downstairs. But I couldn't sit idly forever. For one thing, Lady Vickers would drive me mad with her endless gossiping, and for another, I now had Lincoln to worry about.

Seth provided a welcome distraction when he strode in, dressed in blue overalls like a navvy. His mother clicked her tongue and ordered him not to sit on the furniture.

Gus snickered and made a point of stretching like a languid cat in the armchair by the fire. Instead of sneering back at him, Seth picked up the blanket from the back of the sofa and tucked it around Gus.

"Have a rest, my friend," Seth said quietly.

Gus's smug smile vanished. He nodded soberly.

"How is it back there?" I asked Seth.

"Filthy, but at least the area is secure now and the ceiling won't collapse. Thank goodness that part of the house is only single level."

"How long do you think repairs will take?"

"Weeks. I'll find a builder this afternoon. I know of several who're quite good if they remain sober long enough."

I suspected he knew them from his days as a pugilist but didn't mention as much in front of his mother. She looked horrified enough that her son knew tradesmen.

"I forgot to ask Doyle how Cook is coping without a kitchen," I said, holding up my sandwich.

"Badly, God help me. He's working from the servants' dining room and complaining endlessly. I hope everyone likes sandwiches, because we won't be eating much better for a while."

He went to sit, but his mother scolded him. "Look at you! You're a disgrace."

He rolled his eyes. "Doyle says Fitzroy's unwell," he said to me. "Have you been in this morning?"

I shook my head. "He won't want me to see him like that."

"Are you sure?"

I stared down at my clasped hands in my lap.

Seth crouched in front of me. "He'll be fine. There's no need to worry."

I nodded as my tears welled. "It's just that...Gus said Lincoln was closest to the coachman when the explosion went off. Lincoln was trying to disarm him, wasn't he?"

"Probably." He looked to Gus.

"The man were drunk," Gus said darkly. "He had a gun and a small bomb what looked like he'd made in his stables. I think he was supposed to use it later, when no one were around, as a distraction, maybe. He weren't meant to shoot no one neither, I expect." He touched his side, heavily bandaged beneath his shirt. "Fitzroy tried to calm him down and draw near to overpower him. The coachman panicked and lit the bomb, but he didn't get rid of it fast enough. It all happened so quick."

"Lincoln tried to stop him." I wiped at my cheeks. "He risked his own life to save everyone else. It was a selfless act."

"It was." Seth touched my knee.

"You don't understand," I said, unable to stop crying now. "I accused him of being selfish."

"No, Charlie. Don't blame yourself."

"He would have risked himself no matter what," Gus added.

"The thing is, Charlie," Lady Vickers said, coming to sit by me. "He *is* a selfish man—but only in some matters and not others. I'd say it's because he *thought* he knew what was best for everyone."

"He doesn't," Gus said.

"Both of you, out," Lady Vickers ordered. "I wish to speak to Charlie alone."

"But I'm wounded!"

She stood and pulled me up with her. "Then we'll leave."

I allowed her to lead me out of the sitting room to the base of the staircase. Should I go up and see him?

"I've wanted to tell you something ever since you returned, but it was never the right time," Lady Vickers said, taking hold of both my hands. "I can see the way things are between you and Mr. Fitzroy, and it's creating tension for everyone. It's time to set it aside and move ahead. You must make a decision about him. I'm sure you realize that the choice is up to you."

I was torn between telling her not to meddle and asking her to hug and comfort me. In the end, I said nothing.

"Perhaps what I have to say will help sway your mind. It's the same thing I said to him before he left, and I don't think I'm overstating my influence too much when I tell you my advice led him to bring you back."

I blinked at her. I suddenly felt very small and insignificant. When I lived as a boy, I'd hidden behind my hair and crept into tiny spaces to remove myself from the dangerous streets. I'd been a quiet mouse that had only roared when pushed, and Lincoln had pushed me to my limits when we'd first met. Now, the luxury of anonymity was denied me, but at times like this, I longed for it again. I desperately wanted to crawl away and hide.

"I told him that love is not a choice," Lady Vickers went on, leveling her gaze with mine, "but accepting it into one's life is."

She'd spoken to Lincoln about love? And he'd listened? Or was she fooling herself with regard to her influence? It didn't seem like something Lincoln would want to hear.

And yet *something* had made him change his mind and fetch me.

"Falling in love is a frightening experience for someone used to being in control of one's emotional state. I suspect he felt as if he was losing his self-control, the very thing that made him successful in work, and the thing you yourself fell in love with."

"It's not his self-control I love." I bit my tongue. I'd said more than I wanted to. I glanced up the stairs again, half expecting to see him there, but it was empty.

"Perhaps not, but it is the thing which most people respect about him. It's the thing that makes him unique, and he was losing it with you. His life was heading in a direction he never anticipated, and very quickly, too. He was afraid."

"Lincoln isn't afraid of anything."

"Everyone is afraid of something."

I folded my arms. "How can you know what he feared? You hardly know him."

"We are not that dissimilar. I risked much to be with the man I loved, too."

"You think being with me is a risk for him?"

"Accepting his love for you is. Very much so. Don't belittle his efforts to make everything right between you again. It's difficult for most men, but I suspect it is even harder for him. You said it yourself—he has rarely had to consider the opinions of others."

"I'm not belittling him," I said. "But I haven't been fair on him. I know that."

She drew me into a hug and kissed the top of my head. "After a little persuading from me, your Mr. Fitzroy decided he would rather risk losing control of his life and his emotions than be without you. That, my dear, is quite a statement he made."

I sniffed. "I know."

"There, there. Don't cry, pet." She squeezed me then handed me her handkerchief. "I'm rather good at this mother-daughter thing, aren't I?"

I laughed as I dabbed my cheeks. "You are."

"I've always wanted a daughter who'll listen to her mother, rather than an ungrateful son who will not."

"Seth's not ungrateful. Angry, yes, but that will pass."

"I do hope so," she said on a sigh.

I was about to head up the stairs when the doctor arrived. He stayed with Lincoln for an interminably long time, then wouldn't let anyone except Doyle in to see him afterward.

"He needs to rest and stay calm," the doctor said. "His head aches, and his vision is blurred. I suspect the combination is unsettling his stomach." He did not sound at all confident in his diagnosis.

"Will he be all right?" I asked.

"Let's hope so."

I groaned.

Lady Vickers took my hand. "Thank you, Doctor."

"I'll return tomorrow," he said, eyeing me carefully.

Tomorrow took an awfully long time to arrive. When it finally did, I warred with myself all day about going against the doctor's orders, but Doyle and Seth assured me they would take care of Lincoln when he wasn't sleeping.

"He won't sleep if you go in there," Seth said, as I hovered outside the door. "And he needs to rest. The doctor said it's not just the bump on the head, but he's most likely been suffering exhaustion for some time."

I slumped back against the wall and buried my hands in my hair. I hadn't bothered to fix it that morning, and it hung untidily past my shoulders.

"I knew it," Seth went on with a shake of his head. "I knew he wasn't sleeping while you were away. He was...erratic." He grunted. "I want to say it serves him bloody right."

"But you can't," I finished for him. "Nor can I."

Thank God a distraction arrived in the form of Alice. A hansom delivered her to our door, valise in one hand and the other clamped on her hat as she stared up at Lichfield's central tower.

"I had the same reaction when I first saw it," I said, running down the front steps.

"Charlie!" She dropped her valise and caught me in a hug. "I was beginning to wonder if I had the right place. You spoke so lovingly about it, but it's not at all what I expected."

I took her hands and smiled. "It's so good to see you. You look as pretty as ever, despite the long journey."

"I left at dawn. I think Mrs. Denk was glad to be rid of me." Her smile faded and her eyes shadowed.

I squeezed her hands. "Oh, Alice. I'm so sorry for what your parents have done to you. But you have a home here. Lincoln was adamant that you should be welcomed."

"I want to meet this mysterious gentleman of yours. I admit that I don't know whether to hate him for hurting you or think him wonderful for inviting me to stay."

"Don't hate him." I picked up her valise and headed up the steps. "As to meeting him, it will have to wait. He's unwell."

"Nothing serious, I hope."

"No," I said, unconvincingly. "He received a bad bump on the head the other night when the kitchen caught alight."

She gasped. "Good lord. Is everyone else all right?"

"Gus is a little hurt. We're also short staffed at the moment. Seth and Doyle are taking turns to watch over Lincoln and keep up with chores. That's why I'm carrying this." I indicated her valise.

She went to take it off me, but I refused. I led her upstairs to one of the guest bedrooms and promised to introduce her to the others after she freshened up. "I'm afraid dinner won't be a grand affair, without a kitchen to cook in."

"I'm sorry I've come at such a difficult time," she said with a pained wince. "I feel awful for adding an extra burden. I'll try to help where I can."

"You're not a burden. You're excellent company. And thank you for the offer. You may need to do your own mending, washing, and cleaning for the time being."

"So it'll be just like the school but without Mrs. Denk smacking me on the back with her stick, ordering me to stand straight."

I laughed. God, it felt good to laugh. "She never did that to you. She didn't have to. You have perfect posture." I kissed her cheek. "I am glad you're here."

I introduced her to Gus and Lady Vickers over a dinner of cold salads. I thought poor Lady Vickers was going to have an attack of the vapors, she was so upset that a guest had to dine on such meager offerings.

"At least the setting is elegant," I said, indicating the fine china plates, the same ones we'd used the night of the fire.

"That's because these are the only ones left," she said huffily. "They're fit for roasted meats and salads, and delicious jellies and confections, not salads and sandwiches. I'm heartily sick of this."

"It's hardly been two days," I said.

"If you're sick of it," Gus said, "I'll have yours."

She slapped his hand away. "It'll be a welcome relief when you can resume your duties again, Gus."

"Amen," he muttered.

"Eating without me?" Seth said, strolling in. He stopped short when he spotted Alice. "A guest! Charlie, why didn't you tell me?"

"Because you've been in Lincoln's room, and I'm banished from there. How is he?"

He waved a hand. "Forget him. We have a guest. Lord Vickers," he said, bowing over Alice's hand. "At your service."

"Alice Everheart. Pleased to me you, my lord."

"Bloody hell," Gus muttered with a shake of his head. "Call him Seth or he'll get too big for his boots."

Alice smiled. Seth beamed back and flicked his hair off his forehead with a jerk of his head.

Lady Vickers cleared her throat. "Come sit by me, son," she said, patting the seat beside her.

"I'd rather sit near Miss Everheart," he said, not taking his gaze off Alice.

Lady Vickers looked as if she would order him, but she must have thought better of it. She knew her son wouldn't obey, no matter how much of a scene she made. "We were just asking Miss Everheart about her family and connections."

No one countered her lie. Alice was an extremely unflappable girl and quite capable of navigating the treacherous waters of social politeness. She could cope with concerned mothers of bachelors better than me.

"I'm from Dorset," she said.

"Fascinating." Seth topped up her glass of wine from the carafe. "Go on."

"There's not much to tell. My father is a businessman. He's in cloth, mostly, but trades in other commodities from time to time." She picked up her glass and smiled over the top of it at a horrified Lady Vickers.

I smothered my own smile with my hand. Poor Lady Vickers. She loathed talk of trade and business, particularly at the dinner table. She probably hated even more that her son couldn't take his eyes off the daughter of a merchant.

"Fascinating," Seth said again. "Isn't it, Mother?" he added with a hard edge.

Lady Vickers set down her fork. "Your father sounds very astute, Miss Everheart. I imagine he's quite successful."

Gus and I exchanged glances. We both knew where this was heading. If Alice's father were rich, Lady Vickers would forgive him for being involved in something as "vulgar" as trade.

"You would think so," Alice said. "But he's much too conservative to take risks, and it's really only the risk takers who do well in business. And those who marry off their daughters to more successful men than themselves, of course," she said for what I suspected was my benefit. Her father had tried to do precisely that, until her supernatural affliction presented itself.

"What a shame," Lady Vickers said with genuine sympathy.

Seth glared at his mother.

"Even more of a shame that my parents have disowned me." Alice picked up her glass and sipped elegantly.

I bit my lip to hide my smile. She had taken only a few minutes to get the measure of both Seth and his mother. It was going to be a pleasant diversion watching her settle into our household.

***

Lincoln still did not emerge the next morning. According to Doyle he slept off and on, and he finally managed to keep down some broth that Cook had prepared using a rescued cast iron pot and the hot coals of the dining room fireplace.

"Can I see him yet?" I asked.

"No," Doyle said without looking at me.

"Why not, if he's feeling better?"

"Sorry, Charlie, he specifically said you weren't to be allowed in."

I thrust my hands on my hips, but there was nothing I could do about it. If Lincoln didn't want me in there, I had to accept his wishes. It wasn't easy, however, and by lunch time, I decided to accost Seth and see if he had a different answer. He'd spent most of the morning with Lincoln, giving Alice some much needed breathing space.

"Why not go for a walk?" Alice asked gently as we sat in the sitting room, alone. "It's cool outside but not raining."

I shook my head. "I don't want to be away from the house."

She sat in the window seat and looked out. The sky hung ominously low, but I did long to be in the fresh air. Once I'd seen Lincoln for myself, and knew he was well, I'd walk with her.

I joined her on the window seat. "You should go," I told her. "The estate is lovely at any time of year. The orchard is my favorite place, even without fruit or leaves."

She smiled wistfully and blinked damp eyes.

I touched her hand. "This is hard for you," I said softly. "But you are very welcome here. Perhaps, in time, you will see it as your home too."

She dabbed at the corner of her eyes. "Thank you. I do feel welcome, but I also feel misplaced, like a doll left outside, forgotten."

I put my arm around her but didn't speak. I remembered that feeling all too well, even now, years after my father had thrown me out.

"All I want—all I've ever wanted—is a home where I felt safe." She turned to me. "How did you do it? How did you live for years without knowing if the place you lay your head one night would be the same the following night? How could you live with the uncertainty hanging over you like a guillotine? And you a child, too."

I lifted one shoulder. "I never lost hope, I suppose. I hoped to have a home to call my own again, where I would never have to leave unless I wanted to." I stared out the window, but I saw only my own reflection and that of the room behind me. "You will have your own Lichfield one day, Alice, but until you do, you can share mine."

She leaned her head on my shoulder and stared at our reflections too.

Another face joined ours. I gasped and spun round, knocking Alice on the nose. "Lincoln!" How long had he been there? How much had he heard?

His face was still a little pale and the bump on his head was the size of an egg, but he looked wonderful compared to the last time I'd seen him. His damp hair hung loose to his shoulders, begging to be tucked behind his ears, and his eyes gleamed like polished jet.

"You're better," I said, standing. "I mean, you look better. But you shouldn't be down here. Seth and Doyle were supposed to tell me when you were up and about so I could visit you. Why wouldn't they, if you're better?" I needed to stop rambling, but I couldn't help myself.

"I told them not to," he said.

"Why?"

"I had my reasons." He put out his hand to Alice. "You must be Miss Everheart. Seth has told me all about you."

She shook his hand. "Pleased to meet you."

They exchanged polite pleasantries for a few minutes before Alice excused herself. "I'd like to go for a walk before it rains."

I found myself alone with Lincoln. I'd wanted to be alone with him for days, yet now I didn't know what to say. My tongue felt thick and dry and my heart wouldn't cease its incessant hammering.

He sat on the window seat beside me but didn't speak. After a moment, I hazarded a glance at him. "Do you feel all right? Do you need to return to bed?"

"I've spent enough time in bed. Now I want to spend time with you."

I swallowed and nodded at him to go on.

His fingers tapped on his knee. "I'm trying to think of a way to begin."

"Then I'll begin." I breathed deeply and let it out slowly. "There's something I need to say."

CHAPTER 21

"I accept your birthday gift. The house," I added when he simply stared at me. "I still think it's too generous, but..." I trailed off. Any further comment would probably sound avaricious.

"It's only generous if it's something I cannot afford to give. It's hardly a grand gesture." He sounded disappointed in himself.

"It is grand. You thought of the one thing I wanted above all else, and you gave it to me in the only way you knew how."

"Not the only way, but even by marrying me you wouldn't become an independent woman until after my death." His lips twitched into a crooked smile. "I didn't want to tempt you."

I nudged him with my elbow and laughed softly.

He gently took my hand and turned it over, palm up. He rubbed his thumb along mine. "Charlie—"

"No. Wait. There's something else I have to say first." I closed my hand around his and blinked up at him. "I forgive you, Lincoln."

He looked down at our linked hands. "You shouldn't."

"I should have told you earlier. If you'd died without knowing..." I cleared my throat, but it remained tight. "I understand why you sent me away. I do."

"But I shouldn't have done it." He leaned forward and rested his elbows on his knees. He buried his head in his hands, pushing back his hair. "I heard you and Alice just now, talking about home and belonging... I didn't think about any of that when I sent you away. It never occurred to me that I was doing exactly what Holloway did. That doesn't excuse it; it doesn't absolve me of blame. It *should* have occurred to me." He tilted his head to the side to peer at me. The gleam had vanished from his eyes, replaced with a haunted look. "I profess to love you, yet I don't fully understand you."

My heart tripped. *He loved me.* It was the first time he'd even mentioned the word. I was relieved he at least knew what it meant and that he could identify it within himself. It felt like progress, so I didn't tell him that he'd never actually professed to love me. Not to my face, anyway.

I tucked his hair behind his ear to see him properly. "If men and women understood one another completely, life would be dull. You and I are different, and I can't expect you to know what I'm thinking. You made a mistake, Lincoln, and you regret it. You apologized, and I know you'll never make the same mistake again."

"I won't, but..." He shook his head. "How can you forgive me, Charlie?"

I cupped his cheek, and he sat up straight, his wide-eyed gaze upon me. He seemed to have stopped breathing, whereas my breaths came short and sharp. I had to say this. I had to tell him. I'd never felt surer of anything in my life—never felt more confident of myself and of his feelings for me. We had a future together, as equals—I knew that now. "Not forgiving you hurts me as much as it hurts you. I want you in my life, Lincoln. I want to be with you, and love you, and be loved by you. I want—"

His mouth closed over mine, cutting off my rambling. He kissed how I remembered—confidently, with a little desperation and a lot of heat. But it quickly changed to a more tentative one, as if instinct had suddenly been pushed aside. He was thinking too much. I didn't want him to think, just feel.

I grasped his face with both my hands and touched his lips with my tongue. He smiled briefly, then dug his fingers into my hair. He deepened the kiss and I responded, not holding back. I wanted him to know how much I wanted him, that I forgave him unequivocally, that we should never be apart again. All the intense feelings I'd had in recent months filled me until there was no room left. They flowed out of me with that kiss, dripped down my face, washed over us. Joined us.

He gasped against my mouth and pulled away. He pressed a shaky hand to his forehead and swallowed hard.

"Lincoln? What is it? What's wrong?"

"I'm not sure. Visions, I think."

"You saw the future?"

"I don't know. There were a lot of jumbled images. It's difficult to separate them."

"What did you see?"

"You. Us. The seaside."

I smiled, relieved he hadn't seen awful things. "Does that mean we're going on a holiday together?"

He touched the bruise on his temple. "That was...unexpected."

"You've never experienced anything like it before?"

He shook his head.

I didn't know if I liked our kisses being the trigger for his visions. We'd kissed before and he hadn't experienced them, so perhaps the experience wouldn't be repeated.

He looked a little pale again, so I touched his cheek, but it wasn't overly hot. "Does your head ache?"

"Not too much." He caught my hand and pressed it to his lips. "I'm going to give you time, Charlie. I won't rush you."

"We did progress very quickly last time." Part of me wanted to move forward, very much, but considering the madness of the last weeks, it was perhaps best if we took steady, measured steps.

"Entering into a relationship with me won't be easy," he said.

"I know that."

"I want you to be certain."

I nodded. I felt certain, but I couldn't deny the prudence behind waiting. Last time, there'd been a sense of giddiness about the engagement itself. This time I wanted to be giddy about being engaged to *him*.

"You know where your ring is," he went on. "When you're ready, I want you to put it on."

"I will." I twitched with the effort of remaining seated and not running up the stairs to his room. "Why did you leave it there on your desk and not put it in a drawer or safe?"

"To remind me of what I threw away." He pressed his forehead to mine. "To remind me of the things you said when you gave it back to me."

I winced. "They were awful things. I shouldn't have said them."

"You were angry and had every right."

"I spent too long being angry."

He scooped me round the waist and drew me against his body. I snuggled into him, my head beneath his chin, and listened to the steady throb of his blood through his veins. "It was your anger that gave me hope that I could salvage something from the mess I created."

"What do you mean?"

"Do you remember leaving Bart's Hospital after meeting Dr. Bell for the first time?"

"Not really."

"You were outraged with me for being nice to you. If you hadn't been angry, if you'd been indifferent, I would have known there was little hope for us."

I circled my arms around his waist. "It's fortunate that I don't know how to hide my emotions, then."

He laughed softly. "We balance one another in that regard."

"We work well together." I drew back to look at him. "Speaking of which...about the ministry leadership... are you going to insist you be reinstated?"

"Do you want me to?"

"It's part of you, Lincoln. You really are the best person to be leader. Think of the alternative."

He grunted. "Imagine Gillingham in charge."

"No, thank you. So you'll tell them?"

He nodded. "But not today. Perhaps not tomorrow, either."

I stroked his forehead near the bruise. "Good. You need to rest. Perhaps in the new year, if you're feeling ready."

He tipped his head back against the window frame. "I can't avoid the ministry anyway. I'm also now on the committee."

"You're Eastbrooke's heir?"

"As far as I know." He drew my hand to his lips and kissed my fingers gently. "It doesn't feel right."

"He thought of you as his son."

"I saw little evidence of that."

"Perhaps he had difficulty expressing himself." Of all people, Lincoln should understand that. "He was involved in a disastrous military campaign in Bhutan, many years ago. That affected him, and it led him to search for a remedy for death. Perhaps it affected his ability to love you, too."

"Perhaps."

"He wanted me to tell you that he's sorry. He wants your forgiveness."

He twined his fingers with mine and gently lay our hands over his steadily beating heart. He kissed the top of my head. "I forgive him for his lack of affection for me, but I can't forgive him for trying to kill you."

It was, perhaps, too much to ask. I couldn't forgive the general for the lives he'd taken, and for almost taking Lincoln's, even if the explosion had been an accident.

We sat together on the window seat, the sun warming us, Lincoln's arms around me and my head on his shoulder. I thought about the past, and our future together, and I assumed he was doing the same, but after a while his breathing became even and deep. He'd fallen asleep.

I smiled. Not every woman could make the most active man in England relaxed enough to fall asleep with her. Only me.

***

Cook managed to present a Christmas feast like I'd never experienced. Even Lady Vickers was impressed, although that quickly passed when she realized the entire household was going to eat together in the dining room, not including Bella who had the day off to spend with her parents.

"How did you manage all this without a kitchen?" I asked Cook, helping myself to potatoes. "You're a miracle worker."

He proudly admired the spread of oysters, bouillon, potatoes, sweetbread pâtés, peas, roast turkey with cranberry sauce, and a salad of cold potatoes, beets and celery. "A good cook ain't worth his salt if he let Christmas by without setting a feast on the table for his family."

"You think of us as your family?"

He blushed and dipped his head. "With two annoying brothers."

Seth and Gus beamed at one another across the table.

Lady Vickers' lips pinched. "If you don't put a stop to this, your servants will swindle you blind, Mr. Fitzroy."

"Mother!" Seth stabbed a potato. "No one asked your opinion."

"Do you think they would dare?" I said to Lady Vickers.

She glanced at Lincoln, sitting beside me. "Perhaps you'll be the exception."

"Have you forgotten George so quickly?" Seth asked. "My mother's lover," he said out of the side of his mouth to Alice. "Also our footman."

"Husband," Lady Vickers snapped. "We married in America. And no, I haven't forgotten him. He was a dear fellow, and not at all typical for a servant."

"How decent of you to exclude him from your sweeping judgment." Seth and his mother glared at one another. Their relationship had turned frostier since Alice's arrival. Seth had given our new guest a great deal of his attention, much to Lady Vickers' disapproval. According to her, her son's first marriage ought to be for advancement or money, not for love. Seth disagreed.

Alice didn't seem aware of the fuss at all. She carried herself serenely and effortlessly, more ladylike than Lady Vickers.

"These potatoes are delicious," she said to Cook, as if she hadn't noticed the tug of wills between mother and son.

"*A la maître d'hôtel,*" Cook said with an effortless French accent.

Gus screwed his nose up at the potato on his fork. "What's wrong with English potatoes?"

Cook looked as if he was about to spit back a response, but a glare from Lincoln shut his mouth.

"Have you two discussed costumes yet?" Lady Vickers asked Alice and me. "The ball is only a week away. We must get started on outfits."

An old friend of Lady Vickers' had invited us to a masquerade ball to welcome in the new year. It would be my first in costume, and Alice's too. We were both looking forward to it.

"Princesses," Seth announced. "They should both go as princesses, with highly distinctive masks so we can find them easily amongst the sea of ladies."

"You can't tell the ladies apart if you can't see their faces?" Lincoln asked with genuine curiosity.

"Er." Seth's cheeks reddened. "Of course I can. Some. Usually."

"Let's hope Lady Harcourt decides to stay home," Lady Vickers said, lifting her gaze to meet mine. "Apparently she has been invited." It was a warning, and one I appreciated. I gave her a nod of thanks.

Not that I was concerned about her hold over Lincoln. She had none. Yet her unpleasant waspishness could prove trying, and I wanted to avoid her, if possible.

I touched Lincoln's knee beneath the table, and he rested his hand over mine. We'd spent the morning hanging ornaments, paper flowers, and little bags of nuts on the tree in the entrance hall with Alice and Lady Vickers, while Seth, Gus and Doyle helped Cook with the meal preparations. The men had already wound ivy and mistletoe up the staircase rail and along the fireplace mantels, giving Lichfield a festive feel. Enjoying dinner altogether, with Lincoln at my side, was more than I'd hoped for mere days before. A year ago...well, I'd hardly allowed myself to hope that I'd ever experience a joyous Christmas again. It had seemed an impossibility.

As if he knew the direction of my thoughts, Lincoln squeezed my hand. "I'm sorry I didn't have a gift prepared for you," he said, picking up his glass. "But a rather abrasive nurse wouldn't allow me to leave the house. I didn't dare counter her."

"That abrasive nurse doesn't need another gift, thank you." My smile faded. I indicated the others, sitting around the table, talking quietly to one another. "This is all I want. Besides, I didn't get you anything either. I've been busy with a recalcitrant patient who doesn't like to rest."

He placed his arm across the back of my chair and leaned closer. His lips brushed my ear, his fingers skimmed my shoulder. It was as much an announcement to the others as it was an intimate move. "You gave me everything, Charlie. Everything."

THE END

LOOK OUT FOR

Of Fate and Phantoms

the 7th book in the MINISTRY OF CURIOSITIES series.

As Charlie and Lincoln's lives settle into a harmonious pattern, a new threat arises that could have far reaching effects for the royal family and Lincoln's parents.

To be notified when C.J. has a new release, sign up to her newsletter via her website: www.cjarcher.com